LIZZIE
FOX

a novel by

MIKE MURPHY

LIZZIE FOX

For Lora and our amazing family.

A NOTE TO THE READER:

Music has been used to set the atmosphere in movies since the first talkie was filmed way back in 1927. Without exception each chapter's title in *Lizzie Fox* is a popular song from that era that reflects the mood and tone of that chapter. All the songs are available on Amazon Music.

Chapter	Title/Song	Artist	Year
1	La Bamba	Ritchie Valens	1958
2	You're So Fine	The Falcons	1959
3	Yakety Yak	The Coasters	1958
4	Western Movies	Olympics	1958
5	Tragedy	Thomas Wayne	1959
6	Walkin' After Midnight	Patsy Cline	1957
7	Don't Be Cruel	Elvis Presley	1956
8	There's a Moon Out Tonight	The Capris	1960
9	Get A Job	The Silhouettes	1958
10	Put Your Head on My Shoulder	Paul Anka	1959
11	Everybody's Somebody's Fool	Connie Francis	1960
12	Poetry in Motion	Johnny Tillotson	1960
13	When Will I Be Loved	Everly Brothers	1960
14	Love Me Tender	Elvis Presley	1956
15	Devil or Angel	Bobby Vee	1960
16	Tears on My Pillow	Little Anthony & The Imperials	1958
17	I'm Sorry	Brenda Lee	1960
18	This Magic Moment	The Drifters	1960
19	There Goes My Baby	The Drifters	1959
20	Tequila	The Champs	1958
21	Come Go with Me	The Dell Vikings	1959
22	Poison Ivy	The Coasters	1959
23	Jailhouse Rock	Elvis Presley	1957
24	Bye Bye Love	Everly Brothers	1957
25	Who's Sorry Now	Connie Francis	1958
26	All I Have to Do Is Dream	Everly Brothers	1958
Epilogue	Wipeout	The Surfaris	1963

Justice and power must be brought together, so that whatever is just may be powerful, and whatever is powerful may be just.

—BLAISE PASCAL

Chapter One

LA BAMBA

July 1960 — A light drizzle falls as a dark sedan travels down a brick-paved street that winds along fences made of rock and mortar. The car stops inside an entrance guarded by the Mexican police. Loud music resonates from behind a ten-foot-tall stone wall that has shards of broken glass embedded in the top.

This is La Zona Rosa, a seedy place on the outskirts of Nuevo Laredo, Mexico—also known as Boys Town—a favorite hangout for servicemen from the nearby Air Force base and young boys out to lose their virginity.

Sergeant Escobar, a middle-aged policeman with a big belly, pokes his head from inside a small booth in the middle of the entrance. He waves by several cabs loaded with young Air Force cadets, and then pulls the top of a yellow slicker suit up over his shoulders and saunters up beside the sedan. He taps on the driver-side window glass. As the window cranks down, the driver flips the top of a metal Zippo lighter and rolls the flint, igniting a bright-yellow flame. He draws the flame to a Camel cigarette as Escobar leans down and glances inside. Escobar smiles through his mustache as he turns his head to the side, spits a stream of tobacco juice onto the rain-soaked ground and watches it float in a puddle of standing water. Escobar has met the driver many times before.

"Elo, mi amigo."

Elo Turk pulls a long drag on the cigarette and exhales the smoke in Escobar's face. Elo's glass left eye sets him apart in a crowd and makes him look much older than his thirty-eight years. He is quite aware that Sergeant Escobar is really just a slack-jawed local policeman but someone you should never turn your back on. Elo inhales a deep breath through his nose. His instant expression tells us it's a familiar odor that strikes his fancy.

There's just something about this sleazy place that appeals to him. Like an itch that has to be scratched every so often.

"Business or pleasure?" Escobar asks in heavy Tex-Mex accent.

Elo doesn't answer. He reaches his hand out the window and hands Escobar a small envelope.

Escobar opens it and thumbs through a stack of twenty-dollar bills. He's not through counting the money when Elo rolls the window up and shifts the car into gear. Escobar knows he wouldn't have a pot to piss in on a policeman's salary if not for getting a little cut from all the graft and corruption in Boys Town.

"It is almost seven o'clock," shouts Escobar as he attempts to shine a flashlight through the back window of the sedan. "You know the doctor is very punctual." Escobar keeps hollering and waving his flashlight. Elo peers through his driver-side mirror and watches Escobar turn and slosh back to his hut.

A few lights are beginning to flicker on in Boys Town. The place has a small-town carnival appearance at night, but in the light at dusk, it has a more sordid look, especially since brothels and strip joints occupy most of the real estate on both sides of the cobblestone street. There are only five total streets, three east–west streets, and two that cross. The clubs have names like El Papagayo, Marabu, and Bar 1-2-3. On both sides of the main drag, the Mexican police patrol a crowd of regulars and American servicemen that spill out onto the barricaded street.

A couple of cowboys huddle together. One shows the other his empty wallet and says, "The police took all my money. I didn't do nothing." The other cowboy slips him a ten-dollar bill and says, "You got to learn; you can't slap them whores."

Boys Town even has its own small police station and jail. This is not a place a person wants to be locked up in. Many young men found this out the hard way. The police and most of the politicians here are on the take. The only justice is the amount of money someone is willing to pay for their release. If one can't come up with the money, then they are transferred to the main jail in Nuevo Laredo. There, you will be physically assaulted on a daily basis by the hardened criminals who reside there.

Elo strains to see through the windshield of the car as the wipers flip back and forth every so often, sticking to the glass when the rain slows. Up ahead, he makes out the partially lit sign on a stone-and-stucco building that reads, El Clinico. He glances into the rearview mirror and says, "We're almost there."

In the rear seat, a disheveled young Black girl presses her face close to the window. Pearl Lott is very attractive and physically mature for just fifteen years old, but way too young to understand what is about to happen to her. Elo stops the car and turns around facing the rear seat. "Go up and knock on the door. They're expecting you."

Pearl has never been over fifty miles from home, much less all the way to Mexico. She makes out a set of stone steps that lead up to double wooden doors. You can see the absolute terror written on her caramel-toned face.

A sudden gush of fear washes over her. She feels sick to her stomach, her knees are weak, and her hands tremble.

She must make herself open the car door as she looks back at Elo and in a cracking voice asks, "Where are you going to be?"

Elo looks straight ahead. "Never you mind; I'll be back to get you when it's time."

Pearl slides out of the car and climbs the steps to the entrance. The overwhelming sweet-and-sour smell is something very foreign to her. She knocks on the door and waits; nothing happens. Just as she raises her hand to strike the door again, it swings open and now a pungent chemical odor fills her nostrils. She stands face to face with a gray-haired man in his sixties.

He removes a pair of tiny horn-rimmed glasses and wipes the lens on his white medical coat. He speaks in a heavy German accent. "You are late." Pearl knows she has nothing to do with being late. If it was up to her she would be a thousand miles away from here. He grabs her arm and pulls her inside as

4

she glances back over her shoulder and swallows hard, holding back tears when she sees Elo driving away.

The sun has now completely fallen as Elo makes his way along the Main Street of Boys Town. The music has gotten louder. Seems like every club is playing a different tune. Elo's not crazy about the music; in fact, he could do without it. He notices that it's a bigger than usual crowd for a weeknight. He finds an empty space and parks the sedan, steps out, locks the doors, and starts meandering up the street. Up ahead, he notices a group of guys pause under a brick archway with flashing neon lights that reads El Papagayo Club. The young men grin at one another and step inside. This just happens to be Elo's favorite hangout. He decides this must be the place with all the action tonight. He grins, steps up on the curb, and heads toward the entrance.

Elo slips through the saloon-style doors, straddles a stool, and sits sideways to the bar—obviously, a familiar spot for him. He removes a pack of cigarettes from his shirt pocket and his lighter from his khaki pant pocket. He flips out one of the Camels from the pack and lights it with the Zippo. The lighter makes a familiar metal sound when it snaps shut. Elo scans the room for anyone unusual. He has seen most of these women and girls many times before. They range in age from barely legal to way too old to still be doing this.

Inside the El Papagayo is a long wooden bar that sits in the middle of a rather large circular room lined with booths. Cigarette smoke hovers head-high and then slowly rises, leaving a blue haze in the room. A jukebox in the corner spins the latest hits that are completely lost in the rowdy noise of the patrons.

Mexican prostitutes clad in short skirts and high heels work the crowd of men. Some couples sit in booths sipping Tom Collinses and haggling over the price of a few minutes of sex. A mixture of cheap perfume, tobacco, and stale alcohol gives the place a rather unique scent.

Elo watches as an airman folds and slips money inside the bra of a girl who's young enough to have been his prom date. They stand and slide out from a booth. She takes him by the hand as he turns back to his fellow airmen and motions in the air with a closed fist. They all whoop and holler. She grins and then leads him outside to a row of one-room shanties that surround a lush courtyard. The young prostitute slips some pesos to an older woman who unlocks one of the rooms. The young boy wouldn't admit it, but this is his first time and he's nervous as hell. Other than a little touchy-feely in high school, he knows absolutely nothing about sex, but if all goes well and he can perform, he knows that soon he'll be a man among men.

The girl opens the door, steps inside, and motions for the boy to follow. She closes the door behind them. He's embarrassed because he can tell she knows he's a virgin. He glances around the sparse room, noting a bed, a small table with a roll of paper towel on it. Other than those items, the tiny room is empty. She can tell his reluctance by his body language, so she seductively undresses, sits down on the side of the bed and motions for him to approach her. The only women he has ever seen totally naked were in a magazine. This girl doesn't measure up to any of them. She has certain flaws, but he knows he can't back out now. He steps up in front of her, not sure what to do next as he watches her unfasten his belt and unbutton his pants.

Back inside the club, Elo's good eye locks on a teenage prostitute as she approaches the bar. She wears a short skirt and halter top. He obviously recognizes her as his lips curl into a conceited grin. He cuts his eyes her way and exhales a long plume of blue smoke.

She slides up beside him, drops one hand down to his crotch, and whispers in his ear. "Elo, you want to go to the room?" She squeezes his leg. "Only ten dollars for you."

Elo loves the attention. He drops his head, pretends to sniff her cleavage. To Elo, it's that same familiar smell. He pulls a five-dollar bill from his pants pocket and waves it in front of her face, knowing she will refuse it. She jerks back her hand, shakes her head, and in a heavy Tex-Mex accent shouts above the music, "You fucking cheapskate." She walks a few steps, spins around and thrusts her middle finger in the air. "Fuck you, Elo!"

He laughs out loud. It's more of a game than sex for Elo, although if Elo was to ever find love, it would probably be here in Boys Town. He turns to the bartender and slaps a sliver quarter down on the bar.

"*Vargas, drama uno cerveza.*"

Vargas is a tall Mexican man with an extremely long handlebar mustache that curls on the ends. He makes a quick swipe across the top of the bar with a soiled, wet towel and then sets down a bottle of Carta Blanca. He leans across the bar and in his own Tex-Mex accent says, "Elo, my friend, you are never going to get one of the girls acting like that."

Elo sighs like he doesn't care. He turns his attention to a sudden commotion coming from the rear of the club. He snatches up his beer and pushes his way through the crowd toward a back room.

Inside the room stands a man taking money from a long line of patrons. They cheer and holler as they watch a naked woman position herself under a live donkey. Elo spins around and pushes his way back through the crowd. He's seen this show many times before, and it always ends the same way. Elo takes his seat back at the bar and orders another beer. The young airman is already back with his friends and he's holding court. He's going through all the animated motions of the sex act, most of which he probably never even got to. He's proud though, having gone through the rite of passage from a boy to a man, and he has lived to talk about it.

Elo spies Sergeant Escobar standing at the front door and thinks to himself, *Damn! That was quick.* The sergeant motions back over his shoulder toward the street. Elo nods and glances down at his wristwatch. He steps outside the club, pauses on the sidewalk, and lights a cigarette. He looks down at an old, scraggly woman dressed in raggedy clothes, pulling a small wooden wagon. She stops, tugs on his pant leg, and mumbles a few indiscernible words. On a closer look, the woman is missing fingers on both hands and open sores cover her face. Elo jumps back, thinking she has leprosy or something worse. "Don't touch me."

She looks up at him and utters the word, *"Pesos,"* in a high-pitched voice. Her stringy, gray hair looks like a rat has been sucking on it.

Elo shakes his head and then glances inside the wagon and sees two small shoeless toddlers wrapped in filthy blankets shivering in the night air. He digs into his pockets, drops what

8

loose change he can find into the wagon, and then steps off the curb. He makes his way through the crowd and back to his car. Elo maneuvers through the side streets and parks the sedan in front of the medical clinic. He lights another cigarette and slides down in the seat to get comfortable while he waits. Just as he takes the last drag on the cigarette, he hears the rear door open. Elo sits up straight in the seat and looks into the rearview mirror.

Pearly Lott, the young Black girl he dropped off earlier, pulls herself into the car and lies across the back seat. She clutches her abdomen and stifles a cry.

"You okay?" Elo asks.

She doesn't answer. The pain in Pearl's gut is excruciating. It radiates from her stomach to her backbone, taking her breath away. Elo cranks up the engine and flips the cigarette butt out onto the ground. He can hear Pearl begin to sob as he presses the drive button on the automatic transmission. He rolls down his window, thinking the fresh air might make her feel better as he maneuvers the sedan around the barricade and through the throng of men as they stagger from one club to another. The smells of Boys Town carries into the backseat of the car, making Pearl want to vomit.

Elo passes by the guard station and accelerates down the road. He glances up into the rearview mirror. He watches Pearl curl up in the fetal position and press her face against the back of the seat. He wonders why she won't talk to him, at least say something. He lights a cigarette and watches the lights of Boys Town slowly fade away in the distance.

As Elo approaches the Mexican side of the international bridge, he leans around toward the back seat and tries to rouse Pearl. "You need to get up here in the front seat; we're going through immigration." All he can hear is her shallow breathing. He flips on the interior dome light of the sedan and says out loud, "Holy shit!" Elo sees that the rear seat is soaked in bright red blood. Suddenly, his mind begins to race. What he's going to do now? The line of cars has closed in behind him hemming him in. He has nowhere to go but forward. How is he going to make it through both sides of immigration? What's he going to say?

As Elo pulls up in line, a uniformed Mexican officer stops his car and notices Pearl curled up in the rear seat. Elo's heart is pounding a mile a minute. He gestures with his thumb and little finger like she's had too much to drink. To his surprise, the officer waves him through. Now comes the impossible part: getting through the U.S. Border Patrol. Elo travels the short distance across the bridge and uses what little time he has to rehearse his alibi over and over in his head. As he gets closer to the canopy, he is able to make out the unusual confusion at the checkpoint. There are dogs and a slew of agents searching the back of a semi-truck and trailer. They are letting all the other traffic pass through unimpeded. When Elo pulls through the checkpoint, the agent doesn't even attempt to make eye contact with him. After several minutes, he's through downtown Laredo and out on the highway. Elo draws a temporary breath of relief and then floorboards the accelerator. He feels the V-8 engine in the big Chrysler take hold. There's only one thing on his mind and that's getting the hell back to Seclusion.

Chapter Two
YOU'RE SO FINE

One-hundred and forty-miles to the north, a banged-up, green 1952 Dodge Power Wagon with oversized, badly worn tires leaves a dirt road and lumbers out onto a two-lane highway. The pickup truck looks like it belongs in the military instead of on a road in South Texas. The sky is clear and hazy, the kind of haze you get this time of summer when there's a good chance it won't rain for weeks to come. The temperature is already hot and sultry even for this time of morning.

Lizzie Fox, a stunning young woman in her late-twenties, wears boots, jeans, and a plaid blouse with rolled-up sleeves. Lizzie angles the wing window on her door toward her, so it blows outside air into the cab of the truck, and then steers the truck with her knees as she pulls her long, brunette hair back into a ponytail. Why would she be driving a vehicle like this? Because if you knew Lizzie, you would know it was because she can, and it's also the only thing with wheels that she can afford.

Lizzie presses the station buttons on the truck's radio one after the other until she settles in on a song called "You're So Fine." She raps her fingers on the steering wheel to the beat of the music. Just being around Lizzie makes you feel better. She reaches inside a small brown paper sack on the passenger seat, rummages around, and then flips the bag upside down. A pile of Double Bubble gum wrappers falls out. An undeniable expression of disappointment crosses her face. This wasn't what she was hoping to find; she will have to purchase some more gum in town. Lizzie and her family have recently moved to a working cattle ranch outside the small town of Seclusion in search of a fresh start. In fact, they haven't been relocated long enough to have even drawn their first paycheck. Her pickup rolls past a city limit sign that reads "Seclusion Pop. 9129— Public Water Supply Approved."

Up ahead, she spots a fit, muscular, young Black man standing on the corner, thumbing for a ride. Lizzie recognizes him right away. He is one of the cowboys who work on the cattle ranch. Preston Lott is a tall man in his early twenties, wearing a straw hat that shades his chiseled face. Lizzie thinks to herself, *His hand-me-down khaki pants and shirt may be a size too large, but damn, does he wear a cowboy hat well.* He motions to a long line of vehicles and then watches as they all pass him by. He's not annoyed; he's used to it. He turns and continues down the road.

Seconds later, Preston hears the clattering sound of a vehicle right behind him. Unsure what it is, he hurriedly retreats onto the sidewalk, spins around, and watches the Power Wagon thunder up next to the curb.

Lizzie slides across the seat, pokes her head out the passenger side window, and declares, "I wasn't going to hit you."

Preston offers her a look to imply he wasn't so sure.

Lizzie laughs and shakes her head and asks, "What happened to your car?"

"Needs a new battery."

"Jump in. I've got a couple of stops to make ... then I'm headed back to the ranch."

Preston nods and removes his hat. She watches him walk to the rear of the truck, climb over the tailgate, and sit down on the fender well. She wonders what the hell has got into him as she taps on the back glass and motions for him to get inside the cab with her. He shakes his head; Preston knows the good White people of Seclusion wouldn't take too kindly seeing a Black man riding in the front seat with a White woman. Lizzie coaxes the old Power Wagon back onto the road and heads down the highway in search of a service station.

The old truck rumbles under the canopy of a Texaco service station and slows to a stop. A uniformed station attendant moseys over to the driver-side window. The little old man wears a hat with the Texaco logo and carries a red rag in his back pocket. You can tell by his body language that he's proud of his job and feels quite important. He cuts his eyes at Preston and jokingly asks in a very slow, articulate tone, "Fill her up?" Preston gestures in Lizzie's direction. The attendant turns his attention to Lizzie. He stands on his tippy-toes, pokes his head close to the open window, and attempts to peer inside the pickup.

Lizzie pushes him away, hands him a handful of loose change, and in a stern, slow voice says, "Dollar seventy-five of the Sky Chief and check the oil, please."

"We don't service the vehicle for less than five dollars of gas," he says very matter-of-factly.

Lizzie shoves her door open, jumps out, snatches the red rag from his back pocket and then jerks open the hood, removes the dip stick, and wipes the oil from it with his clean rag. She checks the level, stabs it back inside the engine, and pitches him back his rag all in the blink of an eye.

"Oil's okay," she says to him while giving him a side-eye glare.

He is obviously taken aback as he just stands there with his mouth open before spreading the money out in the palm of his hand and methodically counting it with his index finger. He steps over beside the regular pump and asks in a very condescending tone, "You sure you don't want the regular? You get more."

Not to be intimated, Lizzie snaps back, "No, I'm pretty sure I said premium."

The attendant walks back over to the next pump. He keeps his eye on the ticking numbers while Lizzie fiddles with the truck's radio. It doesn't take long to pump five gallons of gasoline. He doesn't want to put a penny more on the register than she called for. He trains his eyes back on Preston as he hangs the nozzle back in the pump.

Lizzie presses on the truck's starter and listens as it hesitates and drags, making a loud grating sound until it finally spins fast enough to fire up the flathead six-cylinder engine.

Lizzie presses the clutch pedal hard against the floorboard and shifts the Power Wagon into first gear. To her surprise the gears, don't grind as loudly as they usually do.

The attendant watches as the Power Wagon thunders out onto the street and fades out of sight into traffic. Lizzie and Preston pass under a large banner stretched across the road that reads, "Seclusion County Fair July 1960." She takes a quick read of the banner before making a U-turn in the middle of the street. She angle parks in front of a two-story building that has a sign with large letters across its facade that spell out, "Seclusion Timely Remarks."

Lizzie climbs out of the truck and motions back to Preston. "I'll just be minute."

Preston shoots her an approving glance and says, "Yes ma'am." Lizzie keeps walking all the while thinking to herself, *What is this ma'am stuff?*

A couple of flyers hanging inside the front door of the newspaper office get her attention. One says, "Help Wanted," and the other reads, "Room for Rent."

She pauses long enough to read them and then hurries to the grocery store next door. Lizzie pulls open the plate glass door to the grocery store and bumps into a hunched-over old Mexican man burdened with several large paper bags full of groceries.

She steps back, holds open the door, and in her best rendition of the Spanish language says, *"Lo siento, señor."*

Obviously surprised by the kind gesture and her Spanish, the old man smiles and steps through the door. He turns back, looks her up and down, and in Spanish, approvingly says, "*Gracias, señorita.*"

Lizzie gestures her thanks to the old man, makes her way inside the store, and begins to stroll down the aisles. Groceries and a few cheap clothes make up many of the wares. Lizzie's first impression of the place, any place, is always how it smells. O'Connor's Grocery gives off an odor of baked goods and freshly popped popcorn, with a subtle hint of a little rancid meat mixed in.

Lizzie picks up a small basket and fills it with a carton of eggs, quart of milk, loaf of bread, and a pound of bacon. She picks up a small bunch of unmarked bananas and motions to the clerk standing by the register.

"How much?"

The clerk and owner, a middle-aged man with a splotchy, Irish complexion, doesn't even look her way for a while. When he does raise his head to see where the voice came from, he sees that he doesn't recognize her. In his mind, she's what the good citizens of Seclusion refer to as comers and goers. In other words, they have no roots in the community. They're just here one day and gone the next, so it makes no sense to waste his time on them. He raises his voice in a snotty tone, "If you have to ask, you can't afford 'em."

The comment pisses Lizzie off. She sets the fruit back down, gives him a look from hell, and proceeds toward the register. It's not the first time she's been insulted by an old man. The clerk lifts his head and finds himself staring at Lizzie.

She drops the basket down by the register with a noticeable thud and spies a large glass bowl full of bubble gum sitting on the shelf behind him.

He glances inside the basket at the groceries and then removes the items one by one with one hand and with the other hand adds them up on a hand-cranked adding machine.

"That'll be a buck ninety-five."

Lizzie unfolds two one-dollar bills from her back pocket and digs deep into a front pocket for change. She counts the coins one by one, and then points to the glass bowl on the shelf behind him.

"I also want ten cents worth of the Double Bubble."

He twists around, grabs the bowl and pulls it down to the counter, and then reaches inside, grabs a handful of gum and dumps it into a small paper sack.

Obviously, he's short on patience and wants to make her aware of it. He meticulously folds the bags closed, and then removes his glasses, looks her in the eye, and says in a slow and deliberate tone, "Two dollars and five cents."

He places the groceries inside a brown paper bag. Lizzie spreads two-dollar bills and five pennies on the counter. She picks up the gum-filled sack and peers inside and exclaims, "You shorted me."

He eyes her up and down and says, "You sayin' I cheated you?"

She drags two pennies across the counter, scoops them up in her hand, and stares him in the eye and says, "No, sir! I'm saying I overpaid you."

She grabs up the sack of groceries, marches toward the door, glances back at the clerk, and grumbles under her breath, "Asshole!"

The clerk's eyes may be bad, but his hearing is spot on. He turns his head and stares at Lizzie over his bifocals as she swings open the door and steps out onto the sidewalk. She pauses briefly and then strolls next door to the newspaper office. She opens the door, jerks a blue flyer loose from a tack, and reads it and then folds and stuffs it in her back pocket.

Preston jumps from the bed of the pickup, takes the bag of groceries, and places them on the passenger seat.

Lizzie glances up and down the street. "Looks like I've done all the damage I have money for today." She climbs behind the wheel, takes a quick look in the rearview mirror, sees Preston settle back down on the fender well, and then hits the starter on the truck.

Lizzie slams the truck into reverse, backs out into the middle of Main Street, shifts gears and heads back in the direction she came. She changes the stations on the truck's radio; all she can find are commercials.

She pulls the sack of bubble gum from the grocery bag that sits on the seat beside her and then latches onto a piece and removes the wrapper with her teeth and pops it into her mouth. In no time, she's out of Seclusion and rolling down the highway.

She peers down the road in front of her and then takes a quick glance in the rearview mirror. She notices that for the moment she's alone on a straight stretch of two-lane highway. She whips the truck to the side of the road and stops, turns around in the seat, taps on the back glass and motions for Preston to get up front.

He hops from the truck bed and runs up to the passenger-side window, thinking he was quite comfortable where he was.

"Are you sure?"

Lizzie flashes her eyes and cocks her head to one side, "Hey, it's my truck."

With a reluctant look on his face, he slides inside the truck and shuts the door. "You know what I mean." She doesn't answer, just smiles and shows him the bag of gum. "Want a piece of bubble gum?"

He shakes his head. "No, ma'am."

Lizzie turns her head toward him. "What's this, 'No, ma'am?' I'm not your mother; you call me Lizzie like everyone else."

Still not comfortable, he glances down at the floorboard and says, "Yes, ma'am."

Lizzie shakes her head and sighs, "There you go again."

Chapter Three

YAKETY YAK

Lizzie shifts the truck into first gear; she grimaces when the transmission grinds and makes a sound like it's chewing up metal.

Preston remarks, "Sounds like the clutch is going out."

Lizzie answers, "It's been doing that since I bought her." Then laughing, she adds, "Don't get a helluva lot these days for two-hundred dollars." She presses on the accelerator, the pick-up's rear tires spin and throw gravel as she clips the city limits sign and fishtails back onto the pavement.

Lizzie's hand moves back toward the radio, when she hears the disk jockey in a deep, radio voice say, "I'm Bruce Hathaway and you're listening to the top fifty-five on KTSA, San Antonio. Going back to nineteen fifty-eight, it's The Coasters and, 'Yakety Yak.'" She sings along, strumming her fingers on the steering wheel.

In the side mirror, Lizzie catches the glimpse of a car approaching them from behind at a high rate of speed. Preston sees it, too; he hunches down in the seat so as not to be seen.

Lizzie sees him. "What the hell are you doing? It's just kids." She pokes her arm out of the side window and waves her hand. The car is full of teenagers. They blare their horn, wave, and zoom past Lizzie's old Power Wagon.

"Wonder where they're headed," Lizzie says.

"I bet to the beach."

"You know, I've never been to the beach. Not a real one anyway, not much water in Duncan, Oklahoma," Lizzie says with a slight grin.

"It's less than forty miles from here."

"That's okay. I'm not that crazy about water."

She blows a small bubble. The utter disappointment shows on her face when it pops across her nose.

"Someday, I'm going to learn how to blow a fucking bubble." Coming from her, the language surprises him, but he doesn't let on. She downshifts the pickup, sticks her arm outside the open window, and signals for a left turn.

The Power Wagon veers off the highway, bounces onto a rough, single-lane caliche dirt road. Milkweed and Johnsongrass flourish right up next to the edge of the road. Combined with the overhead willow trees, they seem to form a tunnel of green.

"Hold on," Lizzie says, as she steps on the gas.

A white cloud of caliche dust trails the truck and then quickly disappears as it splashes through a low-water crossing. Lizzie likes to plow through the clear, shallow water, glance into her rearview mirror, and follow the stream as the two sides of parted water join back in the middle. Further down the road, she honks the truck's horn. She and Preston both wave.

They've spotted a couple of mounted cowboys driving a remuda of horses up the bank of a tree-lined creek. She smiles as the cowboys' wave back.

"That little creek is so pretty. What's it called?" she asks.

"Silver Creek. It runs into the Aransas River a few miles from here. That river is full of gators."

Lizzie doesn't comment. She shows her distaste for alligators with a scrunched-up nose and a squinted eye.

The old truck bounces across a steel cattle guard and under a metal arch that stretches above the road. The hand-welded piece of art references a cowboy and cowgirl lassoing a sign that reads, "Nolan Ranch." Further down the road, they approach a two-story, plantation-type home with a wraparound veranda surrounded by live oak trees and date palms. The yard is meticulously groomed with green grass and an assortment of flowers and shrubs. The smell of freshly cut St. Augustine wafts through the cab of the truck. A half-dozen or so men can be seen around the house doing chores.

Among them is Elo Turk. The sunlight reflects in his glass eye as he steadies a paint-smeared ladder against the side of the house. He stares at Lizzie and Preston as they pass in front of the house. Lizzie sets her eyes on a light green, government sedan idling on a circular driveway in front of the house.

She glances out her window and follows two immigration officers as they load a Mexican couple into the backseat of the sedan. She takes her foot from the accelerator and lets the truck slow while she flashes Preston an inquisitive gaze.

"What the hell is that about?"

He clears his throat as if he's hesitant to put the answer into words, but Lizzie persists.

"Well?"

"Wetbacks. The Nolans put them to work for little to nothing, and then call immigration when it's time to pay them."

"That's not right. They're breaking the law, too."

Preston agrees, but she doesn't give him time to acknowledge.

"Well, they are. Someone needs to tell the authorities."

Preston just looks at her and thinks, *She's got a lot to learn.* This is Seclusion where those who break the law and those who enforce the law are usually one and the same.

A mile or so away from the plantation home, the dust from the truck settles in front of a rundown, wood-frame house looking decidedly the worse for wear. Cattle pens, barns, and sheds surround the house. A sagging net-wire fence with crooked cedar posts separates the yard from the pasture; otherwise, you would never know the difference in the barren ground. Lizzie brakes to a stop and kills the engine on the Power Wagon. Preston jumps from the truck and sprints to a large gate that leads to a large corral. He unfastens the latch, swings it open and then jumps back out of the way.

Lizzie steps out onto the truck's running board, shields her eyes from the sun with the back of her hand, and follows each horse as they gallop through the open gate and gather inside the pen.

The horses run in a tight circle, nickering and snorting, before they finally settle down and adjust to the closed pen.

One by one, they gather around a large, circular cement water trough located in the center of the corral. The long drive from an adjacent pasture, not to mention a glaring July sun, has the horses parched and thirsty. They dip their noses completely under the surface and siphon up the cool liquid. Goldfish nibble on the dark green algae, and then dart back and forth under the clear water. Lizzie is fascinated by the makeup of the remuda. There are roans, sorrels, bays, and chestnuts. There is nothing about a horse that she doesn't love. Preston closes the gates, snaps the swivel latch closed on the chain lock, and then cuts the wire on a couple of hay bales. He scatters alfalfa along the fence inside the pen.

Cyrus Jones pulls his horse to a stop beside the pen gate. Cyrus is a middle-aged man whose face and personality tend to reveal someone who has fought more than his share of demons. Lizzie and Cyrus have survived their tumultuous relationship for five years. In Texas, it's sometimes called a common law marriage with some sort of documentation, but Lizzie and Cyrus have done nothing to justify a legal partnership. She's just hoping a new job means a new beginning for them.

Cyrus leads a tall buckskin horse with a nose that is distorted and bleeding from two fang wounds. The horse makes a wheezing sound as he labors to breathe through his bloated nose. "This one and the one Sam's leading are snake-bit," Cyrus says as he removes his sweat-stained, brown felt hat and wipes his brow with his shirt sleeve. Cyrus's thinning hair is wet and matted and his sideburns extend well below his earlobes. He climbs down from his horse and removes his leather chaps that blend in well with his khaki pants and shirt. He hangs the chaps on one of many nails that have been driven into the bark of a large mesquite tree, and then hands off the buckskin to Preston.

"Put him in the barn so we can doctor his nose."

Preston takes hold of the halter's lead rope and walks the injured horse toward the barn while Lizzie steps down from the running board and approaches Cyrus.

"Where's Sam?"

Cyrus points over his shoulder and behind him. "He's coming."

Sam Fox, a lanky twelve-year-old, sits tall in the saddle. His Levi's jeans and long-sleeve shirt help protect form the searing rays of a South Texas sun. Sam is Lizzie's only child, born out of wedlock, but nevertheless the love of her life. Sam leads a limping gelding to the pens. The young horse barely puts any weight on his swollen foot. White and yellow pus oozes from the snakebite wounds.

"Got him good. Looks to have been a week or so ago. Probably would be healing up if not for the goddamn blowflies," Cyrus says as he bends down and picks up a mesquite twig and then scrapes dried blood and puss from the gelding's foot. He digs out a squirmy little white worm from deep inside one of the fang wounds and flicks it onto the ground. "Another week and the screwworms would'a got 'em both." Lizzie ruffles the back of her son's head and hands him a piece of Double Bubble.

Lizzie can smell the rotted flesh from the worms. She rubs the gelding neck. "You think it was rattlers?"

Cyrus nods his head and illustrates with a closed fist showing the probable size of the snake's head. "Both big, like rattlesnakes."

Sam climbs down from his horse, takes the gum, smiles and pats the gelding's back, and asks, "Is Winslow gonna die?"

Cyrus shakes his head. "Nope, but he'll be stove-up for a while."

Sam then unwraps the gum and begins to slowly lead Winslow away in the direction of the barn. Cyrus hollers to him, "I'll be in there shortly. We'll put some medicine on those snakebites." He turns his attention back to Preston.

"Find any cowhands?"

"Yeah, a couple of them are Mexican boys, but they know cattle."

"Is it true what they say about this thicket pasture?" Cyrus asks.

"It's awful brushy … cattle are wild as hell and there's a mean-ass Brahma bull the vaqueros have named Diablo."

Cyrus removes a pack of Lucky Strike cigarettes and a penny box of matches from his shirt pocket. He thumps a cigarette from the pack, lights it, and draws a deep breath. "Guess we'll find out soon enough."

"I told them to be ready in a couple of weeks," Preston adds.

Just then Lizzie interrupts, "Saw lots of banners strung across Main Street. Town's getting ready for a big parade this afternoon."

Preston chimes in. "And the rodeo is tonight." Then he turns to Cyrus and adds, "They have a youth calf-roping Sam can enter."

"Now we're talking," Lizzie says in excitement.

Cyrus shakes his head. "He ain't got no roping horse."

Preston takes Lizzie's side. "He can ride mine."

Lizzie doesn't let it drop. "Why not? I think it would fun."

Cyrus cuts his eyes and frowns at Lizzie. He contorts his face and shakes his head, a look she's seen many times before. The expression tells her to drop it, but this time she doesn't. She stands her ground and says, "I think it will be good for him." She wheels around to Preston. "We'll see you there tonight, after the parade."

She turns and hurries over to the Power Wagon before Cyrus can catch her eye again. She opens the truck's passenger-side door, grabs the sack of groceries, marches through the yard gate, and hops up the steps to a porch with a low-pitched roof.

Then, she jerks open the front screen door with one hand. A spring fastened to the wall makes a twanging sound as it stretches against the open door. She steps inside, lets the door slap-shut behind her. The house has a musty old smell, like no one has lived in it for quite some time.

The interior has a box-like appearance, sparsely furnished with used furniture and secondhand appliances. The icebox shows rust from the humid, salty air. The ceilings throughout the house are so low that she can visualize Cyrus's hat scraping the ceiling of every small room. She welcomes an infrequent breeze blowing through the copper window screens, taking a bite of the stifling heat. Looking around, Lizzie knows it is what it is and she'll make it do because she actually has no other choice.

She sets the sack on the kitchen counter, opens the ice-box door, and notices that it's totally empty. She feels the metal shelves; they're cool but not cold. She places the milk, eggs, and bacon inside, opens the plastic door to the freezer above, and notices a huge chunk of ice that leaves little room for anything else.

She knows it'll have to wait; she won't have time to defrost it today. The kitchen has a small table with three chairs next to a three-burner gas cooking stove. Other than that, there isn't much room for anything else. She looks out the rear window above the sink and notices a hog pen about twenty yards from the back fence. She thinks that should make for a nice smell this coming winter during a Blue Norther.

Lizzie hears the screen door open. She spins around and sees Cyrus walk into the back bedroom. He shouts at her from inside the room's closet. "You got something else to wear? We might run into the Nolans."

Lizzie hollers back at him. "I didn't know we were going this early." He steps into the kitchen wearing a clean shirt and carrying his hat. "I'll be back in a few minutes; you and the boy be ready." He takes a few steps, and then turns back around.

"Next time I tell you no something … you need to listen."

Lizzie doesn't answer; she lets it slide. It's not worth the confrontation right before what could turn out to be a fun day for Sam.

She hears the screen door slap shut, so she hurries into the bathroom and combs her hair while yelling, "Hurry up, Sam. We don't want to make him wait."

She sits back on the bed, slips out of her jeans and blouse and into a yellow sundress with a pleated skirt. She smiles when she glances at a framed picture on the nightstand beside her. It was taken five years ago of her accepting the New Writer Award while she worked at the *Dallas Morning News*. Other than some photos of her and Sam, she doesn't have much to reflect back on her life. Growing up in foster care for the most part didn't allow for many mementos.

Just as she slides on a pair of white flats, she hears Cyrus blaring the horn on the truck. She and Sam run out of the house, dart through the front gate, and jump into the passenger side of the Power Wagon. Cyrus cranks up the engine, flips a cigarette butt out onto the ground and mutters, "I told y'all to be ready."

It's early in the afternoon in Seclusion. The local schools have let out early for the day. People jam the sidewalks on both sides of Main Street as far as the eye can see. In the distance, Lizzie hears the distinct sound of a siren. She is surprised to see this many people show up for a parade.

She looks over the crowd and notices a Black mother and her children step off the curb to let a White family pass on the sidewalk. Lizzie moves out into the street and shields her eyes from the glare of the west sun. Through the heat shimmers, she makes out flags that seem to be waving in a pool of water. She knows that the water is just a mirage, but the flags are the beginning of the parade. "I can see it coming."

Sam is terribly excited. "Is it the horses…? Is it Preston?" Cyrus hears Sam ask about Preston. The one-sided grin on his face reveals a tinge of jealousy on his part.

Lizzie doesn't notice as she steps back onto the sidewalk, grins at Sam, and says, "No, it's not Preston. Sounds like a band."

Cyrus glances back over his shoulder and sees Maude Nolan, the wife of his boss, Phil Nolan. She is a tall woman in her fifties. Cyrus watches her knock on a glass door with gold letters that spell out "Cattlemen's State Bank." The front of the building is red brick with a series of tall, narrow windows facing a courtyard dotted with planters full of green plants and ivy. The place just reeks of money, lots and lots of money.

He nudges Lizzie in her side. "There's Phil Nolan's wife … go say hello."

Lizzie is reluctant and resists. "Now?"

Cyrus is visibly put out with her. "Goddammit, that's my boss's wife. What tha' hell you want, an invitation?"

Lizzie drops her head, weaves through the throng of bodies, hurries over, and extends her hand. "Hello, Mrs. Nolan, I'm Lizzie Fox and I just wanted…" About that same time, someone from inside the bank swings the glass door open. Maude Nolan gives Lizzie a patronizing glance and without a word, steps inside.

Lizzie makes her way back through the crowd, stands between Cyrus and Sam. They watch the U.S. Navy Band from nearby Chase Field lead the parade while playing the familiar song "Anchors Aweigh."

Cyrus leans down to Lizzie and asks. "What'd she say?"

Lizzie doesn't take her eyes from the parade. "Absolutely nothing."

Cyrus looks at Lizzie, and then back in the direction of the bank. "Were you nice?"

Lizzie answers in almost a shout to be heard above the band. "Nicer than she was." As Lizzie surveys the crowd, a little girl about six years old catches her eye. She sits on the curb between her parents and drinks from a paper cup brimming with iced, strawberry soda water. Suddenly, a bystander passes by bumps her arm and she spills the soda out across the pavement.

Lizzie watches as the child's father, a vulgar-looking Mexican man known to the locals as Javelina, snatches her up by her arm and pulls her to the sidewalk. As he jerks off his belt, Lizzie is reminded of her own childhood by the familiar sound the belt makes snapping through the loops on his pants. He spins the little girl around while she screams. "No, Daddy!" Lizzie can tell this isn't the first time she's been whipped by her abusive father. Lizzie's eyes blink with every crack of the leather. Only a slight whimper leaves the little girl's lips as she limps back to the street.

Lizzie is furious. She wants to say something, but as difficult as it is, she holds her tongue.

The little girl is embarrassed and turns her body away from Lizzie. Javelina catches Lizzie's stare as he ambles back to the parade. "What the hell you looking at?" Lizzie doesn't answer. Again, she avoids confrontation and turns her head.

They watch the high school band march up the street toward them playing their fight song, "Dixie," followed by the volunteer fire department's best engine motoring by with children throwing candy from the back of the fire truck. Lizzie snatches a cherry sucker out of mid-air and hands it to Sam. Cyrus grabs the candy out of Sam's hand. "Sweets bad for his teeth. I ain't got money for no dentists." He flips out a cigarette, lights it, and blows a blue smoke ring into the hot air.

Cowboys on horses whoop and holler as they bring up the rear of the parade. Sam recognizes Preston riding with a

group of Black cowboys. "Look there he is ... there's Preston."
Sam puckers up and does his best whistle. Preston and the cowboys wave. Sam turns to his mother. "I'm gonna ride next year."

A proud grin settles on Lizzie's face as she puts her arm around him and pulls him close. "Yes, you are."

The last group of horses passes and turns the corner. Lizzie, Sam, and Cyrus step off the curb and onto the street. Lizzie gets a strange feeling as if someone is staring at her. She glances around and sees nothing. Her eyes roll up to the balcony on the bank building. Maude Nolan chats with a group of men dressed in business suits. Lizzie watches Maude hand a drink to Bishop O'Malley, an obvious man of the cloth and an obvious glass of whiskey. Lizzie's eyes trail over to the corner of the balcony. She feels a cold shiver run up her spine when she spots Maude's husband, Phil Nolan, another red-faced Irishman in his fifties. Nolan sips from a whiskey glass filled with a little ice and a lot of straight bourbon. An insipid grin creeps across his face as he winks at her. Lizzie figures just her run of luck, another pervert to add to the long list she's managed to run across in her life. She quickly breaks eye contact and turns away.

Later that evening, the parade crowd gathers at the fairgrounds located a few miles outside of Seclusion. The lights from the carnival illuminate a vast area of the grounds. It sports rides like the Tilt-a-Whirl, the Zipper, the Scrambler, and of course, a Ferris wheel, with the usual games of chance lined up on both sides and down the middle.

Lizzie, Cyrus, and Sam stroll through the midway. Cyrus makes a disgusting face, shakes his head, "These carny people give me the creeps."

Lizzie leans down, whispers in Sam's ear. "We only have money for one ride, so you need to hurry and pick one." Sam is like all kids his age; one is never enough. He looks at each one several times, and then blurts out, "Tilt-a-Whirl." Lizzie swallows hard; she was afraid he'd choose that one. She takes a breath, takes hold of his hand. "Let's go get in line."

They scoot in one of the cars and pull the safety bar down across their laps. She hears it lock and thinks to herself, *I hope I don't puke on everyone.* The idea of backing out crosses her mind, but hell no, she'll ride the damn thing for her son. She watches the carny release the long-handle brake and rev up the engine. The smell of the exhaust fumes already has her a little woozy. She grabs hold of the bar and thinks to herself, *Fuck me! What have I done?* She takes a quick glance at Sam. He is loving it and laughing out loud.

She makes it about halfway through the ride okay, and then it seems like the car gets caught in a vortex and won't stop spinning. That's when the nausea really kicks in. It starts in her throat, and then moves in both directions, up to her head and down to her gut. She just hopes she can hold it together and not vomit in front of everyone. The ride finally slows and then abruptly stops when the carnival worker sets the brake.

Lizzie can't speak or she will lose it. She's feels terribly dizzy as she staggers down the metal steps. Just when her feet hit solid ground an overpowering sweet smell of cotton candy and candy apples hits her. She fights the urge to upchuck and only manages to beat it back when the spinning in her head stops.

An hour or so later, Lizzie and Cyrus sit among the spectators in the stands at the rodeo arena. Preston and Sam stand behind the closed arena gate. They watch as another young boy and his horse bolt from the chute and sprint up behind a running calf. He casts a long loop with his rope and watches the lasso tumble empty onto the soft sand.

The rodeo announcer's voice echoes on the loudspeaker. "No time for this young cowboy. All he's get is your applause. Next up is Sam Fox." Sam hops up on Preston's horse and asks, "Are you sure?"

Preston slaps the horse on the rump. "You just worry about roping; Poco will take care of the rest."

Lizzie watches Sam and Poco trot out into the arena. She is terribly nervous, but so proud for her young son. She feels her palms turn sweaty, and her stomach, still somewhat churning from the ride, rolls over again. Sam pulls his hat down tight on his head and clinches the pigging string tight between his teeth.

He rides into the roping box and backs Poco in the corner. Preston stands next to the chute beside Poco. He rubs the horse's neck and verbally coaches Sam. Preston watches the calf's head and when everything is right, he gives Sam the word. "Now, Sam." Sam nods his head, the gate opens, and the calf dashes out of the chute. Sam feels a sudden rush as Poco explodes from the roping box and closes the distance to the calf. Sam swings and watches the loop slip snugly around the animal's neck. Poco plants his long legs into the soft sand of the arena, his sudden stop launches Sam down the rope and onto the calf. Sam ties three legs and throws his hands high into the air. The crowd in the bleachers applauds and cheers. Lizzie stands, claps her hands.

She is beside herself and feels overwhelmed with pride. "Oh my, that was so good." She looks over at Cyrus, who sits there stone-faced. "Wasn't that just great?"

Cyrus grinds his cigarette butt into the bleacher floor with the heel of his boot.

"He didn't win no money."

"That's not the point," Lizzie answers.

Cyrus grabs her arm, guides her down the row of seats to the steps. "Let's go."

She pulls back. "Wait, we have to watch Preston."

Cyrus nudges her forward. "That's who you really came to see ... ain't it?"

Lizzie hears the remark, but she doesn't acknowledge it. Disgusted, she shakes her head. No sense getting into a full-fledged fight in this situation. As they make their way down the steps of the bleachers, Lizzie catches glimpses of Preston as he jumps on Poco and makes a couple of practice swings. They exit the stands to the side and Lizzie temporarily loses sight of Preston.

Suddenly, the crowd roars. Lizzie runs to the arena fence and sees Preston stepping back up on Poco as the calf lies firmly tied on the ground.

"Damn, that was so fast, I missed it."

She whistles loudly and claps her hands. Cyrus grabs her elbow and shakes her arm. "Stop that; you're makin' a spectacle of yourself."

Just then, the announcer says. "That's your winner, folks."

Lizzie turns to face Cyrus. "Bet you can't say he didn't win any money."

Cyrus spins around and walks off. It's obvious he didn't like the remark. The announcer continues, "When Preston Lott ain't rodeoing, you can catch him playing semi-pro football over in Victoria for the Blackcats."

Lizzie and Sam hop up into the passenger side of the pickup for the ride home. Cyrus climbs in and starts the engine. There is dead silence. After a few miles, Sam is asleep on his mother's shoulder. Lizzie has her arm extended out the window. A blank expression sets fixed on her face as she stares out into the darkness of the night. She rolls the palm of her hand up and down and lets it ride the gusty breeze like a wing on an airplane. She wonders how much more of Cyrus' abuse she will be able to take. She just doesn't want to give up now for Sam's sake. She doesn't want to be a quitter.

Chapter Four
WESTERN MOVIES

It's straight-up noon. Cyrus and Lizzie sit at the kitchen table. The air feels so thick and humid you could almost cut it with a dull knife. The blue flyer from the newspaper office lies crumpled up on the table. Cyrus wipes up the remaining gravy on his plate with a piece of white bread and stuffs it into his mouth. Lizzie's plate of chicken and rice remains untouched in front of her.

"I just thought it would be chance for us to make a little extra money," Lizzie says as she wipes perspiration from her brow with a dish towel. "Maybe buy a couple of fans so we can all sleep at night."

"We ain't never had fans before. Why we need 'em now?"

"This place gets no breeze with all the barns and sheds so close to the house."

"Well, you can forget about it 'cause we can't afford 'em!"

"That's the whole point," Lizzie snaps back.

Cyrus's bottom lip quivers as he slams his fist down on the table and shouts, "I thought this was gonna be a fresh start for me."

"Just for you … don't you think we deserve a life, too?"

Cyrus abruptly stands. "You the one saying the boy needs a man in the house. What kind of man ain't got no land and makes his woman work? Well, I ain't sorry enough to be both."

Lizzie pitches the dish towel the short distance to the counter. She gets up from the table, picks up her plate, and drops it in the bottom of the empty porcelain sink. It makes a sharp cracking sound like a plate does when it breaks in half. "I don't even have a telephone."

Cyrus is quick to correct her. "There's one over at the camp house."

She feigns a smile. "Yeah, so Phil Nolan can listen to every word. Besides, I don't like the way he looks at me."

Cyrus rolls his eyes. "Oh, goddamn here we go again. Every man you see wants you."

"I said he acts like a lecherous old drunk," she says while thinking to herself, *and I've been around plenty of them.* Lizzie must bite her lip to keep from saying it, but she's learned better over the years.

"You don't have any idea what's he's like," Cyrus says as he scoops up his hat. "Anyway, that's him and not me. I ain't had a drink in a year."

Lizzie doesn't miss the opportunity to jab him. "Won't be a year until next month." She watches his expression turn from anger to a smirk.

"Oh yeah; you be sure and not let me forget."

She thinks she might be going too far, so she changes the subject. "Sam wants to go to the drive-in movie tonight."

Cyrus takes a step and stops. "That's just a bunch of damned foolishness."

She purses her lips and says, "Not to Sam; he's just a kid."

Cyrus pulls his hat tight down on his head, "Sam, my ass." He grins sarcastically. "You the one wants to go." In a huff, he storms out of the room and past Sam sitting in the living room. The young boy plays on one of Lizzie's old typewriters and pretends not to listen. His eyes blink when he hears the screen door slam hard against the doorjamb.

From outside the house, Cyrus hollers back to Sam. "You want to work like a cowboy ... you'd better come on." Sam jumps up, puts on his straw cowboy hat, and bolts out the screen door. He runs and catches up with Cyrus as they walk to the barn where Preston and the other cowhands are busy trimming the hoofs and shearing the manes on the remuda. He watches Preston finish up one of the other horses and asks Cyrus, "Can I give Winslow a haircut?"

Cyrus looks over at Preston and nods his head. "Yeah, go catch him."

Sam grins, picks a rope, and forms a loop. He knows he's getting to do something pretty darn special as he maneuvers slowly through the horses and singles out Winslow from the rest of the bunch. He holds the open loop out in front of his body and slowly eases up to face the horse. Winslow is not afraid, as he almost pokes his head inside the loop like he was ready to be caught. Sam leads him under the shed where the action is taking place. They watch him reach for the electric shearers that are resting in a gallon can that is half full of kerosene. His hand slips off the cutters; they weigh far more than he had anticipated. He shoots them a look like what do I do now?

Preston finally says, "You're going to have to use both hands." One of the vaqueros goes inside the barn and comes back with wooden milk stool for Sam to stand on. A little while later, he's balanced on top of the stool and precariously holding the shears with both hands as he gives Winslow a haircut.

Cyrus bends down and rubs his fingers across Winslow's injured front foot and remarks, "Looks like the snakebite healed up real well."

Preston nods his head in agreement and adds, "The buckskin, too."

One by one, all the horses in the remuda have their manes and hoofs trimmed and suffer through a homemade tried-and-true remedy for ear ticks. Preston grabs a broomstick cut to about two feet in length with a cloth wrapped on one end and tied with twine string. He dips the cloth's covered end inside a bucket that holds a mixture of Peerless worm medicine and axle grease. One sorrel mare is having no part of the ear job. A vaquero picks up a short wooden handle with a small trace chain looped on one end, called a nose twitch. He slips the chain over his wrist, grabs the mare's nose and slides the chain up and over her nose. Then, he twists the handle and applies pressure to the horse's upper lip. The mare stands calmly and lets Preston work the mixture up and down and around in her ears. After all the cutting, trimming, and doctoring, the horses, except for one, are turned out into a small trap for the night.

Cyrus gives the remuda a once-over before saying, "Put the buckskin in a stall, we'll keep him for a night horse."

That evening, Cyrus steers the Power Wagon into the entrance to Seclusion's El Rancho Drive-In Theatre and past a lighted sign with plastic letters that reads, *Rio Bravo.* The ground is covered in pea gravel. The tires on the Power Wagon make a loud crunching sound as he aims the truck into an empty space. Cyrus stops and kills the engine. He pulls a box speaker from a pedestal stand and hangs it on the side window of the truck. A Tom and Jerry cartoon plays on the screen. Sam laughs out loud before saying. "We're late. It's already started." Lizzie nudges Sam's leg and tightens her brow as she motions for him not to agitate Cyrus.

They've been watching the movie for over an hour. Sam is about to doze off when he sees a kid walking back from the concession stand with a soft drink in one hand and popcorn in the other. "Mama, can I have a soda pop and some popcorn?"

She turns to Cyrus, who doesn't acknowledge her. She leans around to face him. "Do you have any money?"

He keeps his eyes on the screen. "Nope ... took everything I had to get us in here."

Lizzie digs into her jean's pockets and counts out several coins. "You can have one or the other, not both."

Sam thinks a moment. "Can I have a root beer?"

Cyrus abruptly sits up straight and seizes on the opportunity to leave. "Drink it on the way home ... it's getting late."

Sam catches his mother eye. "I don't want to leave."

Lizzie knows this is one of those battles that's not worth the time or the effort. She speaks softly in Sam's ear. "You want to work cattle in the morning?" He nods his head.

The humid wind blowing through the pickup's windows is hot from the afternoon sun. The young boy chugs a big gulp of soda, wipes his mouth with the front of his sleeved, and hands it to Lizzie. She grins, takes a sip, and offers it to Cyrus. He shakes his head, then guides the pickup under the canopy of a service station. Lizzie hands the soda back to Sam.

"Why are we stopping?" Lizzie asks as he parks the truck and pushes the door open.

"Got to pick up some smokes."

Lizzie turns on the truck's radio. She watches Cyrus mosey up to the counter, pull a folding bill from his wallet, and buy several packs of cigarettes. She glances at the soda pop bottle Sam holds and thinks, *Broke one minute and buying cigarettes the next.* She shakes her head, tunes in her favorite station on the radio, and hears, "KTSA San Antonio, Ricci Ware with you tonight and here are the Olympics with 'Western Movies.'"

Chapter Five
TRAGEDY

Early the next morning finds Cyrus, Sam, Preston, and the rest of the cowhands lined up in front of the ranch's saddle room. Each is busy getting their mount saddled and ready. The sun begins to peek above a dark cloud on the horizon when Milam Avery, the ranch cook, pulls a cowbell from the outside wall of the camp house and bangs it loudly with a huge metal spoon. Milam's weathered black skin might not reflect his true age of sixty years, but his lifetime experience of working cow camps certainly does. He wears a brown paper sack on his head, folded to resemble a chef's hat. In his younger days, they say old Milam killed another Black man during a boxing match set up by the local ranchers. A devastating right hook to the throat crushed his opponent's Adam's apple and ended the fight and the man's life in an early round.

Milam ambles back inside the kitchen and steps up in front of an enormous gas cooking stove. He breaks eggs on the side of a large cast-iron skillet and drops them in hot, smoking grease. Bacon sizzles and crackles in another identical black skillet. He pulls open the oven door and removes a rectangular pan full of freshly baked camp bread. The smell is intoxicating.

Sam leads the cowboys into the ranch hands' dining area of the camp house. The sound of boots and spurs jangling against the wooden plank floor blend with the chatter of the cowboys. Sam feels so big and grown up to actually be having breakfast with the older cowhands. He imitates the vaqueros as he spoons molasses from a gallon can and smears it across his bread. He's really not all that hungry this early in the morning, but this is what cowboys do. Milam turns off the gas burners on the stove top and settles down in a straight chair placed by the door.

Later, as the men finish the meal, they all pick up their tin plates and scrape the food scraps into two five-gallon buckets under a large standalone, porcelain sink. As Preston walks by Milam, he grins from ear to ear and says, "Now, Milam, don't be like old Stiff Finger Percy and get too close to them hogs." Milam just grumbles at him.

Sam looks up at Preston and asks, "What do you mean?"

You can tell Preston is eager to tell the story. "Well, you see when those buckets get full of garbage, Milam hauls them over to the hog pens where he slops those big sows; one time a few years back, a guy called Stiff Finger Perkins was doing that and he dropped his hat into the pen. When he climbed over the fence to get his hat, one of them big sows grabbed him and ate him." Sam's eyes grow as he stares back at the big cans of slop.

Milam snickers. "You know that ain't true. He had a heart attack and fell in the pen."

44

Preston laughs and gets the last word in. "He had a heart attack all right, right after that big old hog took the first bite." Sam doesn't know whom to believe. Preston catches Sam's eye and winks at him.

They make their way back to the pens where the horses are saddled and tied under the mesquite tree. They mount up and head down a long dirt ranch road that leads to the thicket pasture.

Later in the day, a jackrabbit nibbles on a blade of grass in an open pipeline right-of-way. Thick brush lines both sides of the opening that seems to go on forever. The rabbit's enormously long ears are laid back. Suddenly, his head pops up. No doubt something has his attention, as his sensitive little paws feel the vibrations in the ground. He looks all around, like his head is on a swivel as he sniffs the air and finds the familiar musky odor of persimmon shrubs and blackbrush, but there is a feeling of impending danger. Taking no chances, the furry little critter quickly darts off into the undergrowth.

The faint sound of ripping timber builds into a cracking of tree limbs and an explosion of hoofs and horns as a herd of cattle bulldoze into the clearing. The ground quakes and quivers as they plow into the brush on the other side of the clearing, and as quickly as they came, they're gone.

Preston and his horse battle through the brush, ducking and dodging tree limbs as they break into the narrow opening. He pulls his mount to a stop, stands up in his stirrups, and whistles. He listens and can hear Cyrus answer his whistle with a cowboy yell. A few minutes later, Cyrus and Sam break into the right-of-way. Their horses' breaths are rapid with flared nostrils and their hides are lathered in sweat. Cat-claw thorns hang from their legs. Preston glances at Sam's horse. "He all right?"

Cyrus leans over, check out the scar on Winslow's front foot. "He'll be okay." They all turn and gallop down the opening and soon fade out of sight into a thick mott of live oaks.

Back in Seclusion, Lizzie steers her pickup into a parking spot in front of the Seclusion *Timely Remarks*. The radio blares through the open windows. She glances into the rearview mirror, attempts another bubble and again watches it pop across her face. "Well, shit." She takes the gum out of her mouth and sticks it on the side of the steering column and climbs out of the truck.

As she pushes open the door to the newspaper office, she hears a bell chime. She steps inside and surveys the room. A musty odor like old cardboard and ink greets her. The office is in a state of disarray; files and old newspapers are stacked throughout the place.

Lizzie picks up a framed picture of a young military pilot, a handsome young man flashing a proud smile, sitting in the cockpit of a WWII P-51 fighter plane.

A frail man with yellowish-white hair emerges from the back. He wears a rumpled beige jacket and a loose striped tie. Bud Harkins' square-jawed face reveals a man that has witnessed a lot in his sixty-odd years in Seclusion.

It's hard for even him to believe that he's already pushing eighty. He slowly makes his way to a long glass-top counter and places his hands palms down on the glass. He looks Lizzie in the eyes and with a strong, deep voice asks, "Can I help you, young lady?"

Lizzie extends her hand. "I'm Lizzie Fox. I spoke with you on the phone about the job." Bud nods his head, shakes her hand, and then points to the picture she holds in her other hand. "That was our son. Afraid he didn't make it back. Shot down December 10, 1944, somewhere over Germany."

Lizzie places the photo back on the shelf. "I'm so sorry."

Bud reaches in his pocket and pulls out a smoking pipe. "You mind?" Lizzie shakes her head. "No, sir."

He fumbles inside the side pocket of his coat and pulls out a pouch of Sir Walter Raleigh tobacco and a box of matches. "Said you had some experience at a newspaper in Dallas?"

Lizzie responds. "Yes sir, five years."

He stuffs the bowl of his pipe with a pinch of tobacco using one hand and then tamps it down with his index finger. You can tell he's done this countless times before. In fact, he's a master. "I'll need you to take the paper over to Victoria to be printed."

"But Mr. Harkins…"

He interrupts her before she can finish. "You can use my Chevy." He strikes a match, draws the flame deep inside the pipe. "It pays six-bits an hour. When can you start?"

Lizzie stammers at first, trying to find the right words. "I'm … I'm afraid I'm going to have to turn down the offer."

He is obviously surprised by her statement. "I know it doesn't pay much."

She quickly chimes in, "It not that. It's my husband, he … he's got it in his head that I shouldn't work."

Bud inhales a long draw on the pipe and blows smoke out the side of his mouth. "Well, if you don't need the money..." Lizzie glances around, takes in the room: empty desks with typewriters sitting on them, a typesetting machine in the corner. She grins approvingly and thinks how great it would be to be able to whip this place into shape.

His previous words suddenly register in her brain. "Oh, believe me; we could sure use the money."

Bud is obviously disappointed; he extends his hand. "Well, if you change your mind in the next few days..."

Lizzie smiles. "Thank you, Mr. Harkins, but it's what's best for my family right now." Lizzie shakes his hand as she glances around and says, "You'll never know how much I would love to work here."

Bud nods his head, watches her slow-walk to the door, giving the room one more look around before leaving.

She crosses the sidewalk, takes a long step off the curb, and jumps up behind the wheel of her truck. She cranks up the motor, tunes into the radio, and pulls the door shut. Lizzie inhales a deep breath, places her hands on the steering wheel, and for a brief moment, pauses to absorb what she has just done. Was it the right decision or not? Well, it's too late now to change her mind; what's done is done.

She reaches inside her sack of gum and then remembers the old piece she left stuck to the steering column. She peels the bubble gum off and plops it into her mouth. The heat has made the gum like dried putty. Her jaws tire fast as she works the gum to get it pliable enough to chew. Her hand goes to her cheek as she opens her mouth to relieve the sudden muscle pain.

Back at the thicket pasture, it's late in the morning as cowboys on horseback surround a large herd of cattle. The loud bellowing of the cows and calves makes it almost impossible for the cowboys to communicate with one another. Cyrus hollers, "Don't crowd 'em," as they push the cattle slowly along. The dust is dense and sticks to the sweat on the horses. The smell in the air is now a familiar mixture of sweet chaparral and fresh manure. A large black Brahma bull with white spots that blanket his broad face paces back and forth. The two vaquero glance at one another just as Preston spots the bull.

"Watch that motley-faced bull. He wants to run!" Preston yells.

Cyrus hollers back to Preston. "Is this the famous Diablo?"

"In the flesh," Preston answers as he spurs his horse and turns back the bull. Diablo repeatedly paws at the ground with his front feet, sending a cloud of dust flying over his back and into the air.

Cyrus yells to the rest of the cow crowd. "If he gets by us, we'll lose 'em all."

Preston drives the bull back into the center of the herd and yells, "Let 'em blow, let 'em calm down."

Lizzie's truck splashes through the low-water crossing. Water flies up into the air and falls back onto the truck. She flips on the windshield wipers for a couple of swipes, changes the station on the radio, and then sings along to the tune, "Tragedy."

Back at the thicket pasture, the cowboys cautiously move the cattle along. The big Brahma bull paces from side to side at the herd. He lowers his head close to the ground, snorts, and blows loose dirt into the air. Cyrus knows that the Brahma is a hardy breed, but he is also quite aware they are very ill-tempered to say the least. No one sees Sam untie his rope and form a loop. Winslow stumbles, but quickly regains his footing. His snakebite wound is open, blood trickles down his leg onto his hoof.

The double gates are open to the cattle pens. Lizzie maneuvers her pickup beside the plank pens and stops. She climbs into the bed of the truck, stands behind the cab, and watches the cowboys drive the herd toward the opening. They're almost there when the bull charges in one last attempt to escape. Preston and a vaquero team up, and side by side they force him through the open gates and then push the rest of cattle inside the pen with him.

Wanting no part of being confined, Diablo leaps into the fence, splintering the wooden planks, making a loud cracking sound. Blood and snot spew from his nose. Seemingly out of nowhere, Sam spurs Winslow up behind the bull, whips out his rope, and swings the loop above his head.

Preston suddenly sees him. "No, let him go, son."

Cyrus spins his horse around. "Sam, no, goddammit!"

Everything seems to go into slow motion as Preston watches the loop float over the bull's horns and around his neck. Preston mutters under his breath. "Oh, shit."

Diablo bolts forward and hits the end of the rope and the top of the fence at the same time. The force and weight of the beast jerks Winslow to his knees. The young horse struggles to get back on his feet. Sam pulls slack in the rope, tries desperately to untie it from the saddle horn. Winslow's injured leg collapses as Sam works to free himself and the horse. Suddenly, the bull drops his head, charges, and hooks Winslow under the flanks.

Lizzie leaps from the bed of the pickup and climbs to the top of the fence. The bull lifts Winslow high into the air and then rolls him to the ground. Sam, his leg now caught in the rope, is dragged down with the injured horse. Lizzie screams, "Someone, cut the rope; get him out of there!"

Cyrus freezes; he can't move. He watches as the bull throws himself into the planks on the fence and then turns back for Sam and Winslow. Preston jumps from his mount and dives beside the boy, uses one hand and his teeth and jerks open his pocketknife. Lizzie leaps from the top of the fence and dashes in front of the bull. One of his massive horns catches her in the side, spinning her to the ground. Preston slices through the rope, grabs Sam, but not in time as the bull slams into the boy.

Preston kicks at the bull's face in a frantic attempt to rescue Sam. With the rope cut, the bull feels his freedom. Diablo turns and explodes through the splintered planks on the corral and disappears into the brush.

Preston and Cyrus load Sam in the bed of a ranch pickup. Lizzie cradles her son's head in her lap. Preston jumps behind the wheel of the truck and speeds off toward the highway. He keeps both hands on the steering wheel as he turns and glances through the back glass. Lizzie holds her son as blood seeps from the corners of his mouth.

"Am I gonna die?" Sam asks in a fragile voice.

"You know ... I won't let you die," Lizzie says as a steady stream of tears flow down her cheeks.

Back at the cow pens, a vaquero walks toward the injured horse as he cocks the lever on a Winchester rifle. Winslow lies on his side. He thrashes his head to one side as he tries to get to his feet, but his back is broken, and he can't move his hind legs. A soft moaning comes from the injured horse as he repeatedly slams his head against the ground.

Inside the bed of the pickup, blood now pools beside the young boy. He coughs and his voice gurgles as he struggles to get the words out. "What about Winslow?" Just then they hear the cracking sound of a rifle shot echo in the distance.

Preston barely slows for the ranch cattle guard, plows through the low-water crossing and accelerates out onto the highway. Preston knows in his heart they don't have time to get to the hospital in Victoria, so he makes a beeline to Doctor Finn's office in Seclusion.

In what seems like an eternity, the ranch truck finally screeches to a stop out in front of a one-story brick building. Preston jumps out of the driver-side of the truck, sprints to the front door, opens it, and disappears inside. Lizzie's jeans and hands are covered with her son's blood. She screams, "Oh God, please hurry!"

A few moments later, the doctor, an attractive man in his forties, trots out to the street and up behind the tailgate of the truck. He motions for Cyrus to step aside as he climbs up inside the bed of the pickup.

Sam's eyes are fixed, and his lips are a deep purple. The blood seeping from the corners of his mouth has mixed with the dirt that covers his cheeks and neck. Doctor Finn lifts Sam's shirt and examines a gaping puncture wound in his ribcage.

He feels for a pulse, then takes his stethoscope and listens to Sam's chest. His medical skills assure him that the young boy has passed, but those same skills didn't prepare him for finding the right words to tell his distraught mother. Lizzie still cradles his head in her lap. The doctor looks at Cyrus and then Lizzie. "Ma'am, there is nothing anyone can do for your boy; I'm afraid he's gone."

Lizzie just stares at him, hoping that if she doesn't speak, he'll say something different. This just can't happen. She won't let it. This is not how it ends.

Doctor Finn turns to Preston, "Go inside and tell my wife to call the funeral home and get her to give you a clean sheet."

The realization of events catches up to Lizzie. The overwhelming darkness and feeling of doom and gloom are setting in. She begins to sob and rock back and forth. Cyrus and Doctor Finn step down from the bed of the truck. The doctor speaking softly asks Cyrus, "What happened?"

Cyrus's hands tremble, he fumbles for his cigarettes and matches. "Working cattle, I told him not to ... but he didn't listen."

"Not to what?" Doctor Finn inquires.

Cyrus finally gets his cigarette lit. He takes a drag, walks off repeating the same words. "I told him no ... it's not my fault."

A white Chevrolet station wagon modified to resemble an ambulance with a single red light affixed to the roof rounds the corner and heads their way. Doctor Finn turns toward Preston and asks, "What the hell happened?"

"He got hung up in a rope that was tied to his horse and a big Brahma bull."

Doctor Finn glances over at Cyrus standing all by himself, then turns back to Preston, shakes his head, and remarks, "That boy was awful young to be doing that kind of work. He bled to death."

Preston and the doctor climb up in the bed of the pickup and try to drape a white sheet over the boy. Lizzie won't let them cover his face. She shakes her head and repeats over and over, "No, no, no."

The heavy-set Mexican man pulls a gurney from the back of the ambulance and rolls it up behind the truck. Preston takes hold of Lizzie's arm and nudges her to let go of Sam. After a few minutes, she reluctantly lets him help her down from the truck. For a moment, Preston forgets that the bull has hooked Lizzie in her side as he grabs her around the waist with both hands. He lifts her from the bed of the truck and eases her down to the pavement. Doctor Finn notices Lizzie grimace and reach for her side. He jumps down from the bed of the pickup and approaches Lizzie. "May I have a look?" His words echo through the fog in her head as she watches him lift her shirttail and examine a long deep abrasion just above her waist. The doctor turns to Preston and says, "Take her inside. I need to dress that." Lizzie shakes her head and pulls away from the doctor as he tries sway her decision. "I assure you that wound needs attention. It could easily get infected." She shuffles backward several steps while never taking her eyes from the lifeless body of her only child.

Out of the corner of his eye, Cyrus watches Preston reach out, take Lizzie's hand and guide her to the pickup where he opens the passenger-side door and helps her inside the cab.

Lizzie stares straight ahead as the Mexican man and Doctor Finn lift Sam onto the gurney and then into the back of the ambulance.

Cyrus slowly shuffles over to the pickup and opens the passenger-side door and says to Preston, "You drive." He steps up in the truck and pulls the door closed. Lizzie is staring straight ahead; she's in total shock, still not accepting of what just happened. Preston climbs in and cranks up the engine. Cyrus makes no attempt to console Lizzie; in fact, he doesn't say a word or even touch her. About halfway to the ranch, Lizzie glances down and stares at her blood-smeared hands, as she repeatedly rolls them from one side to the other. She reaches up, presses her hands against to her face, tightly closes her eyes, and softly sobs. Cyrus glances at Lizzie and then over at Preston. Without uttering a word, Cyrus turns back and stares out his side window, while rummaging in his pocket for his cigarettes and matches. Preston turns his head and watches him light a cigarette, then blow out the match and flick it out the open window.

Chapter Six

WALKIN' AFTER
MIDNIGHT

The late-afternoon sun kicks up a brisk breeze that turns the rusted blades on a windmill located in the rear of Oak Mott Cemetery. The metal pump rods bang against the inside of the galvanized pipe in a rhythmic drum-like cadence. A small stream of water spills into a wooden cistern, and then just as quickly as it came, the wind dies and the mill slowly grinds to a stop. A green, canvas funeral tent stands alone on the edge of a sea of tombstones. A long, black hearse sits parked nearby. Preston, Milam, and several other cowhands gather in the shade of a large post oak tree.

A preacher holds a small wooden cross; he looks up to the heavens and recites, "We commit this body to the ground, earth to earth, ashes to ashes, dust to dust, in sure and certain hope of the resurrection to eternal life." He hands the cross to Lizzie, gently pats her on the shoulder, and slowly walks away. Lizzie dressed in a dark, modest dress with a long, black scarf draped over her head doesn't move.

Cyrus follows the preacher, Preston, and the cowhands as they make their way down a grassy hill to several parked vehicles. No one really knows Cyrus and Lizzie, much less Sam, as they've just moved to Seclusion. This leaves Lizzie now sitting alone in front of a simple pine casket. Her face is stolid as she rocks back and forth.

The funeral director, an overweight man in a shabby suit, shuffles over behind her. He places his hands on her shoulders, leans down, and whispers, "Ma'am, the service is over; we're going to have to finish up."

A few hours later, Lizzie is still at the cemetery. She stares through the pickup's open window at a cherry-red sun as it slowly sets behind the windmill. The soft rays reflect in her swollen and expressionless eyes. She hits the starter on the old Dodge truck and prays to herself that the engine will start. She feels like she's slipping into a dark place and now her life will begin cascading into shambles. She's beginning to realize that Sam wasn't just the best thing in her life; he was the only thing. If only she had someone to talk to, someone who could help her make sense of all this. Why, when some people have so little, do they get so much taken away from them? If there is a God, why would he do this? She slowly pulls out onto the highway and heads for her home at the ranch.

Back at the ranch, she pulls up and parks near the front yard gate of the house. The place is dark except for a single porch light. She opens the screen door, steps inside and flips on the light switch, and then pitches her handbag on the couch and slowly takes in the emptiness of the house. She glances over to the table with the old typewriter where Sam once sat. She touches her lips with the back of her hand and just falls to pieces.

Seems like every day since Sam's death has been like the last. Lizzie has pretty much stayed holed up at the house, while Cyrus has been stretching each evening a little longer in Seclusion. Lizzie knows he's drinking again; she can smell the alcohol, but up until now she just didn't have the mental fortitude to comfort him. She realizes now it's up to her; she's got to get her act together and pull herself up by the bootstraps before she drowns in grief. She grabs the keys to the Power Wagon, kicks open the screen door and marches down the steps and out the yard gate.

Inside the Hoot Owl Hollow, one of several beer joints in Seclusion, but definitely the most popular, cigarette smoke drifts and curls toward the ceiling. Lighted neon beer signs hang from the walls, giving the place a dull artificial glow that only adds to the feeling of loneliness and despair. Cyrus sits alone at the bar. He has a cigarette in one hand and a bottle of Pearl beer in the other. A woman with bright-red cheeks and pouty lips drops a quarter into the jukebox. Cyrus spots her out of the corner of his eye. He taps his empty bottle on the counter and then fumbles with a pack of cigarettes.

A distant lightning bolt temporarily illuminates the inside of Lizzie's Power Wagon as she cruises down the street in front of the Hoot Owl. Lizzie uses her sleeve to wipe the fog from the windshield of her old truck. She surveys a row of cars and pickups parked along the curb and then spots one of the ranch's pickup trucks and figures it must be Cyrus.

Inside the beer joint, pool balls lay motionless on the green felt of a pool table. With a loud crack, Cyrus scatters the balls wildly across the table. Holding a cue stick in one hand and a cigarette in the other, he watches the eight ball disappear into a side pocket. Losing has always seemed to come easily to Cyrus as he staggers up to the bar and slaps down a quarter. The bartender and owner of this popular establishment is a man known simply as Buster. He's always dressed in slacks and a freshly laundered white shirt. Buster pops the cap on a long-neck beer and slides it across the bar. Cyrus scoops up the beer, wanders over to the jukebox and drops in a dime. His glassy eyes follow the arm in the machine reach out, grab a vinyl 45 record and place it on the jukebox's turntable. The record has been played so many times that the needle makes a loud scratching sound before the music starts to play. The woman with pouty lips sashays up next to Cyrus, whispers in his ear, and then pulls him out onto the dance floor. Cyrus pulls her close, closes his eyes. They sway to the country song, "Walkin' After Midnight." Several other couples empty from the booths that line the wall and join in dancing.

Elo Turk strolls through the front door, eases over to the bar, and straddles a stool. He lights a cigarette and surveys the room. You can tell he's a regular, as Buster sets a cold Lone Star beer in front of him without Elo even having to ask. Buster motions toward Cyrus. "Looks like he's got your gal." Elo grins and winks his cloudy glass eye and then lays some change on the bar and points in the direction of the door.

Buster turns and sees Lizzie standing just inside the doorway. Her eyes are fixed on Cyrus as he and the pouty lips gal are almost motionless in the center of the dance floor. Just as the music ends, Cyrus notices Lizzie staring at him. He strains his bleary eyes trying to focus on her, but she turns and leaves. Cyrus doesn't care; he's had enough to drink that he feels invisible. All he cares about now is that the party never ends. He staggers over to the bar, shoves his hand in his pocket. "Give me some quarters." Elo looks him over for a moment and then takes a long swig of his beer.

Lizzie is back at the ranch, staring through the windshield of her truck at the dilapidated and rundown house. She knows in her mind that she can do better than this, much better. She takes several deep breaths and then abruptly shifts the truck in reverse and wheels around.

She drives the short distance to the camp house and slams on the brakes. The big tires on the Power Wagon lock up and slide a few feet on the loose caliche rocks. The place looks dark and empty except for a dim light coming from the rear of the building. Lizzie jumps out of the pickup and scurries up the steps to a long veranda that stretches across the length of the building. A half-dozen rocking chairs sit lined up on the porch. She steps inside the main room and pulls the string on a single light fixture that hangs from the ceiling next to the wall. The light flashes on, blinding her for a split second. She glances around the large room and notices the light reflecting in the lifeless eyes of numerous trophy mounts, which adorn the walls. The place has a distinct smell to it. She can't put her finger on it, but it's not good. She cranks the handle several times on a wall-mounted telephone and says, "Hello, Operator?" She waits for a few seconds for the operator come on the line. "Would you ring Bud Harkins, please?" The light has now drawn every insect in the room. Lizzie slaps a bug against the wall and swats at another, before she hears a voice on the other end of the line.

"Mr. Harkins, this is Lizzie Fox." She listens for a moment as Bud speaks on the other end of the line. "I am fine, sir; thank you for asking." She pauses a few seconds. "Mr. Harkins, is that job still open?" Lizzie pinches her eyes shut as she stands there with one hand on the receiver and the other hand up in the air with fingers crossed. A big sigh of relief streams across her face and then she abruptly blurts out, "I promise, you won't be sorry."

She doesn't see a shadowy figure appear in an adjacent doorway. She swipes at another bug, misses and strikes the light. She turns and faces the wall. "Okay, yes, sir. Thank you."

She hangs up the phone, hikes up her dress, and smashes a mosquito against her leg. Out of nowhere, a hand grabs her thigh. She spins around and falls back against the telephone as she pushes the hand away. The light swings back and forth directly in front of Phil Nolan's face.

Now she recognizes the smell. It's a cross between body odor and alcohol, and now she knows the source. Her eyes dart around, looking for the quickest exit. He takes a step back, almost falling and in a slurred, whiskey-soaked voice, "Need some help?"

Lizzie tries to appear in control of the situation. "No, I'm finished."

He's not giving up that easily and Lizzie knows it. "Let me show you around?"

Lizzie takes a step sideways and maneuvers toward the door. He reaches out, grabs her by both wrists. His repugnant grin reveals a mouthful of stained and missing teeth from chewing tobacco. "You owe me. I gave your husband a job."

Lizzie blurts out, "He's not my husband, and I don't owe you anything."

"Just as I thought; living in sin." He says as he pulls her close and caresses her hair. "Now you don't want him to lose his job?"

She jerks her hands free and pushes back against his shoulders and screams, "Let me go, or I'll tell!"

Lizzie can feel her heart racing in her chest as he grips the back of her neck and slurs, "Who the hell ... you gonna tell?" He uses his weight to shove her back against the wall and then covers her lips with his open mouth. Lizzie abruptly turns her head, coughs and gags, and then she feels him thrust his hand under her dress and between her thighs. His fingers are tearing at her panties.

Lizzie knows she's on the brink of something bad, but she's not going to be violated again, not ever again. She musters all the strength she has and manages to get a little separation and then plunges her knee into his groin. He gasps and falls backward onto the floor. She bolts through the door and races to the Power Wagon.

As she jerks open the door, she hears him shout, "You ain't nothing but goddamn White trash."

She jumps inside the truck and repeats under her breath, "Please start, oh, please start." As if the old Dodge was hearing her, it fires right up. Lizzie throws it in gear and spins the tires as she tears away from the camp house. She glances in the side mirror and then wipes her mouth with the back of her hand.

In the bathroom of her house, Lizzie stands alone and stares at the bottom of the rust-stained sink. She washes her face with a washcloth, glances at herself in the mirror, and begins to sob. Later that evening, she peels off her clothes and slips beneath the bubbles in an old claw-foot, cast-iron bathtub. She slowly drifts off to sleep. Her body begins to twitch and jerk as she dreams of herself as a small six-year-old girl. The child cuddles a stuffed teddy bear tight against her chest as she sits upright in an iron bed that has been pushed into the corner of a sparse, dimly lit room. Her eyes follow the broken shadows of a light under the door. Her rapid breaths turn to muffled sobs and whimpers as she watches the doorknob turn. Light streaks into the room as the outline of a man slowly pushes open the door.

The sudden crack of a lightning strike rattles the window glass and flashes throughout the room. Lizzie gasps for breath as she bolts upward in the tub. Realizing it was a nightmare, she stands and hurriedly wraps a towel around herself. As she pulls down the open window, she breathes in the sweet smell of an approaching thunderstorm. Several knocks sound at the front door. She waits and listens. She hears more knocking. She wonders who it can be. Cyrus wouldn't knock.

Lizzie tiptoes to the edge of the bathroom door and peers down the hall toward the front door. Through the wire screen on the door, she makes out two figures standing on the porch.

As she gets closer, she sees Preston staring at her. "Mr. Buster at the Hoot Owl called me," he says while he steadies a clearly intoxicated Cyrus against a porch post and then adds, "He's in pretty bad shape."

She pushes open the screen door and in all the commotion, she has forgotten that the only thing between her and her birthday suit is a flimsy towel. She thinks for a second and then says, "Hmm, help me get him in bed." Preston's face shows his embarrassment as one of Lizzie's breasts is suddenly fully exposed.

He has never seen a White woman naked, let alone one this beautiful. He points toward the towel. "Ma'am?"

Lizzie glances down at her chest. "Uh-oh!" Her face cringes as she adjusts the towel and tightens her grip. "Sorry, not much I can do about it now." Preston drags Cyrus through the door and down the hall to the bedroom.

Lizzie pulls the covers back, as Preston guides Cyrus onto the bed. Cyrus belches and then passes out as his head falls to one side. Preston looks down at Cyrus then turns to Lizzie. "I best be leaving." Lizzie follows Preston out of the room and shuts the door. "Wait for me on the porch. I'll only be a minute."

Preston stands under the porch roof and gazes out at a steady rain. Lizzie is barefoot and her hair is still wet as she steps outside the house and onto the porch wearing jeans and a sweater.

She steps over beside him and folds her arms against the cool damp air. Off in the distance, a ball of light dances along the shallow bank of the Silver Creek. Lizzie points toward the creek and excitedly says, "Did you see that?"

Preston turns and looks in that direction. They both watch as it stops, fades into the darkness only to reappear and float a few feet above the water. Preston nods his head and says, "Old folks call 'em will-o'-the-wisps." The light flickers, and then as fast as it came it vanishes. "They say if you see a couple of them together, two souls have been reunited in heaven."

Lizzie stares off into the darkness, hoping to catch another glimpse of the wisps of light. "That's beautiful. I wish I could believe it." She turns back toward Preston, slips her hands into the front pockets of her jeans. "Does Phil Nolan spend much time in the camp house?"

Preston chuckles. "He'll hang out over there if he's drinking. He tries to hide from his wife, but ole' Maude is no fool." Preston tips his hat. "Rain has let up; I best be headed back." He steps off the porch and hears Lizzie call his name.

"Preston?" He spins around, catches her eye. She smiles and says, "Thanks!"

She watches him until he's out of sight and then turns, walks back inside the house and into Sam's room. His hat and spurs sit on top of the dresser beside a framed picture of him and Lizzie. She flips off the ceiling light, pulls back the top sheet, and slips into bed. She lies back, turns her head toward the window and stares off into the night. As soon she closes her eyes, the sights and sounds of Sam being gored to death by the bull flash over and over inside her brain. She gets up and walks down the hall, and carefully opens the screen door so as to not make a sound, and then slips into a straight-back wooden rocker on the porch.

She pulls her feet up onto the seat of the chair and stretches her nighty over her knees. She takes in a deep breath of the cool night air as she rocks in the chair and wonders about her first day at a new job. She needs to wear something conservative and business-like. Only problem is she's fresh out of conservative and business-like clothes and tomorrow is Sunday; all the stores are closed, never mind that she doesn't have any money for new clothes. Lizzie leans back and grins at her own joke. She locks her eyes on the creek bottom as she slowly rocks back and forth, hoping to catch another glimpse of the will-o'-the-wisps. She can feel that she's certainly at turning point in her life; she just doesn't know which way.

Chapter Seven

DON'T BE CRUEL

The next morning finds Lizzie in the kitchen pouring herself a cup of coffee. She looks up and sees Cyrus step through the door. He rubs his forehead and plops down in a chair at the table. "What're you gawking at?"

Lizzie pours another cup and sets it down in front of him. "Nothing." She looks him in the eye. "Gone to drinking again?"

His cup rattles the saucer as he sets it down. "Yeah, I had a couple of beers! So what?"

She keeps pressing. "Is this the way it's going to be?"

He's trying to be defensive. "No, I just was having a little fun with some of the boys."

She thinks to herself, *Funny I didn't see him with many boys.*

He looks over at the stove. "What's to eat?"

Lizzie glances at the empty stove. "Want to go into town for lunch? I've got a little money."

Cyrus stands, digs in his pockets. "You think I'm broke. I got lots of fuckin' money," he says as he pulls out some loose change.

Lizzie interrupts him. "I took that job at the newspaper."

Cyrus flings the coins across the room. "Might as well."

"What's that supposed to mean?" Lizzie responds.

The sound of Cyrus's own voice hurts his head, but he doesn't let up. "No sense hangin' around here. I don't need you."

Lizzie is silent. The words hurt, but what else is new?

He grabs his hat, pulls it down on his head, and says, "If you want to eat, let's go."

Outside the house, Lizzie walks to the passenger side of the truck. Cyrus stops her. "You drive; I'll be back in a minute." She watches him walk over and step behind a cowshed. After a while, she can hear him vomiting.

She gets behind the wheel, starts the engine, and then turns on the radio and waits.

After a few minutes, he jerks open the passenger door and slides in. "Turn that fuckin' radio down! Who is that anyway?"

She turns down the radio. "It's Elvis."

Cyrus lights a cigarette and flips the match out the window. "Play some country music."

Lizzie switches the radio off; she hates country music.

Cyrus takes a long drag on his cigarette, blows a smoke ring, and says, "That's even better yet."

The La Rosa Café is a typical diner of the day. It sits across the town square from the Seclusion courthouse. On the side of the building below the name "La Rosa" read the words, "Where

Oil Men … Meet Oil Men." Inside the café, tables and booths crowd a long lunch counter. Lizzie, Cyrus, and the after-church crowd fill every seat. They sit in a booth by the entrance. Cyrus has his back to the door. An elderly woman in a pink waitress uniform stops by their table to take their order. She done this so many times before, she doesn't even look at them as she recites her line of the day. "The special today is baked chicken and dressing with two sides."

Cyrus lights a cigarette and mumbles, "I don't want no yardbird. Tell the cook I want a chicken fried steak."

She looks up from her order pad long enough to acknowledge his rudeness and give him the stank eye before turning her attention to Lizzie. "And you, young lady?"

Lizzie smiles at the old woman and says, "I'll be having the special and thank you." She finishes scribbling down their order, slips the pencil into the tight, gray hair bun on top of her head, and moseys toward the kitchen. Lizzie glances over at Cyrus as he takes another drag on his cigarette. "Can't you put that out? We're eating."

He waves his open palms and calls her attention to their empty table. "I don't see any food; do you see any food?"

Cyrus finishes his cigarette at the same time the elderly waitress sets their plates of food down on the table. Just as he grabs up his knife and fork to slice into the steak, he notices a couple sitting a few tables away, holding hands and saying grace. Cyrus immediately drops his utensils, reaches over and takes Lizzie's hand and bows his head. The move completely catches her off guard. It takes her a moment to figure out what he's doing. When she realizes that he's going to say grace, the only thing that comes to her mind is, *What a total fucking hypocrite!* Although she has never been fond of public displays of religion, she doesn't want to cause a scene, so she goes along with the charade.

Lizzie bows her head and listens as he mumbles, "Father, we thank you for this food and, Father, we thank you for our wonderful neighbors and, Father, we thank you for my job. Amen."

Lizzie looks up and just stares at him in disbelief. He catches her looking at him and says, "What?" She just shakes her head and begins eating.

A few minutes later, Cyrus is busy stabbing and slicing up the remaining bit of chicken fried steak. With his mouth full of meat and gravy, he turns to Lizzie and says, "If anybody mentions the boy, don't go on about it. Don't want 'em to think we want sympathy."

Lizzie stops eating, places her fork on her plate, and says, "I don't even know anyone here. Why would you even say something like that?" He ignores her question as he gobbles down the last bite of his steak. He quickly lights up another cigarette and doesn't notice Phil and Maude Nolan step inside the entrance of the café. Both have sullen looks on their face as they realize there are no empty seats. Lizzie watches as they stare down an elderly couple that looks to have finished their meal. Two barely eaten desserts of pie and vanilla ice cream sit in front them. The couple jump up and give the Nolans their table. Lizzie can't believe what just happened. Her eyes follow the old couple as they pay their check and exit the café. Cyrus takes a last drag on his cigarette.

"I'm going to catch that goddamn bull. I'm going to do it for Sam."

"That's not what he would want."

He stamps out the cigarette in his plate of leftover gravy.

"You know what I mean."

"Let it go, Cyrus. Wasn't the animal's fault."

Suddenly, Lizzie notices the place go silent. People seem frozen in mid-motion; they stare at the entrance. Oblivious to the situation, Cyrus raises his voice. "No, then whose goddamn fault was it? You sayin' it was mine?" Lizzie kicks his shin under the table and points toward the door. He cranes his head around to see what's going on.

A young well-dressed Black man stands in the doorway. It doesn't take long for the young man to get the attention of Sheriff Vail Taylor, a man in his mid-sixties. Seclusion's sheriff is the quintessential Texas lawman, wearing boots, a short-brim hat and toting a sidearm. Sheriff Taylor pulls his felt hat down on his head, gets up from his table, and saunters over to the man. "What you want, boy?"

The young man responds in calm, polite voice. "I just wanted to get a bite to eat."

The sheriff waves his arm around the room. "Can't you see we're full?"

Lizzie folds her napkin and places it on the table as Sheriff Taylor turns his attention back to the young man. "What do you want me to do, make some of these good White folks get up so you can have their table?"

Lizzie slides out of the booth and stands and in a firm voice says, "We're through; he can have our table."

Lizzie probably couldn't have done anything more egregious than what she just did to piss off Sheriff Taylor anymore. She catches a glimpse of Phil Nolan as he twirls his index finger in the air giving Sheriff Taylor the sign to get the man out of the café. The sheriff's voice now has a little quiver, giving away his building anger.

He looks down at Cyrus. "You got sumpin' to say, too?" Cyrus shakes his head, jumps up, grabs Lizzie by the arm and pulls her out of the café's door.

Lizzie pauses a moment and watches the sheriff escort the young man outside and then point to a sign above the door that reads, "Whites Only."

The young man looks up at the sign as Sheriff Taylor says, "Can't you read, boy?"

Lizzie breaks loose from Cyrus and takes off down the sidewalk. She glances back and watches the sheriff accompany the Black man to the back of the café and point to a grease-stained screen door that leads to the café's kitchen. The young Black man opens the door and steps inside where he's met by two Black cooks and a Mexican dishwasher who stare back at him. He notices a single booth sitting in a corner of the kitchen. He realizes this is the rule and not the exception, but not today. He wheels around and steps back outside where he sees Sheriff Taylor with his eye on Dan Shaw, a very slender, Black man in his early fifties.

Out of the corner of his eye, Sheriff Taylor notices the young Black man leaving the rear of the café. "Lose your appetite?" Sheriff Taylor hollers to the young man who doesn't answer; he just keeps walking toward his car. Under normal circumstances, the sheriff would stop the man and harass him a bit more, but Sheriff Taylor's attention is now on Dan Shaw, and nobody has ever accused the sheriff of being able to do two things at once.

Dan hoists a large, galvanized trash can filled with food scraps onto the back of a flatbed truck. Slop splatters and streams down the side panels and onto the bed. Sheriff Taylor motions to him. "Shaw, get over here."

Dan drops his eyes to the ground and eases over to him like a scolded dog, removes his glove and extends his hand.

"Get that nasty-ass hand away from me. You just ruined my goddamn lunch." Dan drops his hand beside his waist. "Don't let me catch you on Main Street during the day again."

Dan tries to explain. "But I was told by Mr. Grover..." He doesn't get to finish.

"Shut up and get that filthy damned truck outta here," Sheriff Taylor continues.

Dan drops his head and mutters, "Yes, sir."

But the sheriff doesn't let it go. "What?"

Dan speaks up a little louder, "Yes, sir, Sheriff Taylor."

Lizzie stands on the sidewalk, taking it all in. She watches the young Black man get in his car and leave just as Cyrus catches up with her, grabs hold of her elbow, and spins her around to face him. "What the hell gotten into you?"

She jerks her arm free. "I don't like the way these rich people hide behind the law, and the rest just doing what they're told."

Cyrus pivots around to see if anyone could be listening. "Shut up that kind of talk. You want 'em to hear you?"

Neither of them notices Sheriff Taylor hunched down between two parked cars as Lizzie blurts out, "Phil Nolan put his hands on me last night. I was over at the camp house using the phone."

Cyrus drops his head and stares at the ground. "Well, what do you want me to do about it?" She tears up. Cyrus notices and gets up close in her face. "Stop that crying. It makes you look weak."

Lizzie tries to explain. "He had me pinned against the wall with his hand up my dress." Cyrus turns, starts walking away, and mutters loud enough for Lizzie to hear him. "Well, it's not like it hasn't happened before."

Lizzie runs and catches up with him. "Why do you always bring that up?"

He grins from the corner of his mouth. "I don't ... you do."

She pauses and thinks to herself, *How cruel! But what the hell did I expect? I probably did deserve it.*

Cyrus heads off in the direction of their parked truck. He turns back and hollers in her direction. "If you're riding with me, you better load up."

Lizzie thinks, *Where the hell else have I got to go?* She reluctantly follows along behind him.

When they get back to their truck, Cyrus belts out his latest orders, "You drive; drop me off at the Hoot Owl. I'm going to watch football with some of the fellas."

At this point, Lizzie doesn't even care. In the past, she would have challenged him on this, but now all she can think about is an afternoon and maybe night of peace with no verbal abuse. She fires up the engine on the Power Wagon and backs

74

out into the street. A mile down the road she stops in the street out front of the Hoot Owl.

Cyrus shuffles down out of the truck and mumbles, "Don't worry about pickin' me up; I'll catch a ride." He slams the door shut and disappears inside the beer joint.

Lizzie jokingly thinks to herself that if it wasn't Sunday, she'd go shopping. She smiles at her reflection in the mirror and says, "Yeah, window shopping." She tunes in the truck's radio, then turns onto the highway and heads for the ranch.

Inside the Hoot Owl, a black-and-white TV sits on the end of the bar. Cyrus moseys over, focuses on the screen for a moment, and then asks Buster, "Who's playing?"

Buster replies, "Cowboys and the Eagles." Cyrus turns away from the television screen and spreads some change on top of the bar. "Dallas ain't worth a shit ... they give real cowboys a bad name."

Buster chimes in as he sets a cold Pearl beer in front of Cyrus, "How many points would it take for you to like them for, let's say a ten-dollar bill?"

Cyrus takes a whiff of the cold vapor rising from inside the beer bottle and thinks to himself, *There's nothing like it.*

Buster leans across the bar and takes a quick peek at the screen. "Better hurry; it's getting ready to start." Cyrus takes a swig of the beer and says, "Forty points."

Buster, very quickly, "Thirty."

Cyrus follows, "Thirty-five."

Buster reaches across the bar and shakes his hand. "You got a bet, my friend."

In the meanwhile, Lizzie pulls off the highway and onto the narrow road leading to the ranch. As she passes by the barn on the way to her house, she notices Preston leading his horse Poco and the buckskin that was snake-bit to the saddle room. She parks in front of the house and rushes up beside him. "And just what the hell do you think you're doing?"

He laughs at her usual quirkiness. "It's such a pretty day; thought I'd take these two out for a little exercise."

Lizzie glances around like she's waiting for someone to give her permission to ask the question. Finally, she spits it out. "You want some company?"

This time, it's Preston who's trying to figure out how to handle the awkward situation. "Where's Cyrus?"

Lizzie steps up between the two horses and begins to rub their necks. "He's at his new home. I don't look for him to be back until they quit serving beer."

Preston glances down at her sandals and sundress. "Can't ride in that."

A big grin slowly sneaks across her face. "I'll be back in a second." She turns and bolts for the house.

Lizzie isn't gone very long. She runs back from the house and hops over the fence next to the saddle room. Preston checks out her riding wardrobe of boots, jeans, collared shirt, and Sam's cowboy hat. He thinks to himself, *Damn! She looks like a professional barrel racer. Not bad, not bad at all.*

Lizzie sees that Preston has both horses saddled. She moves toward the buckskin. Preston stops her and hands her the reins to his horse Poco. "You ride Poco. This buckskin hasn't been ridden since he was snake-bit."

"You saying I can't handle him?" she quips.

"I'm saying I don't want to have to pick you up off the ground."

In one fluid motion, Lizzie pulls the reins over Poco's head, grabs the saddle horn, hops up on one foot, and stabs the other into the stirrup. She swings herself up and over and settles down in the saddle. Lizzie had forgotten just how damn good it feels to be on a horse.

Preston climbs up on the buckskin, hoping he doesn't decide to start pitching. He looks over at Lizzie and with a smile of relief, says, "All good so far."

Riding side by side, they take off in a long trot down a dirt road marked only by the trail of tire tracks from vehicles. "Where are we going?" Lizzie asks.

Preston looks her way and notices her body moving in complete rhythm with Poco. "You sit a horse well."

She loves the compliment. They have been few and far between in her life. "Well, thank you. I'll take that."

"We're headed to a special place on the ranch called Artesian Falls."

"Sounds interesting. I can't wait."

After about an hour and a couple more gates that separate the different pastures, Preston points up ahead and says, "See that rocky spot ahead of us?"

Lizzie nods, "I do see it."

"It's one of the prettiest places I know. Nolans don't want anybody knowing, so it's not much talked about."

"That figures, knowing them," Lizzie says as she pulls back on the reins and stops Poco. Her eyes grow wider trying to let as much of the sight that is ahead of her register in her brain. "Oh, my God! Where did this come from?"

Lizzie is mystified by the beauty as she follows a large stream of beautiful, clear water cascading down a fifty-foot rocky slope and then spilling over a ten-foot waterfall into a crystal-clear pool half the size of a football field. Lizzie taps Poco in the flanks with her heels and moves forward for a closer look. The friction of the limestone rocks and the deep drop into the pond causes a fine mist to hover around the falls, giving birth to a perfectly formed rainbow.

"So, this is Artesian Falls? Heaven would'a been a good name, too," she says as she steps off Poco without taking her eyes off the falls.

Back at the Hoot Owl, the football game is counting down the last seconds, with Cyrus winning the bet. The game ends and Cyrus runs up to the bar and Buster with the palm of his hand up saying, "You owe me ten-dollars."

Buster laughs, "I applied it to your tab. Now we're almost even."

Cyrus is proud that he's finally won something. "Then how about another cold beer?" he asks while lining up a rack of pool balls.

In a grassy meadow by Artesian Falls, Poco and the buckskin's reins are tied around their necks. They freely graze on the green, tender buffalo grass. Lizzie sits on a limestone rock and watches Preston pick mustang grapes from some nearby vines that weave through the branches of the oak trees. Lizzie stands and then steps sideways along the edge of the pond. Normally, she is afraid of water. She squats, swishes the water with her hand, and then bobs her head from side to side and exclaims, "It's so clear, I can see the bottom."

"This is the headwaters of the creek that runs by the ranch. The clear spring water is why they call it Silver Creek."

"How deep is it?"

"Shallow; there might be a few spots over your head."

"I can see fish." She points to another spot, "Look at all the fish! What kind are they?"

"Bass and piggy perch."

Preston strolls over with a handful of grapes and hands her a small bunch. "They might be a little bitter at first."

Lizzie pops one in her mouth and bites down. Her cheeks contort and her lips pucker up, making a terrible face. "That's what you call a little bitter?"

Preston laughs out loud at her expense. "They actually make good wine."

Lizzie turns her attention back to the pond. She wipes her forehead with the back of her hand. "That water sure looks inviting."

Preston hears her and in a barely audible voice says, "I hope you're not thinking what I think you're thinking."

Lizzie spins around and faces him. "I heard that and hell yeah that's what I'm thinking and don't tell me you haven't been skinny-dipping."

Preston shakes his head. "Not like this. It ain't gonna happen."

Lizzie doesn't give up. "There's nobody within twenty miles of here; you said so yourself. I'll probably never be here again." She makes a sweet pouty face. "Please?"

Preston thinks for a moment. He knows he must make some sort of a stand.

"Okay, but no skinny-dipping."

"Why? You saw most of me the other night."

He doesn't dispute that as the scene flashes back before his eyes.

"That was different; it was an accident."

"Okay; I'll leave on my panties and bra. You do whatever makes you feel right." Lizzie begins to unbutton her blouse and notices Preston is unsure what to do with himself. "Well, turn around until I'm in the water." He quickly and awkwardly spins around. Lizzie pulls off her boots and jeans and, now dressed in white silk panties and a simple cotton bra, she slips carefully into the cool spring waters. A quick shiver quickly runs up her spine; goosebumps appear on her arms.

"Whoa, this water is cold!" she declares as she slips deeper into the water. "Okay, you can turn around." Preston takes a quick look at her pile of clothes, relieved and a little disappointed at the same time to see that they're not all lying on the ground.

"Are you coming in?"

Preston thinks, *Damn! She is persistent.* He sits down, pulls off his boots, socks and shirt. He stands, places his wallet and clothes in a tree fork, and then gingerly steps across the rocks toward the pond.

"You're kidding me. You're going to ride home in wet jeans? Look at me, I'm turning around and hiding my eyes." He takes a deep breath, swallows and pulls off his jeans one leg at a time and places them in the tree fork. His white boxers and muscles on muscles make him look like the professional boxer Cassius Clay.

Before he can slip into the water, Lizzie spins around and for what seems like an eternity, she is actually speechless. Finally, she utters just one word, "Wow."

"I didn't say turn around," he says right before he dives under the water and surfaces several feet away from her.

"Well, hell, I thought you were already in. What took you so long?"

Preston just shakes his head. He's thinking what would happen if he got caught swimming in Artesian Falls and then to make it worse with an almost-naked White woman. None of it would be good. She's going to end up being the death of him.

Lizzie moves slowly about the pool. The soft, sandy bottom feels good on the soles of her feet. Her chin is barely above the surface. She swings her arms back and forth to balance herself in the still waters. She decides to move toward the center of the pond, when suddenly without any warning the sandy bottom falls away like a trap door. She feels her body plunge under the water like a rock. She panics and wildly flails her arms and legs, but to no avail. Finally, she feels her feet touch bottom again. She glances up and can only see distorted flashes of light coming from the sun. *Is this how I'm going to die?* Lizzie thinks and thrashes her arms about. It feels like her feet are glued to the bottom. She quickly tires and her hands fall to her side. She can't hold her breath any longer, but then all of a sudden, a pair of hands, very strong hands, grips her waist and rockets her upward. She breaks the surface of the water, coughs, sputters, and opens her eyes. She is face to face with Preston, his hands still tight around her waist. She can't find words. She just stares into his beautiful green eyes reflecting the dancing waters of the falls.

"Looks like you found one of the deep holes. Why didn't you tell me you couldn't swim?"

She coughs and spits out a mouthful of water. "You didn't ask."

He looks deep into her gorgeous brown eyes. Lizzie wants him to kiss her so badly, she can taste it. For the first time in her life, she feels safe and protected. She wishes this moment would last forever. She closes her eyes and lets her lips drift close to his. She pulls him toward her until their bodies touch. Preston peers through the sparkling, clear water at her white, flawless skin shimmering below the surface with the dancing rays of the sun.

Then, a warning light goes off in his brain and he spins her around in the water and propels her toward the edge of the pool. The sudden rush of water on her face brings her back into the world of reality. Preston climbs out of the water, keeping his back to Lizzie. "Enough excitement for one day."

"Agh, I don't want to leave," she answers in a very disappointed tone.

"It'll take just as long to ride back as it took us to get here," he says with a certain amount of emphasis.

Lizzie glances down at her water-soaked bra and panties that are now almost totally see-through and leaving nothing to the imagination. If she is embarrassed, she's certainly not showing it. She pulls herself up and out of the pond and gathers up her clothes.

Lizzie and Preston quickly get dressed and capture Poco and the buckskin. Lizzie swings up in the saddle, places her hat on the saddle horn and digs into one of her pockets, and then pulls her long, wet hair back into a ponytail and secures it in place with a rubber band.

"I'll never forget this place or this day," she reaches over and pats him on the leg. "Thanks."

"You mean the day you almost drowned?"

She chuckles. "Well, that, too, but you know what I mean." She pulls Sam's old hat down tight on her head, points to the pasture gate several hundred yards ahead.

"I'll race you to the gate," Preston kicks the buckskin in the flanks and gets a quick jump on her and Poco.

Chapter Eight

THERE'S A MOON
OUT TONIGHT

The next day inside the *Timely Remarks* newspaper office, Bud sits at his desk, working hard to light his pipe. This is Lizzie's first day on the job. Bud blows a puff of smoke from the corner of his mouth and remarks, "Nobody wants to read the newspaper anymore. Too much television. Hell, you know that ninety percent of homes in the country have at least one television. I've run out of things to say anyway."

Lizzie seizes on the opportunity. "I can write some if you want."

Bud grins. "You think you've got something to say?"

Lizzie calls Bud over to check out the front page of the upcoming edition of the *Timely Remarks*. "I believe I do."

He pulls himself up, moseys over to the glass-top counter. Lizzie maneuvers up beside him. "Like the layout? I didn't think you'd mind if I worked on it while you napped."

He slowly nods his head. "I do … I really do." He puffs on his pipe and turns to her. "Mildred, my late wife, did work like that."

"How long has it been, Mr. Harkins?"

"Ten years, and you can call me Bud. It was never the same after our son died. She became a different person, quiet, withdrawn, pretty much kept to herself." His chin drops. "I'm so sorry. I shouldn't be telling you all this. You know better than I about losing a child."

"It's okay, Bud," Lizzie sheepishly grins at hearing herself call Mr. Harkins by his first name.

"I think it was worse when he was missing for so long and we didn't know if he was dead or captured. Sometimes, I prayed at night that it would just all be over, one way or the other." He plops down in his chair and glances around. "And remember don't throw anything else away without consulting with me first."

The place is somewhat tidier after Lizzie has spent the last few hours straightening up. She nods and in an assuring voice says, "I promise."

Bud continues, "Now where was I? Oh, yeah, Phil Nolan is what they call a periodic drunkard." His notices that his pipe has gone out. He pulls a box of matches from his pocket. "He may go two or three months without a drink and then have a couple and pretty soon he's barricaded up in that camp house, drinking himself into a stupor."

Lizzie asks. "And Maude Nolan?"

"She turns a blind eye to a lot more than his drinking. This place for the most part is made of two kinds of Catholics, the ones who do penance for their sins and the sinners who can afford to buy their absolution."

Lizzie raises an eyebrow; her curiosity is now showing. "Meaning?"

Bud's getting on a roll now. "Just one example: Maude gets a new Cadillac every year when the new models come out. Her old one is handed down to Bishop O'Malley and his now two-year-old model is given to one of the monsignors in the diocese."

Lizzie shakes her head in disbelief as Bud continues, "Oh, and did I mention? They pay to send him back home to County Cork, Ireland, every so often for a sabbatical." Bud gets up out of his chair. "There's a lot more going on with that Catholic diocese and Bishop O'Malley than they want known. But that's another story for another day."

"I suppose they never run out of money?" Lizzie inquires.

"The church or the Nolans?"

"Both," Lizzie adds.

Bud quips, "There's enough oil under the ground here in Seclusion County to last several lifetimes and a few rich families happen to own all of the land where there's oil. And don't leave out the church when it comes to owning oil and land."

"Is that what's going on at the ranch?" Lizzie asks.

"I don't know. What did you see?"

"Lot of men and equipment building some kind of steel frame."

"That would be an oil derrick. Just another straw in the ground to suck up more money."

Bud runs his hand through his hair. "Think we'd get caught if we went snooping around?"

"I ain't never seen a real live oil well," Lizzie jokes in country hick tone. "I say we go take a look." Bud pushes himself up from his chair. "Best take your truck. My car might arouse suspicion."

Lizzie has the Power Wagon zipping down the highway a little faster than Bud is used to traveling. He spies the speedometer, all the while trying to keep his eyes focused on the highway.

"Not to worry; that rig will still be there."

Lizzie catches the subtext in his comment. She lets off the accelerator and lets the pickup slow down a bit. "Have you ever seen Artesian Falls?"

Bud is surprised by the question. "Yeah, once many years ago. How did you know about that place?"

"Preston and I were exercising horses yesterday and we rode out to it. I don't think I've seen a place quite so beautiful."

"Not many have had the pleasure."

"Why?" Lizzie inquires.

"The Nolans are afraid if too many people find out about it, the State might condemn the land, turn it into a park or the like, and share it with all the common folk."

"What's wrong with that?"

"Nothing, far as I'm concerned, but I don't own it. They say the pond was formed when, back in the 1700s, the Karankawa Indians excavated the limestone below the falls to build the original mission. The site where the Mexican church is now."

"It's such a beautiful place not to be shared," Lizzie says.

"The last thing the Nolans want is a highway running through the middle of their ranch. Believe me, it'll never happen!"

Lizzie barely slows the pickup before plowing through the low-water crossing. Bud places his hands on the dashboard to steady himself. Then a few moments later, the Power Wagon's tires make a repeated thumping sound as they roll over the steel rails of the cattle guard. They pass under the arched Nolan Ranch sign, and no more than a couple hundred yards off in the distance, they spot the looming derrick of a drilling rig. Bud leans forward for a closer look. "Looks like they've already spudded the well and started drilling."

He glances through the back glass, making sure they haven't been spotted. "Let's ease over there for a better view. Don't get too close or they'll make us leave."

Lizzie shifts into first gear and slowly moves forward. "Who are all these people?"

Bud doesn't take his eyes off the rig. "They're roughnecks; some are boiler men. This is a steam rig; you see those steel tanks over there?" Lizzie locates tanks lined up beside the rig and nods. "That's what powers this whole operation. That and money, lots of money." As they inch closer, Lizzie notices several earthen pits dug deep into the soil next to the rig.

"What are those used for?"

"The big one is a slush-pit; the others hold mud and chemicals."

Suddenly, Bud's hand flies up in the air. "Whoa, stop the truck!" He points toward a short man dressed in khakis and a white shirt climbing out of a Cadillac sedan.

"He'll recognize me."

"Who is that?"

"That, my dear, is Joseph P. Hamilton, owner and the hooking bull of Hamilton Oil Company." Just as soon as soon as he says it, he realizes how the words "hooking bull" must have sounded. He quickly apologizes.

"Oh, Lizzie, I'm sorry. I didn't mean to…"

She cuts him off. "Bud, you know me better than that. Forget it."

Bud continues. "He owns the tallest building in Corpus Christi, Texas, and most of the judges and politicians. So, you see how things get done around here."

You can see things starting to add up in Lizzie's head. "You scratch my back and I'll scratch yours."

Bud smacks his lips together. "Exactly."

"Should we leave?" Lizzie asks.

"Yeah, better he doesn't spot me."

On the way out, Bud points over toward the ranch camp house. "If history repeats itself, they'll be having a high-stakes poker game in there tonight."

Lizzie is curious. "They?"

"Well, not for sure, but if I was betting man, I'd say Phil Nolan, Joe Hamilton, the sheriff, Grover Giles, and a man from Houston, named M. Hassan."

Lizzie recognizes all the names but one. She glances over at Bud. "M. Hassan?"

Bud places his hands back on the dashboard as Lizzie approaches the cattle guard. His voice quivers to the beat of the steel rails as she rockets across the cattle guard and into the low-water crossing.

"He's originally from Saudi Arabia; he owns an import business and sells antiques to all these rich old women around here. You can hardly walk inside some of the homes for the clutter. Personally, I wouldn't give two cents for the whole damn lot."

"For some reason, antiques don't seem to fit this bunch," Lizzie jokes.

"A lot of the old wives stay in their silk nightgowns all day. A few never get out of bed. They have a saying for it, called, 'She's gone in.' I guess the antiques keep them company. That's when these reprobates come out to play."

Lizzie shoots Bud another inquisitive look.

"Ever wonder why Catholics have so many children?"

Lizzie has no answer and Bud is more than happy to give her one.

"Once the wife becomes pregnant, she starts dressing in maternity clothes and all love-making ceases; the husbands are then free to run their traps."

Lizzie barely slows as she approaches the end of the caliche road. Bud's eyes grow large as Lizzie blows pass the stop sign and pulls out onto the highway. He clears his throat and continues. "And when they get older, the wives are convinced that they have some sort of illness, and then with a little help from some illicit drugs, they're content being at home."

She presses the accelerator to the floor. "Looks like they've got it all figured out."

The old Dodge's engine sputters and stalls. Bud glances in the truck's side mirror to see if they're about to be run over before saying, "The only exception is Maude Nolan. She definitely has her ducks in a row. Old Phil will be the one who's gone in."

The engine in the Power Wagon suddenly gets a drink of gasoline, backfires and blows a black cloud of soot mixed with smoke from the tailpipe. Bud puts his arm out the window and grabs a hold of the door frame to steady himself as the truck rapidly gains speed down the highway. He glances over at Lizzie; she's awfully quiet. He notices the hot wind blowing her long hair in all directions and wonders what the hell she might be conjuring up in that head of hers now.

Night finds Lizzie in her kitchen. She grabs a hot pad and opens the stove's oven door. A sudden rush of heat smacks her in the face. She blinks her eyes, slides out a roasting pan, and jabs a long fork into a small, charred chuck roast. A few carrots and potatoes floating in thick, brown gravy surround the meat. She stares at the meal, thinking, *What's the point of it all? Why waste time?* She slides the pan back into the oven, turns off the gas on the stove, and glances at the wall clock. It reads 8:45 p.m.

She steps out on the front porch. Cyrus is nowhere to be seen. It's not a mystery; she knows exactly where he is—there's no sense lying to herself. She also hates to admit it, but she really doesn't care anymore. She eases down the porch steps onto the cool Bermuda grass and looks up to the stars. Her eyes are quickly drawn to the full moon. It seems so much closer than usual, bright and larger than life, almost romantic. She gazes at it for a while, lost in dreams of what might have been, before heading back into the house, stepping into the bath-room and closing the door.

Inside the Hoot Owl are the familiar crowd of oil field hands, cowboys, and the usual riffraff. Oh, and of course, Cyrus is there. He's more than accepted now, no threat, just one of them, and he feels quite comfortable. The gal with the pouty, red lips sits in a booth draining the last swallow of beer from a longneck as Cyrus plays pool with some of his newfound friends. She taps the bottle on the top of the table and then drops a lipstick-stained Salem cigarette into the neck of the empty bottle. Her bloodshot eyes follow the fiery ash as it trails smoke to the bottom of the bottle. She hears it hiss when it hits the leftover brew; her eyes trail to several couples dancing to the music coming from the jukebox. Cyrus lights a cigarette and plops down in the booth beside her. She playfully bites him on the ear and then takes a drag from his cigarette.

At the ranch, Lizzie strolls out of the bathroom and into Sam's room wearing a cotton nightie and her hair wrapped in a towel. She lets her long hair fall across her shoulders and then lies back on the bed. The night is hot and very humid. She tosses and turns, flipping the pillow over and over. She gets up, goes back to the bathroom, and runs cool water on a wash-cloth. She wrings it out and then drapes it across the back of her neck and heads back to Sam's room. Inside the room, she grabs hold of the single bed and drags it over next to the open window and lies down. She places the pillow inside the open window frame, searching for some cool air.

She rolls over on her stomach, folds her arms, rests her chin on her hands, and pushes deeper into the window. She inhales a deep breath, scrunches up her nose. The metal screen is choked with lint and has a musty odor. Her eyes open wide; she cocks her head to one side as she spies the drilling rig lights sparkling in the clear night air. The air is so still; she can hear the sounds of muffled voices and clanging iron.

Her curiosity gets the better of her. She sits straight up in bed, slips on her cowboy boots, and heads for the front door.

Lizzie pauses a few yards from the house as the thought of stepping on a rattlesnake runs through her mind, but as her eyes adjust to the bright light from the moon and stars, she keeps going. As she approaches the road in front of the camp house, she can make out the silhouettes of individuals inside the dining room. This must be the famous high-stakes poker game Bud was referring to. She veers from the road and slips behind a couple of parked cars to get a better look.

She crouches behind one of the vehicles. Peering all the way through the back glass and windshield of the car, she sees Phil Nolan, Sheriff Taylor, Joe Hamilton, Grover Giles, and a strange-looking man she has not seen before. This must be the man from Saudi Arabia, M. Hassan. Lizzie laughs under her breath, thinking, *I bet I couldn't even find Saudi Arabia on a map.*

Inside the room, the men sit at a large dining table, covered with a green felt blanket. The table legs sit inside empty molasses cans filled halfway with water to keep the ants and other insects from crawling on the felt.

Phil Nolan abruptly stands, shuffles over and opens one side of a double-door cooler. He reaches inside, grabs an opened bottle of Seagram's 7 bourbon and pours a whiskey glass, three-quarters full. He pops the cap on a bottle of 7 Up and adds a splash, careful not to bruise the whiskey with too much soda. The other men share a drink with Nolan, all except the antique dealer. M. Hassan only acts like he's joining in the drinking, but he sneakily pours his drink into the almost empty molasses can by his feet. He really doesn't seem to fit into this crowd. A heavyset man with a perfectly trimmed salt-and-pepper mustache that seems almost drawn across his top lip. Large, gaudy rings adorn every other stubby finger on his hands.

Lizzie watches M. Hassan light up a short, fat cigar and then start dealing a round of cards. He surely seems to know what he's doing. She watches for a while and then moves unseen down the road. As she gets closer to the rig, the mixture of sounds from the whining of motors, roaring boilers, and clanging metal drown out everything else.

The rig lights run up and down all four sides of the derrick, making it as bright as noon on a clear day. Her nostrils fill with a blend of burnt gas from the boilers and the acidic odor of drilling fluids. She finds herself being drawn closer and closer, mesmerized by the turning drill pipe slowly sinking deeper and deeper into the earth. She is fascinated by every part of it. The intrigue, excitement, and most of all the adventure it represents.

Suddenly, she feels two hands grab her around the waist. She spins around, finds herself staring Javelina in the face. He wears an aluminum hardhat and a jumpsuit covered in drilling mud.

"You don't want to get too close, sweetie," he says in a cocky tone. Startled, she breaks away from his hold and takes a couple of steps back.

"I was just looking."

"Looking for me?" he says, with body language showing the epitome of conceit.

She moves sideways from him, staring at the rig, running scenarios in her mind on how best to get out of this situation.

He positions himself behind her again, leans down close to her ear. Lizzie can feel his hot breath on her neck. And in a cavalier tone, he says, "You know you want me. I'll have you throwing rocks at that colored boy." He places a lot of emphasis on the words "colored boy."

Lizzie glances back at her house and thanks God she left the porch light on. She spins around to face him, knowing that she had better get in control.

"My husband is sitting on the front porch watching you."

Javelina laughs out loud. "I saw your husband at the Hoot Owl; sure he's way drunk by now."

Three short blasts from an air horn can be heard over the rig noise.

"I got to go to work now, sweetie." He takes a few steps and turns back toward her and says, "I ain't done with you." And with a smutty grin, adds, "Yet!"

Lizzie keeps her eyes on him until he's out of sight up on the rig floor. She slowly backs away from the rig, turns, and with long strides makes her way into the shadows. She puts as much distance as she can between her and the rig.

As she passes back by the camp house, she sees all the cars still parked out front. She takes a quick glimpse inside the dining room, sees that the poker game is still in full swing.

Later that night, Lizzie lies in bed thinking of the night's events when she hears the screen door open with a familiar thang. She waits a few minutes, sees the doorknob turn, and the door begin to open. She closes her eyes, pretends to be asleep until she hears the door close. She opens her eyes and listens as the stumbling footsteps fade off to the other bedroom. Cyrus is home. She rolls over to the edge of the bed, grabs Sam's little transistor radio, positions it on the windowsill, and tunes in her favorite station.

She listens as the DJ on the radio says, "This is KTSA, San Antonio, and I'm Ricci Ware. Here are The Capris and, "There's A Moon Out Tonight." Lizzie scoots forward, folds her arms on her pillow next to the radio. She stares out at the moon hovering above the lights of the distant rig, but all she can see is a silhouetted image of Preston. She closes her eyes and sways her head to the song.

Chapter Nine

GET A JOB

Lizzie sits at her desk. She rolls a sheet of paper into her typewriter. Bud rummages through the drawers of his desk until he finds a page out of a Dallas newspaper. He slings it over onto Lizzie's desk. "This is what I was talking about."

Lizzie snatches up the paper and reads aloud, "Bishop O'Malley becomes a friend of the court." She glances at Bud and then continues, "Bishop O'Malley of the Corpus Christi Diocese injects himself into the court proceedings of the Rita E. West estate trial." She flips the paper over and finds a date. "This is recent."

Bud nods his head and can feel the all-inclusive look of curiosity on her face. "It's all about money. We're talking about millions of dollars. It's a very large ranch with oil and gas production southwest of San Antonio. The late Miss West was the sole heir to the ranch. Seems they'd been courting Miss West for over ten years before she died, sending priests and nuns over there to convince her the only way into heaven is by giving her estate to the Catholic Church. And more specifically, the diocese of Corpus Christi, which in turn set up a foundation to administer the money. Just so happens, Joe Hamilton and Maude Nolan are board members."

"It's all starting to make sense," Lizzie says.

She reads more of the article and asks, "Says here the suit is about an illegitimate child of Mike West, her deceased son, claiming to be a rightful heir to the ranch and money?"

"That's right," replies Bud. "Seems Mike West got one of the maids pregnant and they sent her to a home for pregnant girls run by the Sisters of Mercy."

A hot wave of memories rushes through Lizzie. Bud notices her expression change. "What's wrong?"

Her palms are wringing wet. She rubs them across her jeans.

"I had my own experience with the nuns at a home for unwed mothers, but that's another story," Lizzie adds, picking up on one of Bud's quotes.

He doesn't pursue the subject; he can tell now is not the time, so he continues with the story. "The Supreme Court of Texas ruled in favor of the child, now a grown man, and against the lawyers for the foundation. So, Bishop O'Malley came in as a friend of the court to start the whole thing all over again."

"They never give up, do they?" Lizzie asks.

"No; actually it's pretty commonplace even around here. The diocese's lawyers money-whip the rightful heirs and they end up just settling for a paltry amount of the estate. In other words, they just keep it in court until the common folks run out of money to fight it."

Something has stirred Bud's attention outside. He eases over to the large plate glass window. "Wonder what that's all about?"

Lizzie steps up beside him. They see Sheriff Taylor standing on the front steps of the La Rosa Café. A crowd begins to gather as Elo Turk makes his way up beside the sheriff. Then, the courthouse door opens, and they watch Preston escort a distraught middle-aged Black woman down the steps. Lizzie blurts out, "That's Preston Lott. And that's his Aunt Hattie."

Bud interjects as he moves toward the door and reaches for the handle, but Lizzie beats him to it.

Bud tries to stop her. "Whoa, you better let me check..." The door slams shut before he can finish. He watches Lizzie cross the street and maneuver her way through the bystanders.

On the street, people are all talking over one another. Sheriff Taylor raises his hands above his head. "Now pipe down and listen up." The chatter slowly subsides. "Elo found the body early this morning."

Lizzie pushes her way to the front. "Whose body?" The crowd turns and stares at Lizzie. Some wonder about what a newcomer is doing messing in their affairs.

"Her name's Pearl Lott," Sheriff Taylor says in matter-of-fact tone of voice.

Lizzie notices a woman dressed in a waitress uniform pause just before stepping into the café. Laverne Tuttle is a tall, bleached-blonde woman you can tell is dreading turning forty. Laverne in a loud voice for everyone to hear says, "Hell, she was just a child."

The sheriff gives Laverne a stern, hard look. Lizzie can tell there's not a lot of love lost between them.

Lizzie hollers out. "What happened to her?"

A familiar voice rings out. "Why don't you shut up and listen?" Lizzie spins around and notices that Javelina has joined the crowd. He's rolled up his short sleeves to magnify his tattoos and huge biceps. He shoots her a filthy little grin and then winks at her.

"She jumped off the old river bridge, been missin' 'bout a week. Coyotes tore up the body pretty bad," Sheriff Taylor continues to inform the crowd.

"How do know she jumped…. Did somebody see her?" Lizzie shouts in defiance to Javelina.

The sheriff and Javelina ignore her completely. "No more questions…. I'll get to the bottom of this."

Laverne turns in the direction of the café's front door, chuckles, and says, "I'll bet you will."

Sheriff Taylor doesn't like Laverne's statement and frowns at her before motioning for Elo and Javelina to follow him to the courthouse. Lizzie glances at the La Rosa's large picture window and sees Laverne standing inside staring at her through the glass.

Lizzie walks back to the newspaper office. She steps inside and stands in the open doorway. Bud notices the vacant look in her eyes. "Well?"

She spins around and looks back across the street. She watches as the crowd breaks up, splinters off into small groups that chat and whisper to one another. "Preston Lott's cousin: she's dead."

She motions across the street. "Look at them … just going on like nothing happened."

Lost in thought, she watches Preston help his aunt into a car. Preston turns. He and Lizzie lock eyes for an instant until he looks away and hurries around to the driver-side door.

Lizzie shuts the door as Bud sits down at his desk.

"What did they say happened?" Bud asks.

"Said she jumped off the old river bridge."

He relights his pipe, takes a couple of quick puffs, and nonchalantly asks, "Who found her?" His tone is like he already knows the answer before Lizzie speaks.

"Some guy named Elo Turk. Wonder what would make a young girl do that?"

Bud rubs his jaw and stares down at the floor. "Well, looks like we have a headline for this week's edition. Might want to go out to the river bridge, get a feel for the story, and take a few pictures."

He doesn't have to tell her twice. She grabs her purse and glances around the room. Bud reads her mind, opens the side drawer on this desk, and pulls out his camera and car keys. "It's a few miles south of town on the cutoff road. Take the side road before the bridge. Used to be a park next to the river many years ago."

Later that morning, Lizzie strolls along the riverbank. She follows the current as the water spills over a concrete dam and then pours onto the rocks below. She looks up at the narrow, steel-framed bridge above. Very few vehicles cross the rough asphalt deck as she snaps several photos.

She notices that the marked area where they found the body has been thoroughly cleaned, and there is strong smell of bleach permeating the whole area. She trudges up the roadway to the bridge and sees that there's less than a foot of space between the bridge railing and the edge of the roadway. She positions herself where she thinks Pearl might have stood before leaping. She cocks her head and surveys the ground below. Things just don't add up in her mind. The highest part of the bridge is the other end where the river flows. She snaps more pictures.

Catching her by surprise, a black Buick sedan with a single, flashing red light and a long whip radio antenna on each fender is upon her. Sheriff Taylor lowers his driver-side window.

"The sign says no pedestrian crossing."

Lizzie leans down level with the sheriff's line of sight. "I wasn't planning on crossing."

He decides to play along. "Then what the hell are you doing up here?"

"Taking pictures."

He flips a switch on the dash, kills the flashing red light. "Pictures for who?" The sheriff's sedan has several cars backed up in both directions on the one-way bridge.

"Bud Harkins; I work for the newspaper," Lizzie says in a stern, confident voice.

He glances into the rearview mirror. "Get in."

Lizzie decides confrontation at this moment probably wouldn't be in her best interest, as she pulls the camera from around her neck and climbs into the passenger side of the sedan.

"You ever been in a police vehicle before?"

She chuckles and in a soft voice says, "Once or twice."

An insipid grin cuts across his face. "I figured as much." The ride is short as he pulls up and parks beside Bud's Chevy. He turns and stares at her for moment. Lizzie can feel what's coming. The old mind your business lecture. "A little advice; don't go poking your nose into things that don't concern you."

She opens the door. "Is that it?"

He grins, shifts the Buick into reverse, twitches his nose, and says, "For now."

Lizzie walks in the back door of the newspaper as Bud rocks back in his desk chair.

"Well, what did you find?"

Lizzie sits down at her desk. She rolls a sheet of paper into her typewriter. "Something is going on here.... Something's not right."

She begins to type as Bud leans forward in his chair and asks, "Did I say you could start writing?"

Lizzie doesn't stop typing or look up from the page. "You never said I couldn't."

Chapter Ten

PUT YOUR HEAD ON
MY SHOULDER

Across the railroad tracks and several blocks from the center of Seclusion stands a wood-framed, single-story church. Out front is a faded sign nestled in trampled weeds and grass that reads Mount Pilgrim Baptist Church.

Several members of the overflow crowd that stand outside observe Lizzie as she walks up the steps to the front door. She can hear piano music and singing coming from inside. She's wearing the same dress and black scarf that she wore to her son's funeral. She presses down on the door's handle and pushes. It doesn't budge.

Inside the small church, a Black preacher stands by the podium. A closed, pine casket lies in front of him with a casket piece made of white chrysanthemums draped over the top. Hattie Lott, Pearl's aunt, sits next to Preston. Hattie is a rather large, but fit woman. The song finishes and the preacher begins to address the mourners. "We gather to ask ourselves again…." Lizzie places her other hand against the door and pushes harder.

The church door opens with a loud creak, interrupting the minister. In a slow continuous wave, the all-Black congregation leans around to face the door and sees Lizzie standing in the back of the church. Preston catches her eye. Hattie sees what's going on and nudges Preston to turn his attention back to the preacher who is continuing with his eulogy. "Why another one of our children is dead and there is no concern in the community."

A frail Black man sits next to the aisle in the back row. His crepey and wrinkled skin tells on his eighty years of hard work. He stands, gives Lizzie his seat, and then shows her a small photo. Lizzie focuses on a grainy picture of Pearl Lott, and then looks around and surveys the crowd of mourners. Other than the funeral director, she's the only White person there. She notices an attractive Black woman sitting at an upright piano wearing a bright-yellow dress with a pillbox hat to match. She begins to play one of a slew of gospel songs without any sheet music as the crowd belts out the tunes.

Later that morning, the crowd of mourners slowly makes their way from the grave site. Preston sees Lizzie slowly ambling along. She wipes away tears as she passes Pearl's casket resting beside a mound of bare earth. She continues down a row of tombstones with names like Avery, Williams, Lewis, Harris, and on and on. She bets in her heart they all had a very interesting story or two to tell.

Preston eases up beside her. When she sees him and without saying a word, she pulls him close, kisses him on the cheek. "Lizzie, you can't do that." Surprised by the move, he looks around to see if anyone witnessed them.

"Why not?" she asks.

He gives her a serious look. "You know why not."

He escorts her along a winding dirt path through the graveyard. Unseen by the two, the sheriff's car sits idling on the highway above the cemetery. Inside the car, Sheriff Taylor presses a pair of binoculars to his eyes, a sinister grin festers across his face.

It's late in the afternoon; out front of the newspaper office, Bud helps Lizzie load the negatives for the latest edition of the *Timely Remarks* into the back seat of his Chevy sedan.

"You be careful now; she's got a V-8 engine with a four-barrel. Little more zip than your old truck."

"You know a lot about engines?" she asks.

Bud shrugs his shoulders and answers, "Naw; they told me that when I bought her."

A few minutes later, Lizzie passes the outskirts of Seclusion and merges onto a two-lane highway. She presses down on the accelerator and zooms past a couple of slower vehicles. She whips back into the right-hand lane and grins. She unwraps a piece of bubble gum with her teeth, and then spins the dial on the radio until she hears the song "Put Your Head On My Shoulder," one of her favorite tunes. She smiles and sings along to the radio for the next forty miles.

In the city of Victoria, Lizzie slows in front of a single-story brick building that's home to the Victoria County

Press. She locates the gated entrance to the rear of the office, pulls in, and parks next to the dock. Inside the building, she follows the directions to a small cubicle and steps inside. She hears printing presses rumbling in the background. A pimply faced college-age boy enters the room and says, "Pull up next to the dock and I'll get you unloaded."

Lizzie points outside to the loading dock and says, "I already have."

He glances up at a wall clock. "It'll take me a couple of hours. You got time to go to the picture show. That what the other fella did."

Lizzie nods, hands him the keys to the Chevy, and strolls outside. She spots the Rialto Theater on the opposite side of the street. She hurries across the asphalt pavement that is still warm from the afternoon sun and goes up to the ticket window. She hands the cashier a quarter and watches a single ticket stub roll out of a metal slot in the counter. The marquee above her head reads, "Now Showing—*The Time Machine*."

Lizzie steps inside, runs face to face into Preston. The smell of fresh popcorn and fountain drinks bring back a few good memories of her childhood. She notices Preston balancing a drink and a bag of popcorn in his hands and a surprised look on his face when he says, "You over here at the newspaper?"

"Yeah, got a few hours to kill. Looks like we're together?"

He gestures with his eyes to a small sign above a narrow staircase that says, "Negro Section." She glances up at the sign, shrugs her shoulders and says, "I'm right behind you."

He briefly hesitates before taking the stairs. "You know this isn't a good idea."

She rolls her eyes, cocks her head to one side. "What are they going to do? Arrest me?"

He turns and leads the way. She's right on his heels up the flight of stairs. "Can I have a sip of your Coke, or should I get my own?"

He turns back, glances down at her and says, "One sip."

In the theater's balcony, a handful of Black moviegoers are scattered out in the first several rows. Preston and Lizzie sit down together on the very back row. A couple of Black ladies turn around, stare and then whisper to one another. It's not often they see a White woman and a Black man sitting together in the colored section of the balcony.

She takes a drink of his soda and a handful of popcorn. She leans in close, rubs his shoulder with hers. He shies away. She flashes him a quick look. "I'm cold!" she exclaims.

"What if Cyrus was to see us?"

Lizzie laughs, "I guarantee you this is one place you'll never see Cyrus."

She snuggles up close and puts her head on his shoulder.

Later in the evening, Lizzie eats ice from his empty drink cup. She listens attentively to Preston. "Hattie told the sheriff she was missing after a couple of days. Same day you gave me the ride back to the ranch. See, she had run away a few times before, but she always showed back up."

He takes the cup from her, turns it upside down. It's completely empty, not even a piece of ice. "I said one sip."

Lizzie smiles, ignores his statement, and then asks, "Why did she run away before?"

Preston stuffs the empty popcorn sack into the paper cup.

"She was very closed-mouth, but she worked for the Nolans. Who knows what may have happened there?"

"We're going to find out the truth," Lizzie says emphatically.

"You don't know these people, Lizzie."

"That doesn't matter."

The same two Black ladies turn back and shush at them. Preston lowers his voice to a whisper.

"It does matter. You don't know what they're capable of."

"They don't know what I'm capable of."

Preston lets her boisterous comment pass. He knows she can be a little naive when it comes to the powers that control Seclusion.

The movie ends and the balcony empties. Preston and Lizzie continue talking as the credits roll on the screen. They finally get up from their seats as the projector ends abruptly and the house lights in the theater come on.

Across the street in the newspaper office, the pimply faced boy stands by an empty desk with his eyes fixed on the Rialto Theatre. All the moviegoers have exited the building and left. He watches as the door opens and Preston and Lizzie emerge and pause briefly out on the sidewalk. The boy picks up a rotary telephone and dials.

A man's voice on the other end of the line says, "Hello?"

The boy speaks softly and slowly into the receiver. "She's been in the Rialto all night with that Lott boy." He hangs up the receiver and moves away from the desk as Preston and Lizzie finish talking and take off in different directions. He's waiting on Lizzie when she walks into the office. "You're all loaded up."

Lizzie smiles, picks up her keys, and says, "Thanks; that was fast."

He stares at her for a minute before asking, "How was the movie?"

She pulls open the door, turns back, "Great; you should go see it."

He doesn't answer and watches her walk the distance to her car.

Chapter Eleven

EVERYBODY'S
SOMEBODY'S FOOL

A rooster's crow signals a breaking dawn and a new day. Cyrus and Lizzie sit at the kitchen table, both already dressed for the workday. They are silent. Lizzie can feel the seething tension between the two is reaching boiling point. She pushes a couple of empty, mismatched coffee cups and a bowl of half-eaten oatmeal to one side of the table and stands up. Blue flames from a lit burner dancing on the stovetop provide the only source of light in the darkened room.

She then moves over to the sink, pulls up the shade of the window, and glances outside. The reflection of the rising sun peaking on the horizon casts a red glow on distant thunderheads.

"Getting light outside," she remarks, causing Cyrus to jump to his feet.

"I'm goin' after that bull. They seen him over at McFadden's place."

Lizzie knows this is all about him and not about Sam or the bull.

"Let it go, Cyrus."

"It sumpin' I got to do."

"Not for me."

"Never said it was for you."

"Not for Sam," she shoots back.

His eyes follow her as she steps over and clears the table.

"You think you're so goddamn smart."

He grabs his hat. "You blame me, don't you? I loved that boy like he was my own." He walks to the door, stops and turns around. "You got lots of people talking."

"I hope so."

He smirks, rolls his eyes. "Ain't 'bout what you think."

"And what's that mean?"

"You know what the hell I'm talking 'bout. You and Preston Lott."

She knows he wants to pick a fight as he steps outside on the porch and hollers back.

"What, I ain't enough of a man for you no more?"

Lizzie knows it would be in her better interest to just ignore him, but she follows him to the front porch and in a stern tone says, "There's nothing's going on with me and Preston Lott."

"Not what I hear. This is a small town and word gets around."

"Is that the gossip you hear at the Hoot Owl?"

Cyrus is in no mood to being reminded about his drinking. "Oh, there you go changing the subject…. You just don't want to admit it."

Lizzie doesn't want to get in a tit for tat with him, but her anger gets the best of her, and she thinks she needs to defend herself.

"You're right about one thing. He's way more of a man than you'll ever be." As soon as the words leave her mouth, she realizes that was probably the wrong thing to say, but it's too late now. The anger instantly builds on his face. She sees him grit his teeth, raise his arm, and with his open palm, slap her hard across the side of her face. The blow knocks her sideways almost off her feet. Although it actually didn't hurt as much as in the past, she thinks maybe she's getting used to it as she drags her fingertips down her cheek, steps back inside the house, and lets the screen door slam shut.

"I'm taking the truck this morning. If you want a ride with me, you better c'mon!" he shouts as he steps off the porch.

Later in Seclusion, Cyrus is behind the wheel of the Dodge pickup; Lizzie sits silent in the passenger seat, staring out her window as Cyrus pulls up and parks parallel to the curb in front of the *Timely Remarks*. Lizzie turns and looks squarely at him, waiting to hear if he has anything to say. She doesn't have to wait long. While impatiently waiting, he races the engine on the truck and says, "Well, hurry up and get out."

That wasn't what she wanted to hear. She wastes no time opening the door and letting her feet slide off the floorboard and hit the pavement in a run to the back of the Power Wagon. Just as she reaches over the tailgate and attempts to lift her typewriter from the back, Cyrus steps on the accelerator, pulls away from the curb and speeds off down the street. Bud stands at the window witnessing the scene unfold outside.

Lizzie hesitates at the front door of the newspaper office and then wheels around, crosses the street, and trots up the steps to the courthouse entrance. Several citizens gathered in the hall and watch as Lizzie marches across the marble floor that leads to a wooden door with frosted glass that is slightly ajar. She jerks open the door and disappears inside. From out in the hall, one can hear Sheriff Taylor's anger grow as his voice gets louder. "Who tha' hell you think you are to come bargin' in here tellin' me what I'm supposed to be doing?"

Inside his office, the sheriff sits at a chipped and scarred wooden desk. On the wall behind him are pictures of Eisenhower and Nixon framed in Old Glory. Lizzie stands in front of him.

"A fifteen-year-old child goes missing and you don't even look for her?"

"I ain't paid to go lookin' after every wetback and colored that goes missin' around here."

"You're supposed to work for everyone in this county."

He stands. He's now red-faced and very angry as he leans across his desk. Lizzie notices a stream of salvia drool from the corner of his mouth.

"I'll work for whom I goddamn well please."

Lizzie doesn't let up. "Why wasn't an autopsy ordered on the body? Isn't it the law?"

He slams his fist on top of his desk, making Lizzie's eyes blink.

"The law is what I make it." He stomps over to the door and flings it open. Lizzie watches it bang hard against the wall, rattling the glass. "Now, get the hell outta' my office."

They engage in a brief staring match as she walks out of his office. Lizzie hurries across the street and into the newspaper office. Bud can tell she's fired up about something. "What's gotten your dander up?"

"Sheriff Taylor, old son-of-a-bitch, just threw me out of his office."

Bud pulls out his pipe. "Now, why doesn't that surprise me?" He strikes a match, lights his pipe, and says, "By the way, the boys have started delivering the paper around town. I just happened to grab a copy."

Lizzie thinks to herself, *Now the shit is fixing to hit the fan.*

He holds up a copy of the newspaper. "You don't mince words."

Lizzie looks up at him. "But it's the truth."

Bud grins. "The truth and what people want to hear aren't usually the same, not in Seclusion anyway."

About twenty miles north of Seclusion, the old Dodge Power Wagon towing a tandem horse trailer pulls off the highway and stops in front of a closed metal gate made with oilfield pipe and sucker rods. A painted sign welded to the top rail of the gate spells out McFadden Ranch. Three horses stand inside the trailer facing the bed of the truck where a lone vaquero lies across a pile of empty saddles and blankets. Cyrus shifts the pickup into low gear as Preston swings open the gate. Preston has figured out what Cyrus is up to. Although he doesn't agree, he's in no position to stop him. Cyrus pulls the truck and trailer through the entrance and waits for Preston to close and lock the gate.

Preston jumps back inside the cab of the truck and asks, "Do we have permission to be in here?"

Cyrus knows he doesn't have to answer to Preston. "What do you think?"

Preston turns around in the seat and looks back at the vaquero and the horses in the trailer and says to Cyrus, "That we're trespassing?"

Cyrus doesn't answer; he pops a cigarette between his lips, strikes a match, and cups both hands to shield the flame against the wind. He inhales a long drag, blows out the match, and drops it on the floorboard.

Back in Seclusion, Grover Giles, the owner of the La Rosa Café, sweeps the front sidewalk in front of his establishment. He uses his broom to block the path of several Black ladies to let a couple of White men enter the café. Grover follows them inside where they join a large group of men that line the counter and pitches a copy of the *Timely Remarks* on top of the counter. "This is the kind of shit I've been warning you about."

The men continue to chat among themselves. Grover snatches up the paper and reads aloud. "A town that separates its citizens by the color of their skin and the depth of their pocketbooks." Grover shakes his head. "Her and that senile old fart are gonna start stirring these coloreds up."

He hands the paper to Javelina and right on cue Javelina blurts out, "Grover's nephew seen her and that Lott boy coming out of the picture show over in Victoria." Idle chatter breaks out among the men.

Grover chimes back in. "We gonna stand idly by and let this be an example for our children and grandchildren?"

"Hell no!" they all say in unison.

A middle-aged, jug-butted man crosses his arms, leans back against the counter, and mouths, "She sure is a looker. I wouldn't mind getting a little of that."

A skinny bald man smirks and says to the jug-butted man, "If that Lott boy been tapping it, doubt you'd do her much good." The other men all laugh out loud.

In the rear of the dining room, Phil Nolan and the sheriff sit huddled at a small table by themselves. Nolan leans across the table as he slides a sealed brown envelope to the sheriff who takes the envelope, flips it up, and sees that it is official stationery from the Diocese of Corpus Christi. He looks at Nolan and says, "What this about?"

"Last payment for services rendered. There's a note inside. Make sure you don't leave any evidence."

"I'll just call it a little early Christmas," Sheriff Taylor smiles as he stuffs it in his hip pocket and together, he and Nolan get up and walk to the front of the café.

Nolan straddles a chair next to the counter. He takes the paper from Javelina and points to the men around the room. "She's talking about you and me. Our families, which have been here for generations."

Nolan is doing a much better job of rousing the men up than Grover did.

"Pretty soon it'll be your daughters or maybe even one of your wives bedding up with a Black buck." Nolan stands, shoves his chair under a nearby table. "Is that what you want?"

The men now talk over one another, puffing out their chests and siding with Nolan.

Across the street in the newspaper office, Bud sits at his desk. Lizzie stands in front of him. She scratches her head with the eraser end of a pencil. "Who is this Elo Turk?"

Bud takes a breath, like this is going to take a while to explain. "Lives with his mother a few miles outside of town. She's kind' a recluse. Nobody goes out there because of the snakes." Lizzie squints her eyes. "Snakes?"

Bud jokes, "Some people have watch dogs; she has snakes."

"What happened to Elo's eye?"

Bud shakes his head. "He was just a youngster playing hide-'n-seek with another little boy."

Bud plops down on the couch. "Elo was peeking through the door's keyhole, when the other boy shoved a pencil through it."

Lizzie hand goes to her mouth. For a second, she wants to throw up.

"It was a terrible accident," Bud says.

Without them seeing, Sheriff Taylor is stomping across the street, marching like a foot soldier toward the front door of the newspaper office. The door chime sounds and before they can look up, he barges in, surprising both of them. He pitches the newspaper on top of the counter. The headline reads, "Seclusion—A Town Without Pity!" He cuts his eyes toward Bud.

"What the hell is this?"

Bud in a calm, direct voice, "Well, Sheriff, in America, it's called freedom of the press."

Not liking the answer, the sheriff says, "You're shittin' me, right? This is Seclusion. They want it stopped."

Lizzie takes her turn, "Who are they?" He quickly flips his attention to Lizzie as he reaches down with both hands, wads the paper into a tight ball, and then smashes it against the countertop.

"Who you think you are to come barging into this peaceful community and start stirring up all this bullshit?"

Bud attempts to assert what little authority he thinks he has and defends Lizzie. "Taylor, you can't tell us what to print."

"Nobody said I was. I'm telling you what not to print."

Sheriff Taylor points his index finger right at Bud. "You don't want to go down this road again. I thought you knew better."

He wheels around and stomps out the front door. Lizzie goes to the window and watches him head across the street. "That's why we sold out of papers; we've hit a nerve." Bud joins her at the window where they watch Sheriff Taylor stop in the middle of the street, turn back in the direction of the newspaper office, and flash another threatening look as Bud quips, "He's so mad; he looks like he's got rocks in his jaws."

Bud turns away from the window, drops his chin against his chest, and cuts his eyes up at Lizzie and says, "Seriously, you know, it's gonna get rough."

"I know."

"No, I don't think you do."

"You want me to stop?"

"I never said that."

Bud ambles over toward the staircase, pauses on the first step, and looks down. "When I was your age, there were two things I never ran from. One was a fair fight and the other, a good drink of bourbon whiskey." He turns, looks over at her, and with a slight grin says, "I still miss the whiskey." He rubs his upper arm as he climbs the stairs. "I'm going to lie down for a little while; wake me at three-forty-five."

In the middle of the McFadden ranch, three mounted cowboys crest the top of a brushy hill and stop. It seems eerily quiet, like the feeling right before a lightning strike ahead of a storm. Cyrus shields his eyes from the sun, peers through the heat shimmers dancing off the ground, and with a sadistic grin on his face says, "There the sonofabitch is."

Down below, the black motley-faced bull stands grazing in a grassy field with a small herd of young heifers. The big bull slings his head from side to side, causing a thick foam of slobber to splatter and settle across his withers, temporarily relieving him from a swarm of blowflies. The vaquero spits his leftover chewing tobacco onto the ground and whispers to himself, "*El Diablo.*"

Cyrus glances at the vaquero and then at Preston before remarking, "Mexicans all superstitious." Cyrus turns around in his saddle, glances behind him, and then up at the sun. "We'll stay upwind and push 'em to that clearing."

Cyrus, Preston, and the vaquero separate. They ride quietly through the underbrush. Each holds a rope with the loop ready. Diablo throws his head up and around sensing something is out of the ordinary. Suddenly, he sees the cowboys. He pivots and in a few steps, he's in full stride. The bull knows if he can make it to the thicker brush along the creek, he can escape. Diablo turns for the creek bottom and is temporarily outrunning Cyrus.

Cyrus spanks his horse on the rump with his loop; the horse stretches out, plows through the scrub brush. The horse's chest and legs bleed from the prickly pear cactus and cat-claw thorns. He finally gains ground and closes behind the bull. Cyrus makes a couple of swings, building a bigger loop before he lets it fly. He watches the rope float over the bull's horns and around his neck.

He hollers to Preston, "Hurry up and get your rope on him." Preston is reluctant but realizes they're at a point of no backing off now. In several long strides, Preston races up on the other side of the bull; his rope barely fits over the bull's massive horns. Cyrus continues to shout out orders. "Stop him before he gets to the brush." The ropes tighten and Diablo whirls around to fight. The bull's tongue is out; he's fighting for what little breath he can get through the noose that is tightening around his neck.

Preston hollers to the vaquero in Spanish, "Rope his heels." The vaquero hears him and spurs his horse up behind the bull. He swings a large loop that snares the hind feet of Diablo.

Cyrus now shouts to Preston. "Get down off your horse and take your rope off and then get a half-hitch around that tree. We'll neck the sonafabitch."

Preston argues with Cyrus. "Shouldn't we take off your rope? It's choking him down."

Cyrus fires back. "Do what the hell I told you." Preston climbs down from his horse, motions to the vaquero and says, "Don't let him have any slack."

The vaquero pulls back on his reins, tightens the rope around the bull's hind legs. One of the strands of the manila rope near the saddle horn snaps and then unravels. The vaquero glances down at his saddle and notices the fraying rope just as Preston sneaks up beside the bull. The vaquero screams at Preston in Spanish, "*Cuerda, cuerda!*"

Preston hears a sharp crack as the vaquero's rope snaps in two. Diablo gets a sudden breath of air, lunges at Preston and slams him to the ground. Preston crawls on his hands and knees, trying desperately to regain his feet. The bull lowers his head and snorts. The breath from his nostrils stirs the dust. Diablo charges, rolls Preston along the ground like a heap of rags. The vaquero reaches down, grabs the severed rope and takes several wraps around his saddle horn. Cyrus' spurs dig into the sides of his horse. The loop tightens again around the bull's neck. Cyrus continues to circle around the animal, wrapping his rope around Diablo's legs.

The massive Brahma bull chokes and gasps and then crumbles to the ground. Cyrus's saddle leans to one side. The vaquero pulls Preston to his feet. Dirt covers him from head to toe. His eyes are glassy. He struggles to focus as he attempts to shake the cobwebs from his brain. The image of Cyrus and Diablo is blurred and foggy.

"Turn him loose, Cyrus. Can't you hear him … he's dying?"

Cyrus continues to jab the metal rowels into his horse's now bloody flanks. Preston digs into his jeans, pulls out his pocketknife and slices through the rope

"What the hell you doing?" With the slack now in the rope, Cyrus's horse stumbles forward. "He deserves to die!" hollers Cyrus.

Preston can tell by looking at the animal that he's taking his last breaths. "Never like this."

Diablo heaves and makes a deep gurgling sound. He takes several shallow breaths, and then his massive body quivers and goes silent. Cyrus slides off his horse, falls to the ground on his knees. "Get away from him. Let the bastard suffer."

Preston shakes his head. It's hard for him to believe what has just happened. "He's done all the suffering he's going to do, Cyrus."

Preston looks around at all the carnage, sees the vaquero staring back at him. He turns to Cyrus and says, "All this pain isn't going to change what happened."

Cyrus struggles to his feet. "You need to mind your own fuckin' business."

"I thought we were friends, Cyrus."

Cyrus laughs, "A friend wouldn't be fuckin' my old lady."

"You're crazy. You know that's not true."

Cyrus points his index finger at Preston. "Don't shit me. I know what's going on."

Cyrus struggles to his feet, drags his palms across his khaki pants, and in a seething expression of resentment blurts, "You want her … you can have her."

Preston shakes his head, picks up the reins of his horse, and starts leading him away. The vaquero stares down at the dead bull for a moment and then slowly falls in line behind Preston.

It's late afternoon in Seclusion as Bud eases down the stairs, pulls off a note that is taped to the back of his chair. He lights his pipe, strolls over to the window and gazes across the street at the courthouse.

Inside the county clerk's office at the courthouse, a couple of female employees watch Lizzie flop two large books down on a conference table. One hurries out the door and hotfoots it down to the sheriff's office.

Bud hears a loud tapping on the window glass. He glances up to see Preston with his hands cupped, framing his face against the window. Bud motions for him to come in. He pushes open the door and in a very anxious voice, asks, "Where's Lizzie?" Bud notices his face and arms are covered in cuts and abrasions as he points in the direction of the courthouse.

Before Bud can question him, Preston races across the street. Bud moves closer to the window and sees Preston run into Lizzie on the steps of the courthouse. He notices Preston's hands and arms flailing as someone telling a very animated story. After a short while, they separate. Lizzie is visibly upset as she crosses the street and steps back into the *Timely Remarks*. For a moment, she just stares at Bud without speaking.

"Trouble?" Bud asks. Lizzie begins to pace back and forth, rubbing her hands together.

"There was a cattle working accident. Cyrus killed that bull on someone else's property." She takes deep breath. "Phil Nolan fired him."

Lizzie steps over to the window and looks out with a blank stare.

"He's been drinking all afternoon at the beer joint, telling everyone how he got revenge on Diablo."

Just then, they both hear screeching tires resonating from around the street corner. Lizzie continues, "And now he's coming over here to tell me that's he's leaving me."

Lizzie steps away from the window as the old Power Wagon bounces up on the curb in front of the office. Steam from the radiator pours from under the hood. Cyrus slings the driver-side door open, grabs the door frame, pulls himself upright and props himself against the side of the truck bed, and then shuffles around the back of the truck and across the sidewalk to the front door of the office.

Lizzie moves toward the door. Bud grabs her arm, points to a group of bystanders who stare. "Best let him come on in," Bud says as Lizzie steps back. She's ashamed, but not surprised. She wonders which way her life is going to turn from here.

"He's awful damn drunk," Bud says.

The office door slams against the wall. Cyrus staggers inside, steadies himself against the counter, and slurring his words at best says, "Bull's dead."

Lizzie face is expressionless. "I know. Was it worth it?" she snaps back.

Cyrus attempts to taunt her as he knows the only one who could have told her what happened would be Preston.

"You been talkin' to your new lover?" He weaves to one side. "Load up. We're gettin' outta here."

Lizzie tries to speak, but he cuts her off. "Ain't that what you said you wanted?"

She stands her ground and doesn't respond. He coughs, falls backward, barely catching himself. "Hell, I'm better off without you. I already told him he can have you." He turns, stumbles toward the door, looks back, and yells, "This is all your fault!"

Cyrus spits on the sidewalk and then makes his way to the back of his truck, grabs the top of the tailgate, leans down, and vomits all over his boots. As he raises his head, he wipes his mouth with the back of his hand, and notices Lizzie's typewriter lying in the bed of the truck. He picks it up, raises it high above his head, and flings it down onto the concrete. The typewriter smashes into a dozen pieces, with the carriage skipping along the sidewalk to the front of the building next door. From the window, Lizzie watches the spectacle unfold on the street. She and Cyrus's past years together quickly roll by in her mind and she now realizes that if there was any real love, she somehow took a wrong turn at one of the many forks in the road along the way. She eases over to the door and removes what's left of the "Room for rent" flyers and glances over at Bud for his approval. He nods as they both watch Cyrus crank up the truck, make a U-turn, and careen down the street.

"You'll have to carry me for a little while. I don't have the money for the first month's rent. I'm still paying for Sam's funeral."

Bud hates to have to witness her going through more strife and pain in her life. "Lizzie, I'd rather have your credit than most people's cash." Then, Bud gets serious and looks her in the eye. "Divorces can be messy and expensive."

He sees the embarrassment begin to roll across her face as she says, "We were never married."

"I wondered, but I never said anything. That's your business. If you ever need someone to talk to, I'm here."

Lizzie seizes the opportunity to open up and finally release her pent-up feelings. She feels Bud is someone she trusts to listen to her, and like a dam with words flowing over a spillway, she lets go.

"I never knew my father and mother. My mother's folks were strict Catholics, and they were ashamed of her for getting pregnant with me. Soon after I was born, I was shipped away to foster care and I guess she resumed a normal life. Whatever normal meant at the time. When I was about fifteen, she was killed in a car wreck." Lizzie voice begins to crack. "As far as I know she never married and never tried to find me. I found this all out later."

Her eyes turn glassy. Bud hands her his handkerchief. "I was shuffled from one foster home to another until I got old enough to try and escape. That just made it worse when I got caught." She dabs her eyes. "I've had my share of men slipping into my room at night."

She takes a deep breath. "Finally, at age sixteen I was raped and became pregnant by my foster father who was also a big shot in the local Catholic Church."

Bud interjects. "Why didn't you go to the authorities?"

"I did," Lizzie replies. "His wife swore to the police that I was possessed by Satan and that I had seduced him. So, to save shame and humiliation, they sent me off to one of those Catholic homes for unwed mothers called Magdalene Laundries. It was really a prison where we did laundry day in and day out for no pay. The nuns called it doing penance for the sin of fornication, but that wasn't the worst part. They had strict rules and if you broke them, you were severely punished. It was a hellhole. They would lock us girls in a small closet for days at a time or make us kneel on a stone floor for hours for simple things like speaking or smiling at one another." Lizzie dabs her eyes with the handkerchief.

"You stayed there until you had your baby, and then after a couple of months, they sold the baby for adoption. I saw this with several other girls, and I swore it wasn't going to happen to me and my baby. I planned my escape, and one night when the time was right, I started a fire in the laundry area and in all the confusion I grabbed Sam and slipped outside and through the gates."

Bud rubs his chin and shakes his head. "Lizzie, I'm so sorry."

She grabs her purse. "Oh, there were others that had it much worse than me." She looks around the room to see if she's forgotten anything. "I guess I never knew what good people acted like, but that's no excuse for me ending up with someone like Cyrus." Lizzie glances up at the wall clock. "I better head on out." Bud opens his desk drawer and pitches her the keys.

"I'd tell you to be careful, but you already know that! Don't you?"

She just smiles at him, though it was not the affirmative answer he was looking for.

"After I get back from Victoria … okay if I run out to the ranch and get my stuff?"

"Keep them. I don't plan on driving anywhere soon," Bud says as he follows her to the door and adds, "Wake me, so I know you're home safe."

Chapter Twelve

POETRY IN MOTION

Bud's Chevy zips across a series of wooden causeways that span a large bayou dotted with lily pads. Lizzie surveys the murky water below. She's never been fond of a body of water. A river, ocean, or lake, they all scare her, and what could be in the water frightens her even more. Not to mention the little incident at Artesian Falls where she though she was drowning.

Behind the wheel, Lizzie unwraps a piece of Double Bubble and then spins the dial on the radio until she picks up the local Victoria, Texas, radio station and hears, "In tonight's semipro game, Preston Lott will quarterback the all-Negro Blackcats against the undefeated Houston Roughnecks." She pauses a moment and then keeps turning the dial until she finds one of her new favorite songs. She mouths the words to the song "Poetry in Motion," until she catches an image of herself in the rearview mirror. She watches her eyes cross as she sees a small bubble emerge from her lips and pop and stick to the end of her nose. A curtain of disappointment drops across her face.

Later in the evening, Lizzie stands on the sidewalk in front of the Victoria County Press. She glances across the street at the movie theater, and then remembers what the radio announcer said on the way over here. She turns and looks up and down the street. In the far distance, she makes out the faint glow of stadium lights.

The wheels are turning in Lizzie's head. She struts back into the parking area, climbs into the Chevy, cranks it up, and pulls out onto the street. She travels in the direction of the lights. They seem to draw her like a magnet and grow brighter as she gets closer. After a few miles, the field is just a couple of streets over. She turns onto a side street, pulls into the parking lot next to the stadium, and guides the Chevy into an empty space.

Lizzie makes her way into the stadium, passes an un-manned ticket booth, and then climbs the rickety steps of the wooden bleachers and sits by herself in a row of empty seats. The air has a scent of freshly mowed grass. The stands are about a quarter full. In the section next to her, several rows of White men and women chat among themselves. The larger Black community sits to one side and pretends not to notice her. With the scoreboard showing thirty-one seconds left in the game, Lizzie is sad that she'd apparently missed most of it.

A whistle suddenly blows, and her attention turns to the grass field. Bodies hurl into one another. A heap of football players crash to the turf. Grunts and groans mingle throughout the pile of muscle and pads.

She spots Preston as he calls the Blackcats into the hud-dle. Their uniforms are worn and raggedy with mismatched helmets. Some are missing face masks. Across the line are the

Houston Roughnecks in spanking new red and blue uniforms. The Roughnecks are all-White, all-bad, and led by three-hundred-pound, twenty-five-year-old Butch Markowsky. Butch could have played professional football had it not been for his attitude and criminal record.

The scoreboard reads Victoria 19, Houston 20. Butch signals a timeout and calls his team into a huddle. Inside the Roughneck's huddle, Butch is the boss, and he speaks with authority. Snot mixed with a little blood is dripping from his nose as his teammates watch him draw a play on the grass. "We can't let these jigaboos beat us." They clap their hands, break the huddle, and line up on their own goal line across from the Blackcats.

Preston walks to the line of scrimmage, barks out the signals as he stares across the line at Butch. "Your Black ass is going down," Butch shouts as the center snaps the ball. Preston fakes, then darts outside and dives across the goal line and is met by a host of Roughnecks.

Butch dives on the pile of players, drives his fist hard into Preston's side dislodging the ball. Butch jumps to his feet holding the ball high above his head. The referee signals Roughnecks ball and the end of the game. Preston rushes up to Butch, "Hey, that's cheating."

Butch shoves the ball into Preston's gut, shakes his head and snickers. "Cryin' ass niggers." Preston's eyes follow Butch as he sprints off the field, knowing that the only place he can ever settle this would be on the field. He turns to trot off the field when he notices Lizzie standing on the bottom row of bleachers by the railing. She is waving her arms to get his attention. He jogs over to the sideline in front of the stands.

"I saw the lights," Lizzie says as she eyes him up in his uniform. Preston moves closer to the railing. The cuts and bruises from his encounter with Diablo are still very apparent on his face and hands.

"You over at the newspaper?"

She smiles "Right now, I'm watching you." She glances up at the scoreboard. "You almost won."

Preston nods his head and grumbles just loud enough for Lizzie to hear. "Yeah, if they hadn't cheated."

Lizzie acknowledges his remark and says, "Sometimes, that's the only way some people can win."

"Seems like it's all the time lately…. Been thinking about just quitting."

Lizzie hurriedly makes her way down on the field and over beside him.

"You can't quit." She doubles up her right fist and imitates a boxer's jab. "Remember, the first lick in a fight is always the most important."

"Not as easy as you think," he says as his eyes trail up to the stands where the row of White couples stand and stare. Lizzie can see that he is worried what people might be thinking, but she couldn't care less.

Lizzie gets his attention and says, "Cyrus left."

Preston has a puzzled look on his face. "Left you or left town?" Lizzie shrugs her shoulders. "Both, I hope."

"Stop by the newspaper…. I'll buy you a soda. I owe you one."

He glances back up into the stands. "Don't think that'd be a good idea."

Lizzie follows his eyes. "It'll be fine and quit worrying about them."

He flashes her a look like he doesn't believe her. She counters with, "Really!" She spins around, catches a glimpse of the nosy crowd, makes eye contact with several of the White ladies, and shakes her head.

They quickly turn away and chat among themselves. Preston turns and runs off the field as Lizzie hurries to her car. Just before she makes it out of the gate, the stadium lights go dark. She doesn't recognize Javelina standing behind the fence. His lit cigarette casts an eerie red glow on his face as he follows her in the dark. He stays just out of sight as she gets back into the Chevy and pulls out of the parking lot.

Later in the night, back at the Victoria County Press, Preston's 1949 Ford coupe is parked beside Bud's Chevy. Preston has managed to patch and hide the many rusted-out holes with putty, primer, and a fresh two-tone coat of pink and turquoise. Lizzie pulls a bottled Coke from the drink machine, opens it, and hands it to Preston. He sits uncomfortably on the edge of a couch. He winces when he brings the bottle to his lips and takes a sip. She notices, steps up behind, and rubs his shoulder. Uncomfortable with her intimacy, he shies away. "It's just a stinger."

Lizzie is getting a little put out with his standoffish attitude. "Okay! I was just trying to help." She begins to pace the floor in front of him. "Getting back to Pearl, I'm sure you've been up on that bridge. Mighty hard for someone to get out on the edge." She stops, turns to him, and says, "You can't just let it go."

"Not much I can do. Can't go 'round blaming people," he argues.

"Somebody knows what really happened to Pearl."

"Well, Blacks don't go 'round asking questions. Believe me. It's not healthy."

"There's other ways," Lizzie says.

"Like what?"

"I don't know yet, but I'm going to find out."

The pimply faced boy waltzes in, hands Lizzie the keys to the Chevy. "You're all loaded." Lizzie takes the keys from him. "Thanks, Tommy."

He is visibly insulted and snaps back, "It's Tom!"

Lizzie acknowledges her mistake. "Okay, Tom. See you next week."

Tom is smitten with Lizzie and jealous of the attention she gives Preston. He gives Preston the once-over before he leaves the lobby. Preston finishes the drink and looks around for a place to put the bottle. Lizzie pivots around to face him. "A small favor, well not too small." She folds her hands together as if in prayer. "Will you help me get my stuff from the ranch?"

Preston leans back on the couch. "Tonight?"

"Please?" she begs as she takes the bottle from him and slides it into the empties rack. "You can leave your car at the newspaper office. I don't want to go out there alone."

Preston gets up from the couch and opens the door. "Okay, but we need to get going. Morning going to come early."

Outside in the parking lot, he walks her to the Chevy. "I'll be right behind you. Don't run off and leave me."

Lizzie smiles. It's a good feeling when somebody cares about her well-being. As soon as the two vehicles leave the parking lot and pull out onto the street, Tom, the pimply faced boy can be seen through the window marching straight over to a vacant desk and picking up a telephone.

Back inside the *Timely Remarks*, you can make out the flicker of light coming from the television set upstairs. Bud is fast asleep and as usual, he's left the television on.

Lizzie and Preston each maneuver a handful of empty cardboard boxes through the rear door of the office and shove them onto the backseat of Bud's Chevy. She gets behind the wheel and Preston climbs in on the passenger side. They pull away from the newspaper office and head out on Main Street. Lizzie makes a right-hand turn on a side street. "Checking on Cyrus?" Preston asks.

"I just want to see if he's left town or not." They pass in front of the Hoot Owl and spot the Power Wagon parked out front. "He hasn't gotten very far," Lizzie mutters as she steps on the gas pedal and turns at the next corner.

In the meanwhile, inside the Hoot Owl, Cyrus is on his way to full-fledged inebriation, standing with his back to the bar. His elbows resting on the top of the bar keep his swaying to a minimum and help him maintain some sort of balance. He has an audience of some new patrons and of course the gal with pouty, red lips. He speaks slowly and slurs over his new recollection of the story.

"I knew what I had to do. I wasn't gonna let the death of my son go unavenged. The Mexican and that nigger boy were scared to death of that bull." He turns back to the bar, picks up his beer, and takes a long swig. "After I got my rope on him, I had to fight him off of me for what seemed like thirty minutes. I was all by myself; the other two had run off."

One of the regulars asks, "How did you kill him?"

"I kept circling him till I got his legs wrapped up and he fell to the ground."

"And then what happened?" an old codger seated at the bar asks.

"Well, that's the good part. I got down off my horse, pulled out my pistol." He lights a cigarette, inhales a deep drag, and blows a blue smoke ring. "I look smack dab into old Diablo's cold black eyes and shot him right in the forehead." Some of the regulars gasp and blink their eyes. "Yeah, no sense lettin' him suffer more than I had to." Cyrus grins and turns back to the bar. He's getting to the point of believing the story himself. The only problem is, the next time he tells the story, it will be different.

Lizzie plows through the low-water crossing leading to the ranch. "I'm gonna miss splashing through that little stream every day," she says, just before they cross over the cattle guard to the ranch and approach her old home. With the house in sight, Lizzie notices that the oil rig lights are dark. "What happened to the drilling rig?"

"They're finished; I heard the well came in making over four hundred barrels a day. They're going to skid it to another location and drill another well."

Lizzie shakes her head. "Wow! It just goes on and on. Must be nice." She turns to Preston, "Did you know Javelina works on the rig?"

"Yeah, he's what they call a driller in oilfield talk." He glances over at her. "How'd you know that he works on a rig?"

"I don't remember.... Guess Bud must have told me."

They pull up in front of the house and get out of the car. "Did you leave that light on in the front of the house?" Preston asks.

"I'm sure Cyrus came back to get his clothes." Preston opens the rear door of the Chevy. "I sure don't want to be here with you, if he shows back up," Preston remarks as he pulls the boxes from the rear seat. "What about dishes and the like?"

Lizzie sighs. "We had nothing when we came here. Literally just the clothes on our backs." She chuckles to herself. "And that's what I'm leaving with." She takes a couple of the boxes from Preston. "It won't take long."

Lizzie takes a gander around and then a deep breath and then steps up on the front porch. She almost doesn't want to go inside to have to face another failure. She wonders to herself, *When the hell am I going to get my life together?* Inside the house, she goes to the bedroom and switches on the overhead light. She sees a trail of her clothes leading from the closet and strewn across the bed.

She pokes her head into the bathroom. All her makeup and bath products, some opened and leaking, are scattered across the linoleum floor. She yells at Preston, who's next door in the kitchen. "No need to worry. Cyrus won't be coming back here." They load up what belongings she can salvage and head back to Seclusion.

Out on the highway, Lizzie glances over at Preston and softly says, "I wasn't completely honest with you earlier."

Preston shoots her an inquisitive stare. "I walked out to the rig the other night and ran into Javelina."

"And what happened?" Preston asks.

"Nothing, really. Wasn't anything I couldn't handle. I just don't trust him."

"And well you shouldn't."

They zip past the Seclusion city limit sign and Preston asks, "Going to swing by the Hoot Owl again?"

Lizzie shoots him a wide grin and shakes her head.

Chapter Thirteen

WHEN WILL I BE LOVED

everal nights later, Bud's Chevy sits parked beside the river. Up above on the bridge an occasional car's headlights flash and fade as it passes over in the night. The roar of the water spilling over the dam drowns out any traffic sounds.

Preston is behind the wheel; Lizzie sits across the seat. "We shouldn't be here like this," he says as she nestles closer to him and cradles his hand with both of hers.

"What we do is our business," she whispers while she scoots around sideways to almost face him. "Won't you even kiss me?" she says softly as she moves her face close to his, shutting her eyes, and waiting for their lips to touch.

He pulls away, places both hands on the steering wheel and changes the subject. "Why are you willing to have people risk so much?"

Lizzie gives up on the intimacy. She leans forward, gazes through the windshield at the bridge above. "For the truth." She slides back to the passenger side of the seat. "Will you ask her or not?"

Preston doesn't answer for a while. He's running all the scenarios in his head and most of them are bad. "I'm taking a chance on just being with you."

Preston shakes his head and hits the starter on the Chevy. The headlights cast a long beam across the rippling water. "We'll see what she says. I'm not promising anything." He shifts the car into reverse and backs away from the river. They follow the side road back to the highway and travel the few miles back into town.

Back in Seclusion, they cross a set of railroad tracks, and after a few blocks, turn down a dark alley. A pack of lean and mean barking dogs chase and bite at the tires on the Chevy. They pass several dilapidated house trailers, and then stop in front of a row of shotgun houses. "This is our part of town. It's called Frisco." She shoots him a look. "Don't ask me how it got the name; I really don't know."

Preston gets out of the car first; he scolds the dogs and drives them away. Lizzie gets out and they make their way up several steps and stop under the porch's cedar shingle roof that's lit by a single yellow bug light. It's the last house in a row of shacks that face an unpaved street.

He knocks on the screen door just as the pack of barking dogs race through the alley. "Ms. Hattie; it's Preston." From inside the house, you can hear Hattie Lott say, "Come on in, boy." Preston opens the door and looks back at Lizzie. "Better let me go in first and tell her why we're here."

After a few moments, the door opens, and Preston steps out followed by Hattie. She waddles out and plops down beside the door in an old, hand-me-down chair with the cotton stuffing poking out in spots. She places a large glass bowl and a brown paper sack full of fresh green beans on the floor, removes a Bugler tobacco pouch from a pocket in her dress and glances up at Lizzie and smiles. She's been without her four top teeth as long as she can remember.

"You the young gal from the newspaper?"

Lizzie nods her head. "Yes, ma'am."

Hattie pours a perfect row of tobacco on a cigarette paper. "Pearl was such a sweet girl." She gently rolls it between her fingers. "You knows what you're asking?"

"Yes, ma'am, I do," says Lizzie. Hattie licks down the side of the newly formed cigarette, places it between her lips.

You can certainly tell she's done this before. Hattie takes a deep breath; Lizzie can tell she's weighing her request in her mind. She strikes a kitchen match down the wall and draws the fire to her cigarette. In just an instant, the paper and tobacco burn bright red and leave a long ash. She blows a trail of smoke toward the ground and keeps the cigarette perched between her lips. Hattie closes one eye when the smoke curls up toward her face.

"I'll do it, but if I get caught, you know they'll fire me."

Lizzie measures her words. She knows she can't guarantee anything. "I know, Ms. Hattie. You're doing it for Pearl."

"I wax them floors every Sunday night. Nobody is ever up there then."

Lizzie grins, glances at Preston. "Then, Sunday it is."

You can tell by Preston's expression that he's none too happy. Hattie takes a handful of beans from the sack and begins snapping off the ends and pulling away the strings. She takes another pull on her handmade cigarette while not missing a beat snapping beans.

The next day, Phil Nolan and Sheriff Taylor stand on the top step of the La Rosa Café. Nolan waves a copy of the *Timely Remarks* in front of a large group of men. "I don't know about you, but I've had 'bout all this shit I'm gonna take."

He pitches the newspaper to Javelina, who says, "We need to send this bitch a message."

The usual group of Nolan's ass-kissers follows Javelina's lead. They whoop and holler. Javelina removes the toothpick from the corner of his mouth, raises his clenched fist high in the air, and whistles loudly. Then, he stuffs the paper into a trash can and stares across the street at the newspaper office.

Inside the *Timely Remarks*, Lizzie and Bud watch the show through the office window. Lizzie moves back from the glass. "He's got them whipped into a frenzy."

Bud picks up a copy of the latest edition of the *Remarks*. "I don't suppose this had anything to do with it." He reads out loud. "A local government better described as a cesspool of malfeasance."

Lizzie chuckles. "I'm surprised they understood it." Lizzie hasn't figured out how far she can push the envelope with Bud, but for now she thinks it best to change the subject.

"Did you know Preston Lott is a really good football player?"

"Oh yeah; I've known for some time. I had an old college roommate that played professional football for the New York Giants for a time. I sent him a letter telling him about the boy. I think he's moved and is a coach somewhere now."

Bud opens a desk drawer and begins rummaging around.

"Did you hear back from him?" Lizzie asks.

"It would be in here."

Lizzie knows that would be like sifting sand on a beach.

Bud gives up the hunt. "Anyway, these colored boys are never going to have the chance to find out, especially coming from around here. That boy had an uncle named Algie Lott who played football in a stocking hat. His name is now that of legend."

Bud leans back in his chair. You can tell by the expression on his face that the stories whirling around in his head are good memories.

"Sometimes, it's hard to separate the myths from the truths."

"Like what?" Lizzie asks.

"Like one time he outran a horse in a match race at the fairgrounds, and another time, he stood on his own goal line and overthrew a teammate on the opposite goal line, and it goes on and on."

Bud glances at his watch and then pulls himself up to his feet. "I'm going up and turning on the TV. Nixon and Kennedy are on in a few minutes."

"That's right; this is the big debate!" Lizzie exclaims.

"You want to watch it with me?"

"Sure, maybe for a little while."

Upstairs, Bud flips on the switch to a Philco black-and-white television set and turns the channel selector. He and Lizzie settle back on a brown leather couch. Lizzie leans forward with her elbows resting on her knees as she cradles her head for a closer look.

"Kennedy looks all young and energetic. Nixon looks old and tired."

Bud grins and says, "Just like his policies."

"Kennedy's wife is so beautiful. I wish I looked like her."

"Lizzie, you are just as beautiful or more so."

"You're sweet," she says as she pats him on the knee and then points to Nixon on the TV screen.

"Look at him now. He's actually sweating."

Lizzie and Bud stay glued to the TV for a while longer when Lizzie says, "I don't see how anyone in their right mind could possibly vote for Nixon."

"Eighty-percent of this county will vote for Nixon."

"Why doesn't that surprise me?" Lizzie replies with a smirk. Then she stands up and adds, "I've had enough of politics for one night."

Bud switches the television off and turns for his bedroom.

"I'm going to keep watching on my portable set until I go to sleep. See you in the morning."

Later that evening, Lizzie lies on the bed with her head propped up on a couple of pillows. She glances over at an alarm clock on the nightstand. From her room above the newspaper office, she has a full view of the town square. It's a quiet evening. A few regular patrons go in and out at the La Rosa Café. Lizzie jumps to her feet as she sees Hattie Lott approach the steps to the side entrance of the courthouse. She watches Hattie let herself in. Lizzie takes a deep breath, pulls a sweater over her head and looks back at the clock.

A few minutes later, inside the hall of the courthouse, Hattie sings to herself as she steers a large floor buffer left and right across the marble floor. The machine makes a muffled humming sound as Hattie navigates the wide hallway. She rolls her eyes when she notices Lizzie slip into the hall and open the door to Sheriff Taylor's office. Inside the office, Lizzie switches on a flashlight, pulls open a filing cabinet, rifling through one file after another. She moves to Sheriff Taylor's desk. The top drawer won't budge. She grabs a paperclip, works the lock until it opens, and then thumbs through a stack of letters.

One letter grabs her attention. She examines the envelope under the beam of the flashlight. Then out of nowhere and just her luck, she hears a car door slam shut. She switches off the light, folds the envelope and stuffs it inside her sweater. Lizzie pushes the desk drawer close and fumbles with the paper clip in a futile attempt to relock the drawer. She gives up, races to the office door, and slips into the hallway. Hattie shakes her head as she watches Lizzie disappear down the stairway.

The next morning finds an early Norther has blown in overnight. A brisk, dry wind blows trash down the sidewalk. Lizzie has lined several carved pumpkins along the outside wall of the office. She approaches two White women on the outside of the La Rosa Café. They stop and listen for a moment. One of the women starts to speak, when out of the corner of her eye, she sees Sheriff Taylor stomping down the steps of the court-house. The two women turn and scurry off. Lizzie slips back inside the newspaper office. An anxious look covers her face.

"Looks like the sheriff is headed over here," Lizzie tells Bud.

"Something I should know?" Bud asks while he packs tobacco into his pipe.

The chime sounds before Lizzie can say a word. Sheriff Taylor marches through the door. He places the palms of his hands on the counter, leans across to Bud.

"Someone been snooping around in my office." He cuts his eyes toward Lizzie. "I bet you wouldn't know anything 'bout it?"

Lizzie shakes her head. Sheriff Taylor gives her a hard stare and in a low stern voice says, "Best you let dead dogs lie."

He walks to the door and turns back to face Bud.

"Thought you'd learned your lesson a long time ago." Saying so, he wheels around, marches outside without closing the door.

Lizzie sighs, "Look at him, just leaves the door wide-ass open."

Bud shakes his head in disgust and says, "Only way he could get to be a bigger prick is just get bigger."

Bud plops down in his chair, glares at Lizzie. "Don't tell me."

Lizzie shrugs her shoulders, and Bud can't believe it. "You find what you were looking for?"

Lizzie says in a soft, unsure voice, "Maybe." The sheriff's statement has stirred Lizzie's curiosity. "What did he mean by, 'learned your lesson'?"

Bud rubs his chin and doesn't say anything for a while. She feels that now he's on the defensive and seems reluctant to revisit the subject.

"None of my business?" she asks.

"No, it's not that," Bud replies as he rubs the corner of one eye while he searches for the right way to tell the story. He sucks in a long breath and begins. "Many years ago, I did a series of stories about some not so appealing events involving some migrant children."

Lizzie's expression changes. He now has her full attention. "What events?"

Bud hesitates and gathers his thoughts. "Young girls disappearing suddenly. Some being found dead. Others never heard from again. They put a lot of pressure on me to stop." He looks Lizzie straight in the eye. "I regret it now."

Lizzie can see the pain in his eyes. "Where can I find the articles?"

"Over at the library. It's all on microfilm," Bud replies in a somber voice. "Now, what did you find?" he asks.

Lizzie goes to her purse and pulls out the envelope she stole from Sheriff Taylor's desk. She hands it to Bud. The envelope is on stationery from the Diocese of Corpus Christi. Inside,

Bud finds a handwritten note with the scribbled signature of Bishop O'Malley that reads, "Final per our agreement." Bud flips the note over, hoping to find something, anything.

"This by itself doesn't mean anything."

"Sure looks to me like some sort of payoff," Lizzie declares.

Bud just shakes his head and says, "You have nothing, Lizzie."

She doesn't let it drop. "But why would the bishop be making payments to the sheriff?"

"You're assuming that," Bud fires back.

Bud gets up from his desk like he wants to end the conversation. "You need to drop this before you get way in over your head."

Lizzie can tell Bud is not exactly forthcoming about what he knows. He's certainly holding something back from her. She'll just have to find out the hard way. Lizzie is silent as she watches him make his way to the staircase and without turning around, he says, "I'm going upstairs to stretch out for a little while."

That afternoon, Lizzie walks the two blocks to the library. Inside the single-story, modest, white, brick building, a young girl sits with her elbows propped up on the front desk smacking gum. She is reading from a paperback book and barely notices Lizzie enter through the glass doors and approach her. "Where would I find the microfilm reader and archived *Timely Remarks*?" Lizzie asks politely.

The girl doesn't look up from the book or stop pounding the gum as she points with her index finger to a partitioned room off to the side. All Lizzie can think about at the moment is, *Damn! I hope I don't look like that chewing gum.*

Later, Lizzie sits by herself at a long table. The flicker of a soft light reflects in her eyes as she cranks the handle on the reader. She stops suddenly, reverses, and then slowly turns forward.

The Recordak text reads, "*Timely Remarks*—May 6, 1950—Young Girl Reported Missing From Migrant Farm Community." Lizzie stops, rubs her eyes, and continues to read. "*Timely Remarks*—January 29, 1952—Colored Teenage Girl Reported to Be a Runaway Found Dead."

Lizzie pulls back from the reader, licks her top lip. After taking a long, deep breath, she leans forward and continues to read.

Chapter Fourteen

LOVE ME TENDER

It's close to midnight on a very starry night. Bud's Chevy is parked next to Preston's old Ford under the old river bridge. Inside the Chevy, Preston sits on the driver-side. The radio is turned down so low you can barely hear Elvis singing "Love Me Tender" over the tumbling waters of the dam. Suddenly, a meteorite streaks across the sky, leaving a blue-green trail. Preston and Lizzie both lean forward and follow it as it burns up over the horizon. Preston turns to Lizzie.

"Better make a wish."

"I already have."

He turns the volume completely down on the radio and says, "Hattie almost lost her job. Sheriff Taylor was mad as hell and looking for someone to blame."

Lizzie doesn't answer; she rubs the side of her cheek. She knows he has a right to be upset and it's best to let him get it out of his system.

"Was it worth it?"

"You mean did I find what I was looking for?" she answers with a question.

She looks down at the floorboard, shakes her head, and in a barely audible voice. "I don't know. Not yet anyway."

She turns to him. "All I can say is I'm sorry!"

"Lizzie, that's why we learned to let things be."

"You have to admit; I must have touched a nerve."

"Doesn't matter. You need to give it up; let it go."

"I can't do that. I used to, but not anymore."

She then scoots over closer to him, grabs his wrist, and kisses the back of his hand. "Will you just hold me?"

He glances into the rearview mirror and then slips his arm around her. She leans in closer, rests her head on his shoulder, and turns the volume back up on the radio.

Her breathing is deep and slow as she inhales his clean and musky scent, that of a real man, unlike the unsavory smell of alcohol and stale tobacco she was accustomed to.

A few moments later, she gathers up the nerve, leans around and kisses him deeply on the lips. This time, he doesn't pull away.

She thinks how unfair it is that this feeling of closeness, comfort, and love has eluded her all her life until now. They kiss again, and now she knows deep in her heart that wishes can come true.

The next evening at the *Timely Remarks*, Bud is upstairs watching television. Lizzie is downstairs sitting alone at her desk. The room is dark except for the light from a small lamp. She bangs away on the keys of her electric Underwood typewriter.

An unusual mixture of voices grows into the sound of an unruly mob. Lizzie cautiously makes her way to the window and notices a truck parked the wrong way in the street next to the sidewalk. Men with bandanas covering their faces and a couple with cloth hoods made from flour sacks fill the back. One man hurls a gallon pail and watches it strike the office sign. Black paint splatters, streaks down the window.

From the rear of the truck a male voice hollers, "You like it Black?"

Another pail explodes against the side of the building. One of the men wearing a hood stands up holding a brick and shouts, "Hey, bitch, I got another present for you!"

He heaves the brick at close range and laughs out loud as it smashes into the window, leaving a large hole. A barrage of bricks and stones follows before the truck speeds off down the street.

Broken glass covers the floor. Lizzie stands near the door; her face is frozen in fear. Blood dribbles down her temple from a jagged sliver of glass that is embedded in her forehead.

On the edge of Seclusion, an abandoned gas station sits dark and isolated, trash and broken bottles cover the ground. The pickup carrying the mob of men squeals to a stop beside the building.

The men in the back of the truck bail out and race over to a solid black two-door Pontiac sedan parked under the canopy. A swivel spotlight is mounted on the driver-side next to the outside mirror.

They toss their hoods into the trunk, slam down the lid, and then pile inside the car. The dome light stays on just long enough to highlight Javelina's face as he turns the ignition key. The Pontiac's big engine roars to life. Its twin glass-pack exhausts clamor and rumble. The pickup truck used in the attack leaves the station, turns down a side road, and disappears into the darkness. Javelina races the car's engine, lets off the brakes, and squeals the tires as he burns rubber on the concrete driveway. The Pontiac's loud pipes fade as he races out of sight down the highway.

In the newspaper office, Lizzie sits in a chair as Bud stands over her and applies a cloth to her forehead.

"They were just like the Ku Klux Klan."

Bud chuckles. "They don't know enough about the Klan to spell it." He dabs the cut with Mercurochrome. "Might burn a tad."

She grimaces, pulls back, and just about loses it. "Holy shit, that stuff burns like hell!" Her eyes immediately tear up and her nose runs. He sets the medicine down, and with a shaky hand, applies a Band-Aid.

He sizes up the hole in the window and remarks, "I think we can temporarily cover that with some cardboard and tape."

Lizzie agrees. "I can do it; you just sit down."

Bud sits down at his desk as Lizzie covers the hole. "You know, Lizzie, every time you up the ante, they're going to raise you. I told you it was going to get rough."

"That must mean we're getting close to something."

Bud pulls his pipe and tobacco from his coat pocket. "It's obvious that the whole bunch is crooked. Even if you could prove it, you won't find anybody in Seclusion with a backbone. They're either scared or paid off."

Lizzie touches her forehead, sees blood on her fingertips. Bud jumps up from his desk. "Here, I'll get another Band-Aid; may take two."

The next morning finds Sheriff Taylor in his office reclined in his chair, with his feet propped up on the edge of his desk. He holds the latest weekly edition of *Life Magazine* up close to his face. He lowers the magazine and sees Lizzie standing in front of his desk.

"Run into something?"

"Like you don't know."

"Maybe you shouldn't go pokin' your nose where it don't go."

She leans across the desk and points her finger, "You don't scare me. You're not above the law."

"You're 'bout to run out your welcome here," he counters.

She turns to leave and spins back around.

"Might want to tell your boys, Halloween was last week." Lizzie shakes her head, turns, and stomps out of his office and down the hall.

A few days later, under an overcast, gray sky, Bud's Chevy is parked in front of the arched entrance to Oak Mott Cemetery. Toward the back and close to the old windmill, Lizzie kneels down beside Sam's grave. The Band-Aid is gone from her forehead, but the jagged cut could have used a stitch or two.

The only thing that marks Sam's grave is a tin plate with his name stenciled on it. She smooths the loose dirt with her bare hands. Lizzie hears the crunching of dry leaves behind her. She turns her head and sees Preston staring over her shoulder.

"I thought I'd find you here."

Lizzie doesn't answer. She turns back and keeps spreading the soil. "This is such a lonely place. I thought he might need some company."

Preston squats down beside her, rakes over the soft dirt with the palm of his hand. "I heard what happened."

"Just the good ole boys having a little fun night out."

"You okay, Lizzie?"

"I'm fine."

"You shouldn't come here so often. It's not good for you."

She stands and brushes the dirt from her jeans.

"Sam was the best thing I ever had … the only thing I ever had. Sometimes, this wave of guilt flows through me and I can't get rid of it." She suddenly winces, looks down at her boot.

"I think I've got a rock in my boot." She plops down on the ground and tugs on her boot. Preston grabs the boot and slips it off her foot. He holds her foot in one hand and turns the boot upside down with the other. The tiny stone drops to the ground as he stares at her slender, socked foot for a few seconds before shoving her boot back on.

Neither one notices Sheriff Taylor's car idling on the road above the cemetery. Inside the sedan, the sheriff presses a pair of binoculars to his eyes.

The dry dust clouds the air as they stand and slap the knees of their pants.

"I'll walk with you to your car," Lizzie exhales deeply, blows a kiss to Sam, and with a half-smile and a soft voice says, "Thanks." She notices that for the first time, Preston takes her hand in his as they walk together toward the gate. She loves it.

"One of the vaqueros spotted Cyrus hitchhiking out of town this morning."

Lizzie abruptly stops.

"Really!" Preston continues, "He said Cyrus's face was all swollen and bruised."

"Anyone know what happened?"

"The rumor is he was drunk … got into an argument with that old gal from the Hoot Owl and apparently hit her." Lizzie recalls in her mind all too well what that feels like.

She rolls her eyes and adds, "Doesn't surprise me. He could slap you so hard it felt like it popped your eardrum."

Preston feels for Lizzie, but doesn't say anything; he just continues with the story. "Well, anyway, they say she rolled him up in the bedsheet and worked him over with a mop handle and then threw him out of her house."

Lizzie chuckles. "Well, good for her." She thinks to herself, *Probably what I should have had the courage to do myself.* They stroll out of the cemetery together. Lizzie opens her driver-side door and gets behind the wheel as she waves goodbye to Preston. She turns the ignition key, watches Preston pull away from the cemetery, and then shifts the Chevy into reverse. Then she stops and pauses for a moment, and then leans back against the seat and ponders over her options. She realizes with Cyrus leaving town, that toxic part of her life will not be missed. Now is the time for her to move forward; this time in the right direction with no backward steps.

That afternoon, the La Rosa Café is empty except for Laverne, who stands behind the cash register reading a copy of the *Timely Remarks.*

Nolan and Elo step inside. They don't notice Laverne quickly hide the newspaper under the counter. The two men sit down at a small table. Nolan gestures to Laverne with a couple of fingers in the air.

She leaves the register, pours two cups of coffee and places them on their table, and then walks back behind the counter. Nolan glances at Laverne to make sure she's not listening and then whispers and shakes his index finger in Elo's face.

They don't see Lizzie open the door. She marches up to their table, looks directly at Elo. "I'd like to talk to you."

Elo is suddenly petrified; he doesn't know what to say or do. He turns to Nolan, who motions for him to leave.

"He was just leaving."

Elo doesn't need to be told twice. He jumps up and heads for the door.

"You control everyone in this town?" Lizzie fires at Nolan.

"I usually get what I want."

Nolan looks her up and down. "I was hoping you'd be leaving town with your common law husband."

The statement catches her off guard. She doesn't have an immediate answer.

"You've been living in sin all these years."

Lizzie can't believe he said that. Talk about the kettle calling the pot black.

Nolan senses her weakness and piles on. "You oughta be gettin' a little lonely by now."

He stands, puckers his lips and with a sickening grin says, "Unless you and that Lott boy been doin' more than swapping spit."

Lizzie finally has had enough. "What I do is none of your business."

He stands up and tells her, "Everything that happens in Seclusion is my business." Then he ambles over toward the front door all the while saying, "If you don't have anything else, I have more important things to do than sit here and jaw with you."

Lizzie doesn't take her eyes off him as she follows him toward the door.

Laverne pulls a pencil from behind her ear, scribbles a note on her check pad, tears off the paper, and slips it to Lizzie without Nolan seeing. Lizzie stuffs the note into her pocket while Nolan kicks open the door and shoves his foot against the bottom.

"After you."

"I won't give up. I know more than you think I do," Lizzie says, in as stern a voice as she can muster.

Lizzie glances back at Laverne, and then steps through the open door.

Bud stands at the window of the *Timely Remarks*. He watches Lizzie march across the street, step inside the office, and push the door shut.

"What a sorry bastard. He's covering up something." She notices Bud's inquisitive stare. She reaches into her pocket and removes Laverne's note.

"You know a Father Juan?"

"Yeah, he's one of the good guys. He's the local priest for the Mexicans."

"You mean they have their own priest?"

"And church. It's called St. James. Seems Bishop O'Malley doesn't want them mingling with the Whites."

"What is the name of the church for the Whites?" Lizzie asks.

"It's called Our Lady of Sorrows."

She rolls her shoulders. "Seems appropriate."

"Laverne slipped me this when Nolan wasn't looking."

Bud reads the note. "So, looks like Laverne seems to be on your side."

Without warning, Bud suddenly swallows hard, grabs at his chest.

Lizzie is noticeably alarmed. "You, okay?"

He settles back onto the couch. "Damn indigestion."

He points to his desk. "Open my top drawer and chuck me that bottle of pills."

Lizzie finds the medicine and hands the bottle to him. Before he can get a couple of pills down, he suffers another attack and drops the bottle. Lizzie now feels the seriousness of the situation. "I'm calling an ambulance." She picks up the black rotary telephone and dials the operator.

A little while later, Laverne is finishing up her shift at the La Rosa. She pulls her blonde hair out from under a hair net and notices a crowd gathering in front of the newspaper office. She steps outside the café and observes Bud lying on a stretcher at the rear of the local ambulance with Lizzie standing by his side.

"They're just going to run a few tests," Lizzie says trying to calm his nerves.

"It was those tamales. I'm telling you."

Lizzie nods to the driver. Bud still pleads his case. "Heartburn is all." The driver loads Bud into the back of the ambulance.

Lizzie leans inside. "I'll gather some of your belongings and be over shortly."

He doesn't give up. "I'll be ready to come home ... time you get there."

The ambulance pulls away. Lizzie finds herself alone in the middle of the street. A group of Black ladies mill together across the street. As Lizzie approaches, they mumble to one another, and turn and hurry away. She knows it's going to be a tough sell getting anyone around here to speak with her. They're all so intimidated and fearful of the consequences.

Later that evening, Lizzie paces down the hall of the Victoria General Hospital. She glances at the room numbers as she looks left and right. She finds her destination, stops, and reaches up to knock. The door opens and a professional-looking man wearing a pinstripe suit steps out and bumps into her.

He is very apologetic. "I am terribly sorry."

"That's all right, my fault. How is he?"

"Mean and cantankerous, but I think he'll be around a while longer."

He nods, steps around her, and makes his way down the hall to the elevator. Lizzie lightly taps on the door with her knuckles. From inside the room, Bud says, "Come on in." Lizzie pops into the room and finds Bud propped up in bed.

"I hope you came to get me out of this damn hellhole."

A nurse standing beside Bud's bed inserts a thermometer into his mouth and under his tongue. Lizzie in a reassuring tone, tells Bud, "The doctor said he thought you'd live another day." Bud inaudibly grumbles with the thermometer wedged between his lips.

The nurse informs Lizzie, "He is required to spend the night in the hospital for observation." Lizzie nods her approval to the nurse. Bud is chomping at the bit to talk. The nurse finally removes the thermometer from Bud's mouth. He doesn't waste any time.

"I'm not spending the night in here; we've got a paper to put to bed tomorrow. This is election night."

The nurse is having none of it. "You tell that to the doctor."

Bud shoots back at her. "Hell; he's gone home to watch the returns."

Lizzie attempts to defuse the situation. "Bud, you know I'm fully capable of getting that paper out." He grabs at his chest, putting a temporary scare in the nurse and Lizzie. "Oh God, that's what I'm afraid of."

Later that night back in Seclusion, Lizzie is spending her first night alone at the newspaper office. From the point of view of the street, Lizzie is downstairs turning out the lights. She ambles over by the door and takes a quick look outside, when something catches her eye. She jumps back in and kills the lights inside the office and then peeks around the door for another look and sees a dark figure lurking in the shadows across the street. She checks the locks on the door and slowly backs away and hurries upstairs. Whatever it was, it's gone now. She doesn't see Javelina slip into the alley by the courthouse.

Upstairs, she switches on the television set, opens a bottle of Coca-Cola, and settles down on the couch. The first thing she sees is NBC's Chet Huntley and David Brinkley giving the latest returns. She switches channels and watches Eric Sevareid on CBS. Both talk of a tight race and returns too early to call. She moseys over and opens the icebox door and scans the shelves. She shuts the door, and then rummages through the cabinets until she settles on peanut butter and jelly. She makes a sandwich and keeps switching back and forth between the channels until just before midnight, when she hears that the *New York Times* has called the race for Kennedy. She rushes downstairs, snatches a handful of papers, and picks up her typewriter. She lugs both back upstairs and sets it all down on the kitchen table. Lizzie pulls a chair up to the table, sits down, and begins to type.

The next day, Lizzie is driving slowly down the highway that leads to the Nolan Ranch. She has the palm of her hand covering her brow as she searches in the bright sun for a sign of the drilling rig. After a few miles, up ahead and off to the right, she spots her target. She pulls off the road and parks alongside a barbed wire fence. She picks up her camera, gets out of the Chevy, and carefully wiggles between the tight strands and the sharp barbs of the wire. She slogs across the loose dirt of a fresh drilling location until she spots the oncoming monster bulldozers pulling the metal derrick. She knows she must get close to get a decent photo. Then, she slips around to the side of the location using the cover of some low brush. There she begins to snap one picture after another until she thinks she has enough for a good photograph. Finally, she sneaks out of pasture the same way she came in.

That night, Lizzie pulls under the covered entrance to Victoria General Hospital. She jumps out of the Chevy, leaving it running, and sprints inside to the waiting room. There, she finds Bud and he's none too happy.

"Where the hell have you been?"

"I had to pick up the papers. We have a newspaper to run, don't you know?"

"I've been sitting out here for hours. I've met half the citizens of Victoria, and I don't like a damned one of them."

Lizzie grabs up his duffel bag and tries to assist him outside to the car.

"I don't need any help."

"Can I at least open the door?" she asks, to which Bud nods his approval.

As soon as the passenger door swings open, the first thing he sees is a copy of the latest edition of the *Timely Remarks*. "Oh, damn! I'm afraid to look." He backs himself onto the seat and then swings his legs and feet inside the car. Lizzie shuts the door and hoofs it around to the driver-side. By the time she gets seated behind the wheel, he's already scrutinizing the front page. In a banner headline across the front page reads, Kennedy Trounces Nixon. Bud looks over at Lizzie.

"It was one of the closest elections in history."

"Well, it damn well shouldn't have been." Bud just shakes his head. "I like Kennedy, but I have my doubts about Johnson."

"Why?" Lizzie asks.

"There are people who are convinced that he stole the Democratic primary in 1948. I just don't trust him, and young Kennedy shouldn't either."

"How did he steal it? What happened?"

"Remind me sometime to tell you the story about Box 13 in Duval County," saying so, Bud switches his attention back to the newspaper.

"And this giant photograph?" The photo shows four enormous Caterpillar tractors with heavy steel cables attached to a drilling rig, skidding it from one location to another on the Nolan Ranch.

"I figured people oughta know who's getting all the breaks."

Lizzie exits the hospital's parking lot and pulls out onto the street. Bud rubs his chin and keeps reading until they lose the lights of the city. He folds the paper, places it between them on the seat, and says to Lizzie, "This ought to fire them up again." Lizzie smiles as Bud leans back and lets his head rest against the doorpost. She reaches over and turns the radio on, but just barely loud enough for her to hear. She unwraps a piece of Double Bubble and pops it into her mouth.

Chapter Fifteen

DEVIL OR ANGEL

You can tell by the dilapidated structure of the building that St. James's congregation isn't a part of the affluent Catholic populous of Seclusion.

Lizzie parks on the street in front of the church. Gazing through the windshield of the car, her eyes trail up the tin-covered steeple to a faded wooden cross with chipping white paint. She steps out of the car, strolls over to an old Mexican man toiling in the fresh soil along a walkway, and inquires, "Father Juan?" The old man never looks up. He points to a modest building next door to the church. "Thank you." Lizzie says as she turns and makes her way down the paved brick walk lined with fresh, blooming flowers.

Lizzie knocks on the door and reads a small metal sign that says Rectory. She looks back around and notices that the old man has stopped gardening and is staring at her now. She knocks again and then again.

Just when she is about to give up, the front door swings open. Lizzie finds herself face to face with a gray-haired, stern-looking Mexican woman in her mid-sixties.

The woman asks in Spanish, "Yes?" Lizzie responds, also in Spanish.

"Could I speak with Father Juan?"

The woman is surprised that Lizzie can speak Spanish that well, so she answers Lizzie in English. "He is not here." Lizzie can tell by the woman's eyes that she is confused and is trying to figure her out.

Lizzie pokes her head inside the door as the woman slides her foot over to block any chance of Lizzie stepping inside. Before being pushed back away from the open door, Lizzie witnesses several Mexican families milling about inside doing laundry and preparing food in a large kitchen at the rear of the room. Off to one side, she catches a glimpse of a pregnant teenage girl standing alone folding clothes.

"When will he be back?"

The old woman shrugs her shoulders and attempts to shut the door. Lizzie places her hand against the door just in time to say, "Would it be all right if I come inside and wait?"

The woman shakes her head and closes the door in Lizzie's face. Lizzie backs away from the door, steps out on the walk, and gathers her thoughts. She thinks, *The place seems more like a refugee center than a parish church.*

Back at the town square, Lizzie marches inside the newspaper office, plops down at her desk, and throws her hands up into the air.

"Drove all the way over there and he wasn't there."

Bud flashes his impatient look at her. "Oh, he was there, all right. Might be best to call him first and explain yourself."

Lizzie flips open a phone book, thumbs down several pages, and then dials the number. She places the receiver to her ear and hears a man speak in a very soft voice, "Hello."

"Father Juan, my name is Lizzie Fox."

There is silence on the other end of the line, so Lizzie speaks again. "I would like to talk to you."

Through the phone, Lizzie hears Father Juan say, "Not over the phone."

"La Rosa Café, ten in the morning. Will you meet me?" Lizzie asks.

"I cannot promise," Father Juan responds.

Lizzie gently hangs up the receiver and looks over at Bud. "Well, I guess we'll see."

The next morning, the La Rosa is empty except for an elderly couple eating breakfast. Lizzie sits alone in a booth at the rear of the café. Laverne fills her cup with coffee.

"Honey, he ain't coming."

Lizzie glances at a wall clock that reads 10:20 a.m.

"Beginning to believe you're right," Lizzie says; then, she stands, walks to the front of the café, and pulls open the door just to run into Sheriff Taylor.

Lizzie moves to one side to give him room. He gives her a counterfeit smile as he steps inside. Lizzie continues on across the street and hurries inside the newspaper office.

Inside the *Timely Remarks*, Bud sits on the couch. He watches Lizzie as she begins to pace the floor. "Someone got to him."

"You can't blame people when they're afraid, Lizzie."

"You would think they would want to know the truth."

"They're going to believe what they want to. It doesn't matter if it's the truth or not," Bud states before Lizzie chimes in.

"This is a systemic abuse of children over the years. We have no idea how many."

Bud looks down at the floor. "Or how far up the chain it goes. Rumor is the church is a part of it."

Lizzie figures Bud knows more than he's letting on, so she presses him a bit.

"What do you mean?"

"Oh, you know some of that stuff that is whispered about, but never actually sees the light of day?"

"Like what for instance?"

"Several years ago, there was this lay teacher that taught catechism over at Our Lady of Sorrows. The rumor was that he was queer, and he got caught doing some pretty nasty stuff with a few of the young boys."

"Wow! Who caught him?" Lizzie asks.

"Supposedly, one of the boys' mothers."

"And what happened?"

"Nothing ever became of it. It all got hushed up. They put out the word that the lay teacher got a better job somewhere else."

"See what I mean about a cover-up?" Lizzie says to affirm her suspicion to Bud.

Bud agrees and says, "Yeah, I'm sure money exchanged hands. I'd be willing to bet this kind of abuse is rampant in a lot of these churches."

Lizzie nods her head in agreement while she poses the next question to Bud.

"Don't you think it's strange that Sheriff Taylor shows right after Father Juan was supposed to?" She witnesses the expression on Bud's face change and the wheels begin to turn in his head.

"You think someone is listening in on our phone calls?"

"Nothing would surprise me."

Lizzie snatches up the car keys from her desk.

"Now where are you headed?"

"Think I'll pay Elo a little surprise visit."

"Lizzie, I wouldn't go out there if I were...!" Bud yells, but Lizzie has already left, slamming the door shut behind her.

Lizzie passes the city limit sign and rolls on down the highway. The radio is blaring as she pops a fresh piece of bubble gum in her mouth. She cranks down the side-window glass and extends her arm out of the window. She pivots her hand up and down like a wing in the wind.

Several miles outside Seclusion, Lizzie pulls to the shoulder of the road and stops in front of a rotted wooden gate with a hand-painted sign nailed to the top plank that spells out, "No Trespassers."

She hops out of the car, approaches the gate, steps on the lower plank, and then throws her other leg across the top. Just as she does, a cowbell tied to the gate with baling wire makes a loud clanging sound. Through the mesquite trees, she makes out a ramshackle house barely visible behind all the vegetation. Bed linens attached to a clothesline billow in the gentle breeze.

Several old cars are jacked up and sitting on cement blocks in what would normally be the front yard on most houses. Here, it's hard to tell where the pasture ends and where the yard begins.

Through the thick brush, Lizzie hears a raspy voice resonate that belongs to Emma Turk a no-nonsense, gruff-type women in her late fifties.

"You step off that gate onto my property, and you'll regret it."

Lizzie hears the sound that shotgun shells make when thrown into the gun's chamber.

"Now, what do you want?"

Birds flee from the nearby trees as Lizzie balances on the gate.

"I want to talk to you about Elo."

"What about him?"

"I need some information."

"Ain't got no information. Now, get the hell outta' here."

Lizzie pushes her luck and steps off the gate onto the ground and moves forward a few steps.

"I'm Lizzie Fox. I work for the…"

Before Lizzie can finish the sentence, she hears the distinct sound of a double-barrel, 12-gauge shotgun boom and echo through the countryside.

"I know who the hell you are."

Lizzie runs back to the gate, climbing higher, trying to get a better vantage point. "I'll just take a few minutes of your time."

Emma fires another blast from the shotgun, this time much closer. Pellets strike the ground near the gate, sending a cloud of dust into the air, which covers the gate and Lizzie.

She backs down from the gate and wipes dirt from her eyes as she hotfoots it back to the safety of Bud's Chevy. She wastes no time getting inside the car and slamming the door shut. She takes a quick look at herself in the rearview mirror and thinks, *This woman is a fucking lunatic.*

Later that day, back inside the newspaper office, Bud shuffles down the stairs, jotting on a notepad, when he sees Lizzie sitting at her desk, dabbing her eyes with a washcloth.

"What happened now?"

"Elo Turk's mother: that woman's insane."

"No more insane than you for going out there. I tried to warn you."

"Can you believe she actually shot at me?"

"Yes! What I can't believe is that she missed."

Lizzie picks up the keys to the Chevy and her purse. "I'm headed to Victoria. You okay here by yourself?"

"Thanks, but I've been staying by myself long before you got here. You're the one who needs to be careful."

Chapter Sixteen

TEARS ON MY PILLOW

Lizzie pulls into the parking lot of the Victoria County Press, stops next to the dock, and kills the engine of the Chevy. She climbs out, pulls open the lid on the car's trunk, and then catches Tommy, the pimple-faced boy, staring at her from the other side of the window. She points toward the open trunk on the car and then moseys across the street to the movie theater. Tommy watches her purchase a ticket and disappear inside the movie theater. The marquee above the entrance advertises, "*The Lost World.*"

A few moments later, Preston approaches from the opposite direction. He glances around and steps up to the ticket window. Tommy hasn't left his vantage point inside the County Press.

In the balcony of the theater, Lizzie and Preston sit together on the last row. The flicker of the movie reflects on their faces. They share a fountain Coke and a bag of popcorn.

Preston in almost a whisper tells Lizzie, "You keep prodding them and they're going to bite back."

"I'm not scared of a bunch of local yokels," Lizzie says as she snuggles closer to him and adds, "Quit talking and let's just watch the movie."

In the parking lot of the County Press, Tommy takes a quick look around and then lifts the hood on Bud's Chevy. He takes a pair of wire cutters from his back pocket and slices through the wire on the distributor cap and then eases the hood back down and hurries back to the office.

A couple hours later inside the theatre, Lizzie and Preston watch the credits roll on the screen. The house lights come on as they sit up straight. Lizzie stretches her arms high above her head and yawns. She is sorry that the movie ended so quickly. They are the last two to file out of the theater. Preston points up the street toward his parked car. "I'll meet you in the parking lot and follow you back to Seclusion."

As Lizzie strolls back to the County Press, she sees Tommy push an empty dolly toward the door and notices her newspapers stacked on the dock. Tommy remarks, "I see you have some help tonight." Lizzie spins around and looks behind her; Preston is nowhere to be seen. She thinks, *How would he know that unless he is spying on me?*

She opens the driver-side door, climbs behind the wheel of the Chevy, and turns the ignition key. The starter whines and turns the engine over, but it won't start. She tries again and again. She wonders what's going on; it's never done this before. Finally, after several more attempts, she slams her palms against the steering wheel and exclaims, "Well, shit!" and then hears a light tapping on the roof. She rolls down the side window and hears Preston say, "Don't flood it. Let me get behind the wheel."

Lizzie steps out of the car. "Glad you're here. I don't know what to do."

Preston climbs inside, turns the key, and pumps the accelerator pedal.

The spinning sound of the starter slowly fades and then stops.

"Now the battery's dead." He steps out, shuts the door. "Nothing open this late. We'll have to take my car." Preston pulls his Ford coupe up next to the dock and begins sliding the bundles of newspapers in the truck of his car.

Tommy is inside, out of sight, standing behind the counter and speaking into a telephone.

"I took care of it just like you said," he relays to a person on the other end of the line.

With the receiver still up to his ear, Tommy slips sideways over to the window and peeks outside and says into the phone, "Yes, they're both together in his car."

Preston slides inside behind the wheel as Lizzie turns the dial on the radio. Slightly embarrassed, Preston says, "Doesn't work."

"Oh, that's okay!" Lizzie exclaims.

"I've tried to fix it…. They said I needed a new one."

"It's okay. Really!"

Preston shifts the coupe into first gear and pulls out of the parking lot and onto the street. Soon, they are out on the highway and picking up speed.

Lizzie notices the passenger-side window is not all the way up. She attempts to roll it up the rest of the way, finds the handle is jammed. She slides close to him and away from the cold draft of the open window. He cuts his eyes her way as she snuggles up even closer.

Inside the *Timely Remarks*, kerosene sloshes from a metal can held by someone with black-gloved hands and then a fiery match and a sudden whoosh of flames ignites a saturated couch on the bottom floor of the building.

Back out on the highway, Preston's old coupe zips by a pair of headlights sitting stationary on an unmarked side road. Preston's taillights fade into the distance down the highway until they finally disappear into the lucent blue light of a full moon.

The headlights on the side road go dark as a black sedan rolls onto the highway and chases after Preston's car. Inside the sedan, a bright amber glow reflects on the face of Javelina as he lights a cigarette and with a perverse grin, presses the accelerator to the floor. The rumble of dual exhaust breaks the silence of the still night.

In the *Timely Remarks*, thick white smoke fills the office. There is a strong, overwhelming odor of burning fabric and kerosene. Bud shuffles down the stairs, falling to his knees on the last step. He presses a handkerchief against his nose and mouth. His eyes are watery and burning from the toxic air.

He crawls over to his desk and pulls a brown manila envelope from the bottom drawer. Then, he takes a fountain pen, scratches several words on the cover and grabs the telephone, attempting to dial the operator while coughing and choking on the deadly fumes.

Bud drags himself across the floor before he collapses facedown, a few feet from the door.

Back on the highway and inside Preston's moving car, the wind whistles through the open window. Lizzie nestles closer to Preston. He reaches his arm around her and shields her from the cold. She pulls his face to hers. They're only a breath apart as she takes a deep breath, inhaling his intoxicating masculinity, and then passionately kissing him on the lips.

Suddenly, an intense burst of bright light shines through the rear window and illuminates the inside of the car. Javelina aims the sedan's spotlight and growls to himself. "You nigger-lovin' bitch."

Lizzie shades her eyes with her hand and stares through the rear window. She sees the headlights on the sedan come on and hears him rev the engine.

"He's trying to kill us. Who the hell is it?" Lizzie cries out.

"Javelina!" Preston answers before stomping on the accelerator. Javelina's sedan is too fast for the coupe and it rams into the rear of the old Ford, ripping the back bumper from the frame.

"I knew this was going to happen," Preston mutters.

The metal bumper hangs by a single bolt as it drags along on the pavement, spewing fire like a giant sparkler.

Javelina maneuvers alongside the coupe as they pass a sign that reads Narrow Bridge Ahead.

Javelina shouts through his open side window. "What you gonna' do now, nigger?" The sedan's exhaust pipes sound a deafening roar.

"We can't outrun him."

The spotlight burns into Preston's eyes and he hollers to Lizzie. "Hold on to something." Lizzie grabs a hold of the seat as Preston slams the brake pedal flush against the floorboard.

Smoke engulfs the rear of both cars as their tires screech and burn into the pavement. The sedan slams the coupe against the railing's wooden planks, shattering the windows on the driver-side of the coupe. Broken glass sprays the inside, covering Lizzie and Preston.

Javelina's spotlight bathes Preston's car, the bridge, and the bayou below as his sedan crosses the yellow line, raking the fender of the coupe. The coupe's right headlight shatters and goes dark, followed by the front tire scraping along the concrete curb until it explodes and scatters chunks of rubber into the water below. Preston tries to control the coupe, but Javelina strikes the rear fender of his car, sending it swerving and fishtailing on the narrow bridge before it crashes through the railing.

Splinters of wood and scraps of metal shower down on the murky water below. Then, a giant plume of water rockets into the air as Preston's coupe pancakes into the bayou.

Inside the car, Lizzie is slammed face first against the dashboard, but it doesn't knock her out. She is thankful they're still alive, but her joy is short-lived as she sees water rushing inside the coupe.

"We're sinking!" she cries.

"That's the least of our worries," Preston says as he looks around planning his next move. There is an uncanny quiet except for the distant sound of Javelina's exhaust pipes.

Preston, in a panicky voice, says, "We gotta get out of here."

The exhaust pipes on the sedan idle and then rev to a growl. Lizzie watches the water rise above the windows as the coupe slowly sinks into the dark depths of the bayou. Lizzie thrashes and gulps for air. Preston grabs her and holds her head up against the roof of the car. Her breaths are short and rapid, matching the trembling of her whole body. He can see that she is now in full-blown panic mode.

He cradles her face with both his hands and in a slow, deliberate tone says, "Calm down." Lizzie is doing her best to slow her breathing and is having some success until she hears Preston say, "Now, take a deep breath." She sucks in a breath of air and barely gets the words, "Oh, no," out before he pulls her under the water and spins her around to face the open window.

Preston pushes her through the opening and after what seems like an eternity to Lizzie, she finally feels herself surface outside of the vehicle. She takes several deep breaths as she feels Preston's hands around her waist. Much to her relief, he breaks the water right beside her. She holds on to him for dear life as she gasps and chokes on the fishy smelling water. She never thought that being in the middle of the bayou in the dark of night would be a relief, but the claustrophobic feeling of being trapped in a sinking car was more than she could handle.

The full moon casts a soft, eerie light on the still water. The sound of Javelina's exhaust pipes grows louder. Headlights from his approaching sedan highlight the splintered bridge above.

Preston voice is anxious. "Hurry; he's coming back!"

He points to a small tree-lined island covered with water lilies several yards away. "We gotta swim and take cover in those trees."

Lizzie shakes her head, "No, I can't do it."

He grabs her wrists and swings her around over his back with her arms around his neck. "Just hang on." Preston and Lizzie glide through the water and reach the trees just as the sedan squeals to a stop on the causeway bridge above them.

The spotlight lights up the roof of the coupe and with a sudden gush of spewing air, Preston's car slips under the water like a sinking ship. The beam from Javelina's spotlight skips and dances across the water as Javelina looks for any sign of life.

Preston and Lizzie are motionless and quiet as they listen to a car door slam and then hear the sedan roar away.

"How do we get out of here?"

Preston laughs, "Not the way we came in."

After all the commotion has finally subsided, nature unleashes its voices, with grunts, howls, and hisses filling the night.

"Don't let that scare you."

"It's what I don't hear that scares me," she says, taking a quick peek behind her.

"I bet this place is full of water moccasins."

"Gators probably ate them all."

She shoots him a look. "You're just full of laughs."

He grabs hold of a tree branch and hoists himself up out of the water.

"We find the river; we'll find the way out."

Lizzie begins to shiver, this time from the cold.

"Look over there."

Lizzie sees a ball of light floating along a line of trees.

"Remember the will-o'-the-wisps we saw at the ranch? Means the river's over there."

Lizzie nods her head and asks, "How deep is the river?"

"I think I know where we are; there should be an old swing bridge across it somewhere around here."

Far away on the horizon, cloud-to-cloud lightning bolts dance across the sky as the pair slosh through ankle-deep water.

"Looks like a storm is brewing," Preston says as Lizzie stops and rubs her hands together. Her teeth start to chatter as Preston wraps his arms around her.

"We need to get you some dry clothes," Preston adds.

She presses her body against him, puts her hands behind his back.

"Not now, Lizzie."

She doesn't respond to his statement as she draws him close and covers his mouth with her lips. For an instant, he loses himself before he breaks her embrace.

"Why can't we be together?" she asks.

"We're different, Lizzie."

"It shouldn't be about who you love, but how you love."

He steps back and grabs her hand. "We've got to keep moving."

They wade through a knee-deep ditch and then step up on dry ground.

"There it is. I told you it was here!" he exclaims in a proud tone.

In the soft light of the full moon, Lizzie strains to make out the structure ahead of her. Metal pipe beams support thick steel cables covered with cedar planks that stretch high over the river. Lizzie places one foot onto the bridge's wooden deck and feels the bridge sway. She freezes in her tracks and says, "Can't do it."

Preston in a smug tone says, "Bridge or the water?"

Lizzie is sulking now, holding her ground and chewing on the side of her cheek. "That's not much of a choice."

"Hurry up, sooner we get across ... sooner we warm up."

Lizzie methodically puts one foot in front of the other, careful not to make the bridge bounce or sway. Halfway across, she steadies herself, glances down below and sees water rippling around a flat-bottom skiff loaded with cane poles and fishing nets.

They finally reach the other side and step through a wire gate, from where Lizzie notices lights off in the distance.

"Somebody lives way out here?"

She rakes the back of her hand across her nose. "What's that smell?"

The nearby sound of snorts and squeals stop her in her tracks. The pupils in her eyes grow large to let in as much light as possible as she tries to locate where the sounds are coming from. Just about the time she braces herself for the worst, she sees a long line of tiny piglets march by like little toy soldiers.

Up ahead, Lizzie notices smoke billowing from a steel pipe that rises from the roof of a small house. Rusty, corrugated tin covers the roof, and the walls are made of shiplap lumber. There is absolutely no grass in or around the house; it seems the large population of pigs has seen to that.

Preston points to a panel truck parked in front of the house.

"This is where Dan Shaw, the slop man, lives."

Preston and Lizzie step up on the front porch and knock on the door. The door swings open wide, and Dan's jaw drops as he sees Preston and Lizzie standing in front of him. From the light coming from inside the house, and for the first time, Preston can see that Lizzie has two monster black eyes from her face slamming into the dashboard.

"Holy shit, you have a couple of shiners."

Lizzie is still shaking from the cold as they step inside the home.

Dan's wife, Marge, a hefty Black woman in her fifties, stokes red-hot coals inside a large wood-burning stove. Dan moves over and sits down at a linoleum-covered dining table.

Lizzie and Preston turn their backs to the hot fire and soak up the warmth as Marge motions for Lizzie to follow her into the next room and says, "You best get out of them wet clothes."

Marge soon returns to the stove and dumps a handful of catfish fillets into a deep cast iron skillet. Crackling hot grease rises to an instant quick roar.

"The fish are fresh, caught today," Marge says, raising her voice to be heard above the sizzling sound of fish frying in hot lard.

Preston is over at the table visiting with Dan, when he notices a figure flash in the corner of his eye. He turns his head and sees Lizzie standing in front of the wood fire. Her naked body is silhouetted through a threadbare cotton dress by the flickering light coming from the red-hot coals.

She pulls the towel from her head and shakes out her long hair. Marge notices the glint in Preston's eyes as she flips the fish in the skillet.

A little while later, Marge places a platter of fried fish and potatoes on top of the linoleum dining table and says, "Better dig in while theys hot."

You don't have to tell Preston twice. He grabs a plate. Lizzie is a little more reluctant. She doesn't feel comfortable eating someone else's groceries, although the smell of the crispy fish is almost overwhelming. Marge picks up an empty plate and scoops some fish and potatoes on it and hands it to Lizzie.

"Oh, it wouldn't be right; this is your supper."

"Honey, you don't wanna hurt my feelings."

Lizzie picks up a piece of fish with her fingers and takes a big bite of the white, flaky meat. "Be careful; you gots to watch for bones," Marge cautions her.

Lizzie doesn't know when she's ever had fish that tasted so good. She remembers Dan from his encounter with Sheriff Taylor behind the La Rosa Café. He is quiet and doesn't have much to say. She can't figure out if he's just a shy man or maybe he's used to taking a backseat to Marge.

After the quick supper, Lizzie is clearing the table when Preston eases up beside her, leans down, and whispers, "We better go before old Dan changes his mind."

Lizzie steps back, waits her turn as she watches Preston hug Marge and say, "Thanks; the fish sure was good."

Lizzie puts her arms around her and says, "Don't know when I've had something that tasted so good." Lizzie points out the dress that Marge gave her to wear. "I'll get this back to you."

Marge throws her hand up in the air. "No need, that dress belonged to my daughter. She outgrew it long ago."

Lizzie smiles and steps out the door onto the porch behind Dan. Preston starts to follow, when Marge pulls him back inside the house and whispers to him.

"Boy, I sees how you look at her. You best let that White woman be." Preston is silent as he turns back toward Marge and narrows his eyebrows in a subtle attempt to reassure her.

Outside, they all pile inside the old panel truck. Dan climbs up behind the wheel. Lizzie steps up on the running board and scoots over in the middle as Preston slides in beside her. They travel down a gravel road for a few hundred yards and then turn onto a narrow-paved road for about a mile that then intersects with the highway back to Seclusion.

Dan's old truck putts along on the paved shoulder of the highway. One headlight flickers and almost goes out at times before coming back to life. A set of bright headlights with multicolored lights in the background closes in fast from behind them. Dan steers the truck further to the side of the road as a tractor-trailer blares its horn and then blows past by the old truck. Dan's old truck's steering column has a lot of play in it. He constantly is turning right and left.

A sudden gust of wind makes Dan's truck shudder and stirs the smell of slop. Lizzie covers her mouth and nose with her hand. Dan has been silent the whole night and now he stares straight down the highway as he fights to keep the truck from crossing the center stripe.

Suddenly, he blurts out, "We don't need your kind of help."

The statement surprises Lizzie. For an instant she's not sure who he's talking to until she turns and sees him staring at her. "What?"

Before Dan can say anything, Preston jumps in. "He thinks it's better to leave things be."

"I..."

Preston doesn't let Lizzie finish her thought before he butts in again and says, "He thinks you're just gettin' the White people all riled up."

Lizzie turns and faces Preston. "And you?"

Preston doesn't answer. He tilts his head to one side like he has no comment. Disappointed in his nonanswer, she shakes her head and stares straight ahead.

A lightning strike lights up the inside of the truck and reveals a single tear rolling down Lizzie's cheek. Dan slows the truck, pulls over, and stops next to the curb.

"I can't go no further than this."

Preston opens his door and climbs out of the truck's cab.

Lizzie slides over and places her foot on the running board. She glances at Dan and then looks deep into Preston's eyes and says, "I expected more from you."

"It won't change anything," Preston counters.

"You don't know that."

He reaches for her hand. She ignores the offer and steps off the running board onto the curb.

"Sam and Pearl are gone. You can't bring them back," Preston says.

"Someone needs to pay for Pearl and all the others."

"In time, everyone pays," Preston replies.

"And how much time is that?" Lizzie asks as she fights back tears. "I've waited all my life for justice. It never came for me." Tears now stream down her cheeks. "I'm through waiting."

Preston touches her shoulder and softly says, "Lizzie..."

She doesn't let him finish. She places her fingers against his lips, turns, and walks off down the street.

Chapter Seventeen

I'M SORRY

Lizzie turns the corner and sees a flashing red light reflecting off the street and the sides of the buildings. She picks up her pace, walking faster and faster, before breaking out into an all-out sprint.

A whip-like cracking sound and a simultaneous bright flash of lightning is followed by a loud thunderclap. A driving rain now pelts her face. The air is cold, and large raindrops sting her face. The rainstorm is now in full swing.

A lone firetruck is parked parallel to the curb in front of the *Timely Remarks*. On the sidewalk sits a smoldering, burned-out couch. Lizzie reaches the open door and pauses. She is afraid to go in, scared of what she's going to find. She slowly eases inside and calls out, "Bud?" There is no answer. She scans the inside of the office, contemplating what might have happened and asks herself where is Bud?

She notices a tremendous amount of black soot covering the ceiling where the couch once sat. She is wet and freezing from the drenching rain. She grabs a sweater from her desk chair and slips it on. It smells of smoke. The furniture and files are in disarray. A lone volunteer fireman appears and stops in the doorway. Lizzie turns toward him and asks, "Bud?" The fireman shakes his head.

"I'm sorry ma'am; smoke must have got to him."

Lizzie feels like she's just been kicked in the gut.

"He tried to make it out. We found him here by the door."

She struggles to hold back her anger and frustration. "Where'd they take him?"

"Funeral home, ma'am." The fireman glances around the office.

"It's mostly water and smoke damage." He starts to leave and spins back around and glances down at the floor. He hesitates for a moment and then raises his head and says, "Just want you to know, me and my wife appreciate what you're doing. We would lose our jobs if anyone found out that I said that." Lizzie manages to create the semblance of a smile. She appreciates the gesture but knows quite well that the fight is now over.

The rain lets up just as the fireman steps outside the door. Lizzie eases over to the window and watches the firetruck drive away. She can feel the events of the night and the past few minutes festering inside her, like giant waves of different emotions that are going to explode.

She steps out of the burned-out office, bolts into the middle of the street, and cries, "Goddamn you!" She falls to her knees, buries her face in her hands. "I give up…. You win."

She cries softly to herself. The rain returns in earnest, leaving Lizzie drenched and motionless in the street.

The next morning, Lizzie bursts into the office of Sheriff Taylor. He looks up and sees Lizzie.

"Don't you ever knock?" Then he notices her two black eyes.

"What'd you run into this time?"

"One of your goons!" she fires back.

"I don't know what tha' hell you're takin' about."

"Javelina tried to kill us last night. He ran us off the bridge at Mullen's bayou."

"First I heard about it."

"I suppose you don't know anything about Bud Harkins dying in a fire last night. A fire that was intentionally set?"

"Yeah, I knew Bud passed away and I'm investigating the source of the fire. I tend to believe it was accidental. Bud was always dropping fire from that old pipe of his."

Lizzie just shakes her head; she knows the cover-up is on. The good old boys taking care of each other. Sheriff Taylor looks at her with a smirky grin. "I figure you'll be leaving town now that you don't have a job. I think that'll be in the best interest of everyone."

Lizzie hurls one last insult. "Tell me, Sheriff. How can you stand to look at yourself in the mirror each morning?"

His expression suddenly changes to anger. "Get the hell out of here!"

Days later, Lizzie is cleaning out the icebox. She clears every shelf and throws the contents into a paper grocery bag. She unwraps a package of baloney, smells inside, makes a nasty face, and pitches it into the bag. She shuts the door on the icebox, opens the cabinet and finds a can of Vienna sausage. She mangles the top of the can with an opener, prying it open and then pulls out one of the sausages. She looks inside the can, sees the gooey, clear gel floating in the bottom. She must work hard to surpass her gag reflex. The can of sausages joins the rest of the food in the paper sack. She carries the sack downstairs and out the back where she deposits it into a galvanized trash can.

On Main Street, Seclusion's curious crisscross the street and stare at the charred newspaper office as Lizzie stacks several boxes of her belongings on the sidewalk by the front door.

She locks the door, glances at the set of keys in her hand like she doesn't know what to do with them, and then straightens a purple wreath attached to the door.

She doesn't notice the man in the pinstripe suit that she ran into in the hospital stroll up behind her. He's still in a suit, but he also wears a white felt cowboy hat.

"Miss Fox?"

Startled, Lizzie spins around. The man extends his hand. She is obviously confused. "Doctor?"

"Oh, no, ma'am. I'm Bud's attorney. Name's Albert James." She hands him the set of keys.

"I guess these belong to you."

He points toward the door. "May we step inside for a minute?"

Lizzie is suddenly suspicious. "Hey; it's all in there. Honest; I didn't take anything."

He again motions toward the door. "Please." He pushes open the door and waits on Lizzie to go ahead of him. She moves to the end of the glass counter.

"Miss Fox."

"You can call me, Lizzie."

"Lizzie, Bud thought the world of you. In a way, you replaced his son."

"May I interrupt you?"

He nods his head.

"What about a service for him?"

"Oh, I'm sorry; I thought you knew. Bud said he didn't want any kind of service; just scatter his ashes alongside his wife's on the banks of the Guadalupe River."

Albert removes papers from his briefcase and lays them out on the glass top.

"These documents represent Bud's estate; included is this business, the building, its contents, and a substantial amount of cash."

"Why are you telling me?"

"Because he left it all to you."

He hands her the set of car keys to Bud's Chevy.

This is almost too much for Lizzie to comprehend. This has never happened to her even in her wildest dreams. It seems like her life is suddenly spinning out of control, but in a good way. One minute, she didn't know where her next meal was coming from and now, she has a feast laid out in front of her.

"We had the car towed to a garage. The motor had been tampered with. That's why it wouldn't run."

Then, he pulls a brown manila envelope from his case and hands it to her.

"What is this?" she asks but makes out her name scribbled on the scorched cover.

"It must be awfully important. He sure wanted you to have it."

Lizzie sets both sets of keys on the counter, rips open the flap, and removes the contents.

"None of my business, but if I were you, I'd put a lot of miles between me and this place."

It's like Lizzie doesn't hear him. A smile grows on her face as she reads down the pages. She looks over at Albert. "A short time back, Bud told me that when he was a young man, there were a couple of things he never shied away from." She stuffs the papers back inside the envelope. "Irish whiskey and a good fight."

Lizzie moves closer and looks him squarely in the eyes. "Mr. James, I'm not a drinking woman."

He grins, closes the snaps on his briefcase, ambles over to the door, turns back to Lizzie, and says, "He was also a helluva good judge of character."

Lizzie grins.

"Goodbye, Lizzie." He dons his hat. "And good luck." He steps outside and heads back down the sidewalk the way he came.

That evening, Lizzie is back at the library. She has a stack of papers beside her and the brown manila envelope that Bud left for her. She takes a sip from a bottle of Dr. Pepper and continues to turn the crank on the microfilm reader.

Chapter Eighteen

THAT MAGIC MOMENT

At the rear of St. James's Church, an elderly Mexican man rises from a small window of the confessional. He makes the sign of the cross and shuffles toward the altar. No one sees Lizzie slip through the weathered doors of the old church, hurry over, and kneel at the confessional. A black lace scarf covers her head.

Inside the confessional, a tall, clean-shaven man in his fifties leans close to the curtains that cover the window and says, "Yes?"

Lizzie, in a soft, sweet tone and words that no Catholic ever forgets, says, "Bless me, Father, for I have sinned. It has been years since my last confession."

"Go ahead, my child."

Lizzie rolls her eyes and continues. "I have sinned against my people."

A puzzled look creeps across Father Juan's face.

"I do not understand, my child."

"Turning one's back on injustice only begets more injustice."

Father Juan rubs his chin. "I am still not following you, my child."

"Well, maybe I should be sitting in there and you kneeling out here."

Father Juan jerks back the curtain and sees Lizzie. "What is it that you want?"

Lizzie raises her voice, "I want the truth."

Father Juan steps out of the confessional and glances around. "Walk with me," he says.

Lizzie moves up beside him as they stroll down a wide aisle toward an altar flanked by an assortment of flowers and covered in starched white linens. Lizzie immediately recognizes the distinct aroma of freshly cut roses and candle wax as she observes a small number of loyal parishioners kneeling in the front pews reciting the rosary.

"Do you pray?" Father Juan asks.

Lizzie sighs and then replies rather tartly, "I used to!"

"Why did you stop?"

Lizzie avoids the question. She realizes he's now trying to deflect from the subject.

"Laverne said you have information that I need."

He abruptly stops, turns to her, and says, "Seeking this knowledge will put you in grave danger."

"Bud Harkins is dead. I've swam with gators and water moccasins after almost drowning in a sinking car." She moves closer to him, stares deep into his eyes, and says, "I'm willing to take that chance."

They continue down the church aisle to a votive stand where Father Juan pauses to light a small candle in what seems like a sea of tiny flames. "If only it were that easy."

Lizzie is tired of dancing around the edges and decides it's time to cut to the chase. "You know of La Zona Rosa?"

Father Juan abruptly stops. He bites his top lip; she can tell the words have made him uncomfortable. She asks the question in a different way. "Why would Pearl Lott go to Boys Town?"

He walks away toward the altar. She follows, catches up beside him, and says, "Everyone knows, but no one speaks?"

He seems embarrassed as he stares up at a large crucifix above the altar. "They leave us alone."

Lizzie doesn't let up. "Without the truth, can there ever be justice?"

He doesn't take his eyes from the crucifix as he makes the sign of the cross and continues. "Over the years, this community has been the harbor to many sins and sinners." He turns around and faces her. "Some are only memories in the minds of a few."

"And La Zona Rosa?" Lizzie asks again.

He hesitates for a moment. "There is a place there called El Clinico."

He moves back close to Lizzie, looks deep into her eyes. "This is a vile and dangerous place; you should not go there alone."

Lizzie feels like for the first time a shell has cracked. "Tell me about this El Clinico."

Father Juan reluctantly answers her question. "It is run by an evil man who masquerades as a doctor. The word is that Phil Nolan gave Elo Turk an envelope and mentioned the name Pearl Lott only a short time before the young girl was found dead."

"What would Pearl Lott and this clinic have in common?"

Father Juan genuflects, blesses himself, and turns back to face Lizzie and says, "One can only imagine. The depths of the depraved run deep in Seclusion."

"Father, would I be correct in saying this is not an isolated incident?"

He doesn't answer and the expression on his face doesn't change. Lizzie feels like she's probably got all the information Father Juan is willing or brave enough to share with her for the moment.

"Thank you, Father."

He reaches out and touches the back of her hand and softly says, "I pray the Lord watches over you."

Lizzie smiles, nods her head, turns, and leaves Father Juan standing alone at the altar.

She steps outside and makes her way down the walk toward her car. She passes the same old Mexican gardener pruning the flower beds. He pauses and looks up at her when she passes by him and follows her with his eyes until she opens the door to the Chevy.

Chapter Nineteen

THERE GOES MY BABY

Lizzie bounces down the stairs munching on a hardboiled egg. She skips over the landing, hurries over to her desk, and picks up her keys and a pair of new Ray-Ban sunglasses. The office is clean and almost put back into shape. She steps outside and is greeted by a bright sun high in the sky on a clear day. Lizzie notices Sheriff Taylor and a few of the usual suspects staring at her from the steps of the La Rosa Café. She opens the front door on her Chevy and gets behind the wheel and then digs around in the seat until she finds an unopened piece of Double Bubble.

A little while later, Lizzie pulls off the highway and parks in the bar-ditch next to Emma Turk's gate. She hops out and climbs over the gate, careful not to strike the cowbell and lands on the other side of the gate, with her boots stirring the dust as she spits her chewing gum out onto the ground.

Lizzie spots a sign nailed to a tree that reads "Beware of Snakes." As she trudges through the soft sand of the road, she makes out the outline of Emma's house almost hidden in the mott of mesquite trees.

She carefully makes her way up a stone path to a wood-frame house with boards covering the windows. With her eyes fixed on the house, she walks right up on a large diamondback rattlesnake. The reptile coils and raises its head to strike. Lizzie freezes and watches the snake's head sway from side-to-side and its tail vibrating but making no sound. The rattler's forked tongue darts in and out. She is petrified in fear; she can feel her heart rapidly thumping against her chest. She knows if she makes any sudden moves the big snake will strike. Just the thought of those fangs sinking deep into her leg makes her sick to her stomach.

Out of nowhere, around the corner of the house, a bare arm raises the barrel of a 12-gauge shotgun and fires into the air. Lizzie hears the familiar husky voice of Emma Turk holler, "Get on back." Lizzie isn't sure if Emma is talking to her or the snake.

Relieved, she sees the snake drop its head and slowly slither away into the cover of the weeds and grass. Lizzie clutches her chest, looks up, and sees Emma Turk for the first time.

Emma doesn't fit her surly voice. Lizzie is looking at a neat, petite woman with silver hair that is pulled back in a tight bun. The double-barrel shotgun is almost bigger than she is. Lizzie is at a sudden loss for words, so she blurts out, "He never made a sound."

"Lost his rattlers sticking his nose where it don't belong." Lizzie catches the dig as Emma lowers the gun, points it at her. "You are persistent."

Lizzie finds herself staring down the business end of the gun. "I just want to speak with Elo."

"Elo's not here."

Lizzie points to a sedan parked beside an old, raggedy station wagon. "Isn't that his car?" Lizzie shoots back.

"That don't mean he's here, and besides that my car."

Emma steps up closer and pokes Lizzie in the ribs with the barrel of the gun.

"Now get the hell off my property."

Lizzie backs away several steps.

"I know more than you think. If something happens to me, they'll come for you and Elo."

Emma sarcastically grins. "Now who the hell is they and do I look worried?"

A window curtain slides back inside the house. Elo's glass eye blinks as he peeps through the glass pane. Emma pokes her in the ribs again. "Go on and get."

Feeling defeated again, Lizzie backs away, turns and makes her way back down the path with her tail between her legs, so to speak.

Lizzie's Chevy blows past the Seclusion city limit sign and then down Main Street. It slows as it passes in front of St. James's Church. She stares out her driver-side window and sees Sheriff Taylor motioning to a group of uniformed officers as they march several Mexican families toward an immigration bus.

Lizzie jerks the steering wheel and swerves to the side of the road. The driver-side door flies open as the car bounces off the curb. She leaps out of the car and races across the street. The pregnant teenage girl is pleading with Father Juan as the officers force her and her family onto the bus and then close the doors.

Lizzie steps up on the sidewalk beside Father Juan. "Why that family?"

He turns toward her. "They worked for the Nolans. They have no papers, no home, and no money."

Lizzie sees tears stream down the young pregnant girl's face as she finds a seat on the bus. She stares out the window and catches Lizzie's eye.

"Why her?" Lizzie asks.

Father Juan waves goodbye. "I think that is obvious in her condition. The innocent always have to be the ones to sacrifice."

"Who's the father of her child?"

"It could be one of several outstanding citizens of Seclusion. That is why I tell you that you are putting yourself in grave danger. The sin against these children goes to the very highest."

"Why won't they tell?"

Father Juan shakes his head. "They are all too afraid."

Lizzie keeps asking. "You know ... don't you? You know who abused her."

Father Juan looks down at the ground.

"I can tell you this; the girl and her family were hired help for the Nolans. She's fortunate, if there is such a thing in this case, that they did not know until it was too late that she was with child."

"You saying they would have done something to her?"

He looks up at her. "I've already said too much. You see how they react to you."

Sheriff Taylor shoots Lizzie a sarcastic grin as he motions with hand signals for the bus to depart.

"All this because I talked with you?" Lizzie asks.

"The wealthy and the powerful have many ways to enforce their will."

Father Juan and Lizzie's eyes follow the bus as it pulls away from the rectory.

"I'm so sorry, Father."

Father Juan nods his head like he's witnessed this horrible scene many times before.

"This is not the first time it's happened, and it won't be the last."

Lizzie is at a loss for words; she turns and walks back to her car.

Later that day, Lizzie's Chevy sits parked on the road out front of Hattie's old shotgun house. Lizzie is behind the wheel; Preston is across the seat. He shakes his head and emphatically says, "I'm not going to Nuevo Laredo, and neither should you."

"I'll go without you," Lizzie counters.

"What are you trying to prove?"

She turns away from him and glances out her side window.

"That somebody cares."

"Javelina and the boys had a little talk with me the other night."

Lizzie is silent. She looks down, not knowing or wanting to hear what's coming next.

"Seems they don't take too kindly to a Black man being seen with a White woman."

"It's none of their business."

He unbuttons a cuff on his shirt and jerks up his sleeve.

"They make it their business." Lizzie takes in a sudden breath as she stares at a trail of cigarette burns running down his forearm.

"They said this is just the beginning."

Lizzie reaches over to touch his hand. He pulls away.

"Preston, I care about you." She takes a deep breath, pauses for a second, contemplating her next words. "I'm in love with you." There, she said it; she can feel her stomach knotting up as she waits for a response. She studies his face for a clue, any sign of body language.

He opens the car door. "Lizzie, when are you going to understand? We can never love one another." He steps out, leans down. "Goodbye, Lizzie."

Tears roll down Lizzie's cheeks as she watches him walk away from the car and head back inside Hattie's house.

Chapter Twenty
TEQUILA

It's a little less than two hours from Seclusion to the border—not the most scenic drive one will ever make. Prickly pear cactus and not much else line both sides of the two-lane highway. Lizzie has been driving into an afternoon sun most of the way. Now with the reddish-orange ball of fire finally setting behind the distant mountains of Mexico, she makes out the outskirts of the border town of Laredo.

Darkness has fully descended as she passes the last cross street before the international bridge and a daunting sign that reads, "Last exit before entering Mexico." As she crosses the Rio Grande, her first thought is that it's not much of a river. On the Mexico side, she is stopped at a checkpoint. A Mexican officer briefly shines a flashlight inside the car and motions her on. A few miles inside Nuevo Laredo, she makes out her destination off in the distance. The lights of La Zona Rosa shine against the far horizon.

Lizzie turns onto an isolated gravel road lined with shacks made of cardboard and scraps of wood. She stares through the windshield, keeping her destination in her sight. As she gets closer, she spots an island of neon lights glowing in the midst of the blight and misery. She thinks, *This must be the infamous Boys Town.*

She pulls the Chevy up inside the entrance and stops; Sergeant Escobar eyes her behind the wheel and moves toward her car.

Up ahead, several hundred feet in front of her, she notices a man rush outside onto a street that overflows with American servicemen. He whistles to the police and then points back to the neon-lit entrance of a nightclub. A half-dozen Mexican policemen rush toward the front door of the nightspot. Escobar is seemingly unfazed by all the commotion; he switches on his flashlight and proceeds to inspect the inside of Lizzie's Chevy as he approaches her side window.

Lizzie speaks and gestures with her hands. "I'm looking for the El Clinico." The Sergeant points up the street with the beam of the flashlight. He doesn't see many young women from the States visiting Boys Town, especially by themselves.

"You have business with the doctor?" Sergeant Escobar asks.

Lizzie nods her head. "Nolan sent me."

Escobar rubs the side of his jaw; he acts a little puzzled and asks, "There is nothing for me?"

The sergeant can't figure out exactly what's going down. He knows that usually when Nolan is involved, he gets a little cut of the action. He decides it's best for now if he straightens it out later, so he steps back and motions her through. His eyes follow her car as she drives inside and then turns along the rock wall.

Lizzie parks the Chevy alongside several pickup trucks. Being not at all familiar with her surroundings and trying not to arouse an abundance of suspicion, she decides to check out this part of Boys Town. She gets out of the car, glances around, and must immediately jump back out of the way as a detail of Mexican police throw a bunch of drunken cowboys across the curb and into the middle of the street. The men quickly pick themselves up, scoop up Lizzie, and stagger next door to Club El Papagayo. One of the cowboys puckers up and kisses Lizzie on the side of her cheek and hollers above the music, "Goddamn darling, you can have all my money."

Inside the El Papagayo, the air is thick with cigarette smoke. Loud music blares from a jukebox. Lizzie manages to break away from the cowboys. She notices a crowd gathering in the rear of the club. Curious, she moves closer to the commotion.

Suddenly, a hand grabs her wrist and spins her around. She looks up to see an American soldier. The young man waves a folded ten-dollar bill in front of her face. Lizzie shakes her head. He pulls more money from his pocket and jerks her close to him.

"Baby, I think I love you."

She breaks his hold on her wrist and stumbles backwards into the boisterous crowd, falling to her hands and knees.

Her eyes open wide as the full view of the donkey show comes into focus a few feet from her face. She can't believe what she's witnessing. The look on the woman's face just as the animal mounts her from behind is something she knows she will never unsee. Now all she wants is to get out of there. As she struggles to regain her feet, one of the drunken cowboys grabs her around the waist and then a young soldier slugs the cowboy. Another cowboy punches the soldier. The fight escalates into a melee.

Back at the entrance, a dark sedan pulls up and stops beside Sergeant Escobar. The window slides halfway down, revealing the face of Elo Turk. Escobar grins, squats down beside the car and makes eye contact with Elo and asks, "You have my money?"

Elo shrugs his shoulders, "For what?"

The sergeant points inside the entrance and says, "The girl."

Elo rolls his eye, shakes his head, drives forward, and follows the same route as Lizzie.

Sergeant Escobar is thoroughly confused at this point. He waves his flashlight and motions for another policeman to come relieve him.

Inside the El Papagayo, brawlers spill over onto the stage where they shove the naked woman and the donkey out into the courtyard. Just as the police burst into the club to break up the fight, the bartender snatches Lizzie up from the middle of the fracas. He escorts her to the bar and speaking above all the noise asks, "Señora, what are you looking for here?"

Lizzie straightens her clothes and shouts, "El Clinico!"

He stares at her for a moment and then ushers her through the door outside to the edge of the curb. He points to the far end of the street and then walks back to the club's entrance. He stops, turns around, gives Lizzie another quick look, shakes his head, and disappears back into El Papagayo.

Elo steps out of the shadows and lights a cigarette as he watches Lizzie climb into her Chevy. Lizzie stares out both side windows as she drives. She realizes now there is a darker side to life than she ever dreamed. If one can believe it, the area seems to further deteriorate the farther down the road she travels.

The prostitutes who long ago lost what innocence they might have had occupy this part of Boys Town. They sit out front of shanties that face the street.

A Mexican woman with missing teeth and a sagging body leads a man inside one of the shacks. From the street, Lizzie can see a single bed, a dresser, and the tiny flames from several religious candles.

Lizzie wipes the fog from inside the windshield. She now focuses on a partially burned-out sign that reads El Clinico. Lizzie feels that familiar knot in her stomach arrive on schedule as she stops and parks on the street next to the clinic.

She gets out and pauses for a moment beside her car. She notices an old woman in raggedy clothes pulling a wooden wagon. The woman holds out her hand. Lizzie notices her missing fingers and open face sores. Lizzie shakes her head and says, "*Sin dinero.*"

The woman mumbles a few indiscernible words and frowns at her. Lizzie spots a small boy sitting outside on the steps of the clinic scratching on the concrete with a small rock. He doesn't look up as she climbs the steps and pushes open one side of the double wooden doors. Inside the clinic, Lizzie closes the door and observes a middle-aged Mexican woman dressed in a nurse's uniform.

Nurse Cantu sits on the other side of a counter listening to a small radio. Lizzie surveys the room as she approaches the woman. The place has a unique smell that Lizzie can't exactly put her finger on. It's chemical all right, but not like a hospital; it's more like a veterinary clinic.

The rock walls of the interior give the place a cold and sinister look. Nurse Cantu glances up and notices Lizzie standing in front of her. She turns down the radio and stands and eases over to the counter.

"You want the doctor?"

Lizzie gives the room another quick look and nods. Nurse Cantu stands, walks around the counter and looks Lizzie up and down.

"Who sent you?"

Lizzie pauses for a moment. "Nolan … Nolan sent me."

The woman opens the door, shouts to the young boy on the steps.

"Summon the doctor. He has a patient."

Nurse Cantu motions for Lizzie to follow her as she leads her down a long hall, stops, opens a side door and says, "Wait in here."

Lizzie hesitates for a moment and then steps inside a small room and waits for the woman to close the door. The door to an adjacent much larger room is cracked partially open. Lizzie pushes the door further open and peeks inside before stepping all the way in. Inside, she finds tile walls that are stained and filthy. A large circular fluorescent light hangs from the ceiling directly over an examining table. A blood-splattered cloth hangs from one of the stirrups on the table.

Lizzie steps over to a long counter along one wall. She notices a bottle of Clorox bleach sitting beside a container of clear fluid. Next to the container, she counts several small amber bottles sitting beside a metal tray of medical equipment.

Inside the tray are forceps, scalpels, and a syringe with an abnormally long needle. Lizzie eases down to the far end of the table to a small aluminum chest.

She leans forward and slips the lid back and tilts the chest toward her. Several small clumps of bloody tissue spill out onto the table. A putrid smell of decomposing flesh slaps her in the face, taking her breath away. Her hand flies to her mouth as she gags and coughs and then rushes over to a sink and vomits. She wipes her mouth on her sleeve not wanting to touch anything in the room. In her mind, it's all coming together now. This place is an illegal and filthy abortion clinic stashed away in the wretched streets of Boys Town.

The sound of a man's voice rouses her back to her senses. She races back into the smaller room, cracks open the door and sees a gray-haired man slip on a white medical coat. Lizzie looks down toward the end of the hall and spies a back door. She darts out of the little room, down the hall, and slips out the rear door. She pushes the metal door shut, quickly glances around and finds herself alone in a dark alley. A single light fixture above the door does very little to brighten the area. She bolts from the door and sprints down the alley.

Lizzie reaches the street where she spots a dark sedan pull over and park beside her Chevy. If things couldn't get any worse, they just did. She sees Elo step out of the sedan, size up her car, and then make his way toward the clinic. She ducks back into the alley and listens, trying to slow her breathing so she can hear. In the distance, she makes out the sound of barking dogs and voices shouting in Spanish.

Lizzie finds an open doorway, ducks inside, and feels her way along the walls of a dark hallway. She can hear a faint sound of music mixed with moaning coming from behind closed doors. She finds a door that has been left ajar. She pushes it open, stumbles over the step down, and falls face down on a flimsy single bed. As her eyes adjust to the light, she finds herself in bed with the toothless Mexican prostitute and her male customer whom she had seen earlier. Both are now naked and in the throes of sex. Her face is only inches from the action.

Lizzie immediately pushes herself up and back to her feet. The back of her hand flies to her nose as she inhales the pungent aroma of body odor and sex. Lizzie glances around the room and notices a small altar with flowers and candles surrounding a statue of a skeletal woman clad in a white robe. She backs out of the room and runs back into the alley.

She sneaks in and out of the shadows, bolts across the street and runs face to face into the old woman pulling the wagon.

"Aqui! Aqui!" screams the old woman. Elo turns around and heads toward the woman. Lizzie turns down the alley, sprints past the rear door of the clinic, and catches a glimpse of the doctor standing inside the open doorway. The light fades as she runs further into the darkness before slamming into a dead-end wall.

Lizzie falls to her knees. A hand grabs her arm and pulls her upright. Startled, she looks up to see Sergeant Escobar.

"Senorita, you are in need of help?"

"There is a man after me."

"I did not see any man," says Escobar with a sadistic grin plastered on his face. Lizzie takes a quick glance down the alley and points.

"He was right over there."

Sergeant Escobar grabs her arms from behind, presses a white piece of gauze across her face. She kicks her legs and feet and pulls at the cloth covering her mouth and nose with her hands before she is slowly overcome by the rum-like, sweetish odor of ether.

Her vision blurs. She can hear voices echoing in her head, but she can't make sense of the words. Just before the darkening haze turns to black, she catches a glimpse of the gray-haired doctor motioning from the rear door of El Clinico. The picture of that examining room flashes in her mind. She knows she doesn't want to end up in there.

Lizzie musters up her remaining energy in a futile attempt to escape and then she feels all the life drain from her arms and legs as they go limp.

She comes to and finds herself in her worst nightmare. She opens her eyes and squints from the bright light given off by the fluorescent fixture above the examining table. Nurse Cantu positions her feet in the table's stirrups and secures the leather ties. Except for her white socks, she is completely naked from the waist down. Nurse Cantu drapes a stained sheet across her legs and then picks up an amber-colored bottle from the table and sprinkles several drops of liquid on a piece of gauze.

"Now, doctor?"

Lizzie blinks her eyes and strains to focus as the doctor positions himself at the foot of the examining table. Lizzie notices his piercing steely blue eyes staring at her naked body through horn-rimmed glasses.

He speaks with a thick German accent as he instructs Nurse Cantu. "Not too fast; we want her asleep, not dead."

Lizzie's eyes blink as she hears him remark, "She does not fit Mr. Nolan's penchant for the young girls."

The doctor flips the sheet back across Lizzie's waist and presses on her stomach. His voice echoes inside Lizzie's head.

"And the money?"

"The one-eyed man is here," Nurse Cantu replies.

"Then, we will proceed."

Lizzie strains to focus on the figure standing above her. Groggy and unable to speak, she tries to move her body. She sees him draw fluid from a bottle into the syringe with the long needle. She is remembering the words Father Juan said to her about Boys Town; how she wishes she had taken his advice.

Lizzie lifts her head and sees that her feet are tied with leather straps to the table's stirrups. The doctor picks up a speculum from the dirty tray of surgical tools and leans around to see Lizzie's face.

"It will be over soon, *fräulein*."

He picks up several more tools from the tray and lines them up single file on a table beside him as Nurse Cantu sprinkles more ether on the gauze.

Then, Lizzie sees Elo step into the room. A feeling of all is lost races through her mind along with total regret for going up against the establishment. She is thinking, *If I had just one chance to change something, anything, that would have kept me out of this predicament.*

"You have the money?" the doctor asks.

Elo reaches inside the front pocket of his pants.

Out of the corner of his eye, the doctor sees a blurry image of a man's clenched fist slowly come into focus as Elo strikes him just below his temple with a pair of brass knuckles.

As the doctor crumples to the floor, the nurse makes a break for the door. Elo tackles her, presses the saturated rag of ether against her face.

The nurse's arms fall to her side. Elo hurries over to the table, pulls a pocketknife from a scabbard on his belt and easily slices through the leather straps on the stirrups.

Still quite woozy, Lizzie fumbles with her clothes, finally getting her jeans pulled up around her waist. She's sure Elo has seen most if not all her private parts. At this point, she doesn't care, and by the look on Elo's face, he doesn't either. She follows Elo to the front door clutching her boots tight against her chest. On the way out, she spots Sergeant Escobar unconscious and sprawled out on the floor in the main room.

Lizzie and Elo burst through the double doors. Elo gestures for Lizzie to drive. The young boy leaps up from the steps and hurries inside the clinic. Lizzie jumps behind the wheel of her Chevy as Elo scoots in on the passenger side.

The Chevy squeals away from the curb and careens down the street. Lizzie glances over at Elo. In silence, he stares straight ahead. She shakes her head to clear the cobwebs as he points up ahead to the guard booth and says, "Stop right there."

Elo pushes open the passenger side door as the Chevy screeches to a stop. He pauses and then leans across the seat and switches the engine off. He gives Lizzie a quick glance and then jerks the keys from the ignition. Elo is not sure he can trust Lizzie not to drive off and leave him at the mercy of the Mexican police.

He bails from the car, sprints to the guard booth, reaches inside, and jerks the telephone from the wall. He jumps back into the passenger seat, flips Lizzie the keys, and says, "Drive."

She cranks up the engine and slams the Chevy in gear, spinning the back tires and slinging rocks and gravel as she accelerates away from La Zona Rosa.

Elo turns and glances into the Chevy's side mirror and watches the guard station disappear into the darkness. Lizzie gives him a quick look.

"Why should I trust you?"

Elo doesn't answer; he just looks at her with a blank stare.

"Well, you act like you don't trust me," Lizzie adds.

He doesn't reply as Lizzie presses the accelerator to the floor making the Chevy rocket through the squalid shantytown.

"Is this what happened to Pearl Lott?"

Elo is quiet as he glances into the side mirror and sees two sets of faint headlights.

Back in Boys Town, two jeeps loaded with Sergeant Escobar and a detachment of Mexican police barrel away from the police station.

Lizzie is totally confused. She wonders what the hell is going on. The bad guy turns out to be the good guy or is he still the bad guy? *Why did he save me?*

"Why'd you follow me?' she asks.

He stares into the mirror and doesn't answer. Lizzie jams her foot on the brake pedal. The Chevy's rear wheels smoke. The car skids sideways and comes to rest on the side of the road. Lizzie grips the steering wheel with both hands and stares through the windshield.

"I'm not moving till I get some answers."

Elo spins around and peers through the back glass.

"They're coming."

She takes a quick glance into the rearview mirror. Through the dust and smoke, she sees several sets of headlights. She mashes the pedal to the metal and fishtails back onto the road.

Up ahead, Lizzie sees a horde of tourists wandering the downtown streets of Nuevo Laredo. Lizzie slows the car as it makes its way through the throngs of people. Elo wipes moisture from the window with his sleeve.

"How many young girls have been brought here?"

Elo doesn't answer.

He leans close to the windshield and sees a long trail of taillights snaking toward the International Bridge. Elo knows that they will be captured by the Mexican police if they have to wait in line to cross the border.

He pokes his head out the side window, takes a hard look behind them and says to Lizzie, "We gotta' go on foot. Pull over now."

"What about the car?" she asks.

He gives her a parting glance as he grabs the handle on his door. Lizzie gets the message; she jerks the steering wheel to the right. The Chevy veers to the side of the street and slides to a stop.

They jump out and race down the sidewalk together. Without saying a word, Elo stops and pulls Lizzie inside a liquor store. He digs in his pants pockets and turns to Lizzie.

Lizzie smirks as she says, "You've got to be kidding!" Then, she reaches deep inside her jeans back pocket, retrieves a ten-dollar bill, and hands it to him. A few moments later, Lizzie and Elo hightail it out of the store. He holds a bottle of tequila by the neck as they sprint down the street and then race alongside the long line of cars. Out of breath, they slow down for a few steps. Elo hands the bottle to Lizzie, and says, "Drink some."

Reluctantly, she does and coughs at the harsh taste; she just stares at him, shaking her head as he takes the bottle and douses himself and her with more tequila.

They take off running again as the sound of sirens and honking horns grow louder. After about a hundred yards, they wheel around and see the Mexican police already at the rear of the line of cars.

Between them and the freedom of the United States, they see the Federales roaming under a metal canopy on the Mexican side of the International Bridge. They are questioning the pedestrians and occupants of the vehicles crossing to the American side.

Elo is now sure that Sergeant Escobar has radioed ahead to the Federales. He grabs Lizzie by the arm and spins her around. "Act drunk ... real drunk."

Lizzie and Elo stagger arm and arm to the head of the line. Several of the Federales approach them and then point to the rear of the line.

Lizzie heaves and gags.

Elo tells them in Spanish. "She's drunk; she's going to vomit."

They snatch the bottle of tequila from Elo and pitch it into a trash can. Then, they turn their attention to Lizzie and stare at her for a moment before motioning them both along. Elo doesn't waste any time getting onto the bridge and putting some distance between him and his old buddy Sergeant Escobar.

He spins around to see Lizzie still standing under the canopy. She looks at Elo and then back at Sergeant Escobar who's leading the detail of Mexican police charging through the line, pushing people to one side as they sprint toward her. It doesn't take her very long to figure out that Elo is certainly the lesser of two evils.

She spins around and races after Elo. Halfway across, she stops, catches her breath, and then glances back and sees Sergeant Escobar stop and throw his hat onto the ground. Then, they both turn and hoof it across the Rio Grande and back into Texas.

Just after they make it across, Elo motions in the direction of a side street and says, "Follow me." Lizzie has no choice but to follow him now. They walk about a half a block down the street where Lizzie finds herself standing dead still and staring up at a sign that reads, "La Posada Motor Hotel." She doesn't remember seeing it when she crossed the bridge earlier. She follows Elo inside and watches as he locates a pay telephone and slips inside the booth. He drops in a dime and waits for a while; no one is answering on the other end of the line.

Elo steps out of the phone booth and approaches Lizzie and says, "No answer. She must be on her way."

Lizzie studies his face for an expression or anything to understand what's going on. "Who's on their way?" Lizzie asks.

"Emma."

"Emma sent you?"

"She'll explain when she gets here."

Elo surveys the lobby and spots the restrooms.

"I'll be right back."

Lizzie glances around the lobby; through the windows, she can see a beautiful outdoor patio with a large swimming pool surrounded by date palms and banana trees. In a few minutes, Elo emerges from the bathroom and scoots back on a plush brown leather couch.

"It might be a while."

Lizzie looks up at a wall clock. It reads 11:05 p.m.

"Okay if I go to the restroom?"

Elo nods his head. Lizzie really doesn't know if she's being held captive or if she's free to go, although she has no means of going anywhere.

Inside the ladies restroom, she stares at herself in the mirror. She feels nauseated and has a ripping headache from the ether. She washes her face and hands. It's been a scary evening, and as far as she knows, it's not over. Lizzie wanders out of the restroom and begins to stroll around the lobby. The hotel is suddenly crowded with tourists coming back from dinner in Mexico. She thinks, *I could use something to eat myself.* She finds a soft, comfortable-looking chair and falls back in it. It doesn't take long before she feels her eyelids getting heavy as she muffles a yawn, but quickly decides falling asleep right now would not be a good idea. She keeps nodding off and then waking herself up, but after several minutes, she drifts off into a deep sleep.

In what seemed like no time, she is awakened by Elo tugging on her arm. "Let's go. She's here." As Lizzie pulls herself up and out of the chair, she takes a parting glance at the wall clock and sees that it's straight-up midnight. Lizzie follows Elo outside to the hotel's porte cochere.

Idling in the driveway is Emma's pea-green 1953 Plymouth station wagon with sketchy—at best—white-wall tires. There is a mangled and shredded tire tied to the luggage rack on the roof of the car.

Inside the car, Emma motions for Elo to get behind the wheel as she scoots across the seat to the passenger side. Emma is wearing a baseball cap and has an automatic pistol strapped to her side. With a bit of hesitancy, Lizzie opens the back door and crawls in to sit behind Elo. Emma slowly leans around and throws her arm across the back of the front seat.

"As I said before, you are damn persistent."

"How did you know?" Lizzie asks.

"That you were in trouble? That Lott boy got worried 'bout you. Evidently, you told him where you were going. He ran to Father Juan who came to me. I guess the guilt finally caught up with me. So, I sent Elo after you."

"Guilt?"

"Later," Emma says, cutting her off, and then turns back around but continues talking. "Then, you all didn't show back up. So, here I am. I'd 've been here sooner, but I had a blowout right outside of Freer."

The cool night air blowing through the open windows has almost put Lizzie to sleep again.

"Damn wonder you weren't bad hurt or something worse."

Lizzie's headache is better, but the grogginess from the ether lingers like a bad hangover. Lizzie's voice grows weak and slow. "Where are we going?"

"Seclusion. Back to my house. We've got a lot of talking to do."

Lizzie barely hears Emma's voice, like its fading away in the background. She dozes off and catnaps on the drive back to Seclusion, catching a glimpse of lights every now and then as they pass through the small towns.

Lizzie feels the car stop; she doesn't open her eyes but figures this must be the gate leading to Emma's place. She hears Emma open the passenger-side door.

"Better give me that flashlight; not all these snakes like me."

Elo pulls up and stops inside the pasture as Emma swings the gate closed. Lizzie pushes herself upright against the seat's back as they pull up and park in front of Emma's house.

Chapter Twenty-One

COME AND GO
WITH ME

Emma, Lizzie, and Elo pile out of the old station wagon and head toward Emma's house. Lizzie hears Emma tell Elo, "Put on a pot of coffee and fry up some bacon and eggs."

Emma turns to Lizzie, "I bet you're hungry, aren't you, honey?"

Lizzie nods her head. She doesn't exactly know why the sudden change in Emma's attitude, but she's not about to question it. Emma pushes open the front door and motions her inside. Lizzie makes her way down a narrow foyer into a large, beautiful solarium. She thinks to herself, *Who knew?* You would have never envisioned this by the appearance of the outside of the house.

Tall, green bird-of-paradise plants bloom in terra-cotta clay pots. Two massive air conditioner units mounted in the wall rumble and hum while blowing cool air. A floor-to-ceiling wire cage located in the center of the room is home to hundreds of multicolored parakeets. The walls are covered with countless watercolor portraits of brightly colored birds. Lizzie's eyes pause on several easels that hold works in progress.

"These are really good. You could sell these."

"Agh, you think? What you say we have an early breakfast and coffee out here?" Lizzie nods her approval as Elo sets down a large tray full of scrambled eggs and crisp bacon on a tile-inlaid coffee table.

Elo returns with a monster pot of coffee and sets it down on the table. Emma takes note of Lizzie sizing up her large coffee pot.

"That's boiled coffee, the way my momma used to make it," Emma says as she reaches for the pot. Lizzie notices that it takes both of Emma's hands to lift and pour the coffee. Lizzie watches the coffee spill into her cup. If it was any blacker, it would be blue.

"Hope you like it strong," Emma says as Lizzie picks up her cup and rotates it in her hand, studying Emma's artwork. "I paint birds on everything," Emma informs her with a proud grin.

Emma hands Lizzie an empty plate. "Better grab you some eggs before Elo eats 'em all."

Lizzie scoots the chair closer to the table and dumps a couple of spoonful of eggs and several pieces of bacon on her plate. She wraps a piece of burnt toast around a slice of bacon and takes a whiff before she bites it down. She honestly can't remember when bacon has tasted so good.

"Don't get much company out here anymore."

"I wouldn't think you would, with all the snakes."

Emma grins. "The birds draw 'em. They do a pretty good job of keeping away trespassers." Emma cocks her head to one side, looks directly at Lizzie and clears her throat. "Most of the time." Lizzie catches Emma's attempt to poke a little fun her way and manages a smile as she watches her light a Camel cigarette.

"I read what you wrote about Bud. He was ashamed of this town, but more ashamed that he quit standin' up to the sumbitches."

"I'm sure they found a way to get to him."

"Oh, hell yeah; they threatened to ruin him and at the time Mildred was in poor health."

A little while later, the plates and tray are gone. Emma wipes the seat of her chair and sits down as Lizzie scoots her chair back away from the table. Emma takes a sip of coffee. "You want another cup?"

Lizzie shakes her head. "No, thank you."

"Now, where was I?" Emma asks.

"Phil Nolan?"

Emma morphs her expression into a phony smile. "That bastard! Or as I like to say, he went broke prospecting for silver down in Mexico ... came up here and stuck his dick in a gold mine."

"Maude Nolan?" Lizzie asks.

"Uh-huh, that's one mean bitch; part of that Irish Impresario legacy that they all cling to. She's the one that runs the show."

Emma takes another sip of her coffee and makes an ugly face.

"I hate cold coffee," she says and sets the cup down on the table before continuing.

"Phil Nolan is nothing but a trifling old womanizer with no scruples. Got a teenage girl pregnant this spring. I know the parents were hiding her out over at St. James for a while. Then, Maude Nolan calls the border patrol and has them all picked up."

Lizzie clenches her teeth and says, "I know. Unfortunately, I was there when they were picked up."

Emma nods her head like she knew and then continues with her stories.

"Just like old Grover Giles down there sweeping the sidewalk in front of his café with that shit-eating grin on his face. He'll stab right between the shoulder blades if he gets a chance."

Emma uses her cigarette to stir the ashes in a large, round ashtray already overflowing with butts.

"They think it's all owed to them, like some unwritten law."

She folds her hands, mocking someone in prayer. "Come Sunday morning, all of the uppity bastards are down in front of the church, hands folded, eyes closed, gettin' that absolution."

"Forgive and forget are two different words," Lizzie says. "So, what happens now?"

"You mean 'cause Bud's dead?" Lizzie asks.

"Bud Harkins was the best thing this town ever had, but they broke him down."

"I know," Lizzie agrees.

"Let me tell you what, young lady; they'll do the same to you, if you let 'em."

"That's why I kept coming out here. Bud said you'd help me."

Emma lights a cigarette.

"It's a way of life for these people. You own the sheriff; you own the town … and it doesn't hurt to have the Catholic Bishop on your side, taking up any slack."

"And Elo?"

Emma gets serious, leans across the table, and lowers her voice.

"Elo's a good boy. He's just … a little slow."

Emma flicks the ash on her cigarette and misses the ashtray completely.

"That so-called clinic in Boys Town was built to keep tabs on the whores."

"VD?" Lizzie asks.

"Yeah, mostly gonorrhea or the Clap as they call it around these parts. But like everything else in the government, the doctors are on the take and abortions became a profitable sideline."

"Boys Town is such a grungy and sleazy place, yet the people all seem so religious," Lizzie remarks.

"That the hold of Catholicism on the Mexicans," Emma answers.

"I saw the same scary statue over and over down there." Lizzie rubs the side of her cheek, like she's pulling the image up in her mind. "The skeleton of a woman dressed in a white robe."

Emma takes a drag on her cigarette and says, "Oh, that's La Santa Muerte or as they say, the saint of death. She's the patron saint of prisoners, prostitutes, and underworld figures.

They believe she gives them the right to do the things they do. The Catholic Church forbids the Mexicans to worship her, but they do anyway."

"The German doctor? Talk about a scary son-of-a-bitch. What's his story?" Lizzie asks.

"The rumor is he's in Mexico hiding from the Jews. Supposedly, during the war, he was doing some real nasty stuff for the Nazis."

"And Pearl Lott?"

She was household help for Maude Nolan. Emma answers and then adds, "I'm sure Phil Nolan had his way with her, and I mean not in a nice way, and then got her pregnant."

She puts out her cigarette in the ashtray; butts and ashes are all over the table.

"They conned Elo into making the trip to Mexico."

Emma lights another cigarette. "When he picked her up from the clinic, she was already crying when she got into the car. Before he crossed the bridge, he switched on the dome light, and he could see blood all over her and the backseat. Her eyes were really glassy, and she wasn't responsive."

She takes a long drag on the cigarette. "Elo tried to reassure her that they were almost home, but hell! They had almost two hours."

"So, she bled to death?" asks Lizzie.

Emma nods. "Elo didn't know what to do, so he runs to Grover Giles. Together, they run and get the sheriff. The sheriff and Maude Nolan hatch up this cockamamie suicide story."

"The boy that put out Elo's eye, that was Bud's son?"

"Bud tell you that?"

"And more. He wrote me a letter that I got after he died."

"It was an accident, but Bud always blamed himself. What else did he say in that letter?"

"That Nolan is Elo's father. Not by any choice of yours."

Lizzie has touched on painful memories for Emma; you can tell this is not something she's wanting to have to rehash.

"I was ashamed and alone in this rinky-dink ass town, but I wasn't gonna give up my baby. Bud was the only one who stood by me."

Emma picks a speck of tobacco from her lip.

"Even my own sister, Laverne, turned against me."

Emma's face shows her searching for the right words to describe this arduous chapter in her life.

"Yeah, hurts real bad when your own kinfolk disown you. I should've got out of here years ago, but I didn't have the courage. Back then, I tried to sell the place, but the bank wouldn't give anyone a loan. As you well know, Maude Nolan owns the bank."

She gives Lizzie a hard stare. "Why you doing all this? You've been down this road. Somebody hurt you, didn't they?"

Lizzie evades the question. "I can prove a lot of this and I'm going to print what I know is the truth."

"Well, if you're lookin' for justice, you'll be damn lucky to find any in Seclusion."

"Every wrong should have a price to pay," Lizzie replies as she ambles over and stares inside the bird cage.

"Bud told me about two old maid sisters that died about a year ago; you remember?"

"Yeah, the old Dorsey girls. They died a few months apart."

"Is it true that they left all their land and money to the Catholic Diocese of Corpus Christi?"

"Well, I remember there was a big trial and it involved Bishop O'Malley."

"Bud has evidence of witness tampering in that trial. At that point in his life, I'm sure he just wasn't up to the fight, but I sure the hell am!"

Emma exhales a long plume of smoke. "The damn hypocrites." She stamps out the cigarette. "I'd rather be hit in the face with a sack of shit than be lied to by a goddamn hypocrite."

A sly grin appears on Lizzie's face. "Well, it so happens that the statute of limitations has not run out in this case."

Lizzie turns back to face her. "Well one fight at a time, but with your help, we're going to bring these people down. You've got to chip away at the bottom to bring down even the tallest tree."

"I don't cotton much to religion, but I do like the part about the eye for an eye and a bullet, or however it goes."

Lizzie laughs. "Close enough."

Emma stands and picks up the cups.

"They don't give a damn. Hell, they're throwing a big highfalutin' Christmas party tomorrow night."

Lizzie whirls back around to Emma and with a broad grin says, "Think they'll mind if I stop in? Just for a minute."

Emma laughs out loud.

"Don't even think 'bout it. They wouldn't let you within a mile of that house."

Lizzie and Emma step out of the house onto the front porch.

"I forgot you was on foot." Emma glances over at her station wagon. "Drive my old wagon, till you find something. We ain't never getting those cars back from Mexico. Hell, I bet Bud's old Chevy is halfway to Guadalajara by now."

"Oh, I couldn't."

"Sure, you can. I got several more junkers 'round back." She hollers back inside the house to Elo. "Get a spare tire out of the shed for my wagon, preferably one that's got air in it."

Just for a little fun and meanness, during the wee hours of the morning, Lizzie has parked Emma's old Plymouth wagon directly in front of the *Timely Remarks*. She knows she can count on this stirring up the good old boys when they see it and it doesn't take long for the trap to spring.

She stands back from the window and soon spots Sheriff Taylor cruising down Main Street headed toward the courthouse. She laughs to herself while she witnesses him swerve to miss a parked car as he does a double take on seeing Emma's station wagon parked across from the town square.

Chapter Twenty-Two
POISON IVY

A long line of cars on both sides of the road snakes up to the driveway to Phil and Maude Nolan's colonial home. Cadillacs and Chryslers make up most of the late model vehicles, the reason being the Nolans just happen to own the dealership. Lizzie steers Emma's old station wagon off the road and parks beside a late model Cadillac. A spare tire with little to no tread showing is secured to the old Plymouth's roof rack with baling wire.

Lizzie hops out of the wagon and runs to catch up to a couple of men dressed in all black. Slightly out of breath, she says, "May I walk with you?"

Bishop O'Malley turns back, smiles, and stops. His young assistant glances back at her, walks a few steps, and also stops.

"My pleasure. How long have you known the Nolans?" Bishop O'Malley says as he gestures with his hand for Lizzie to proceed ahead of him.

"Seems like a lifetime," Lizzie says with a made-up smile.

"They are fine people, wonderful benefactors to the church."

"That's what I hear," Lizzie adds.

They walk up the steps to the plantation-style home; Lizzie takes a step back and lets Bishop O'Malley ring the doorbell. She peeks through a side window and sees a large lit Christmas tree standing in the center of the room. Men in suits and women in fancy dresses mingle and make idle conversation. She thinks to herself, *This is going be interesting at the very least.*

A huge smile appears on Maude Nolan's face as she peeks through the side curtain and spots Bishop O'Malley. She swings the door open wide and in a very animated voice says, "Bishop O'Malley, please come in."

Her expression sours when she recognizes Lizzie standing there with a perky little grin fixed on her face. Bishop O'Malley gestures in Lizzie's direction.

"And you know Miss Fox?"

Maude smiles as the Bishop and his assistant step inside.

"Well, of course," Maude replies with a narrow brow and a look from hell.

She glares at Lizzie and then turns back to the Bishop, "Step over to the bar and Phil will pour you some eggnog."

In the corner of the room, Phil Nolan pours straight whiskey into a large bowl and then swirls the contents with a ladle. Sheriff Taylor and Grover Giles stand in the kitchen where Joe Hamilton, the oilman, is holding court.

Maude takes Lizzie by the arm and ushers her over beside the Christmas tree. Not just any Christmas tree, but an eighteen-foot, blue spruce, with multicolored lights and hundreds of shiny ornaments.

"I don't make a habit of inviting White trash into my home. In lieu of embarrassing Bishop O'Malley, I'm not going to throw you out, right now."

"Now, I want you to know … you don't have to do me any favors," Lizzie states very politely and tongue-in-cheek.

Lizzie jerks her arm from Maude's grasp, bends down, and waves her hand over the numerous presents under the tree, so many presents that it looks just downright gaudy. Lizzie thinks there's enough gifts for everyone in Seclusion to have one. That is, except for herself.

"Which one of these have you marked for the Bishop?"

She picks up a small envelope wrapped in red.

"I bet it's this one, red on the outside and lots of green on the inside."

"What the hell is that supposed to mean?"

"You people actually do think you can buy your way into heaven."

Maude tries to snatch the present from Lizzie's grasp. Lizzie jerks her hand back, out of Maude's range.

She then shrugs her shoulders, pitches the present back under the tree. "Hell, for all I know, you probably can."

"You gonna accuse my husband of having an affair with some little chocolate drop?"

Lizzie gets much closer and raises the pitch of her voice.

"No; I promise you it's going to be much worse than that."

Maude glances around to see if anyone is listening. Lizzie notices most of the guests are silent and staring her way. Maude, in a voice barely above a whisper, says, "If I were you, I'd think twice about it." With that comment, Maude storms off.

Later, as Lizzie meanders from room to room, she witnesses the good citizens of Seclusion go out of their way to avoid her. She ambles over to the bar where Phil Nolan fills a whiskey glass with Seagram's 7 bourbon.

"That's your idea of holiday spirit?" she asks with a light smirk framed on her face. He takes a long swallow of the bourbon, flashes her a lecherous wink, and walks away.

A short time later, Lizzie sees Sheriff Taylor eyeing her from across the room and then notices Bishop O'Malley saying his good-byes to Maude.

She hurries to the door and grabs the Bishop's arm.

"Looks like we're together again."

They step out onto the veranda. The Bishop turns to Lizzie, "Now, what is it you do?"

"I am the editor of the local newspaper, the *Timely Remarks*."

The fake smile on Maude's face withers away as she closes the door and peeks through the side curtains.

Outside, the Bishop and Lizzie make their way along the circular driveway.

"How much do they pay you, Bishop O'Malley?"

The Bishop abruptly stops, turns, and faces Lizzie as his assistant steps up beside their black Cadillac Fleetwood and opens the rear door.

"Are you accusing me of something, Miss Fox?"

Lizzie looks right into his eyes.

"Not yet, but if I were you, I'd be looking over my shoulder for what's coming."

"I don't know what you're talking about," saying so, the Bishop turns and walks to the limo and settles back onto the rear seat. His assistant gives Lizzie a quick stare, shuts the car door, and walks around to the other side of the car. Lizzie stands beside Emma's wagon and watches the Cadillac's taillights fade out of sight. She thinks if nothing else she's got them worried and at the very least, she must keep the pressure on.

The next morning finds the good White citizens of Seclusion headed to Sunday Mass at Our Lady of Sorrows Catholic Church. Lizzie is a little late; she must park Emma's old wagon on a side street. She gets out of the car, grabs her purse, and presses the wrinkles from her navy-blue dress. She glances into the side mirror and straightens the matching scarf draped over her head. She thinks to herself that it really is a beautiful church building, although probably wasted on this crowd. It certainly lives up to the descriptions she found in her research, built in 1911 on land donated by Maude Nolan's father. Then, it had to be rebuilt after the hurricane of 1919 took off the roof. She climbs the steps up to the ten-foot-tall, thick, double wooden doors. Lizzie glances up at the top of the steeple just as the bells begin to ring.

The door creaks as she pushes it open. She thinks to herself, *Thank God for the bells or everyone would have certainly turned around.* Much to her chagrin, the only remaining empty seats are down front. Sheriff Taylor, Grover Giles, and a few others have occupied the last row or as it's sometime called sinner's row. She hasn't located the Nolans. They must be closer to the front. The pipes on the organ suddenly blare, startling Lizzie for a moment and then it seems like the whole congregation turns around and stares at her. She thinks, *Why the hell are they all staring at me?* Couldn't have been worst timing on her part. She can feel the eyes of the crowd, not to mention the cold stare of Sheriff Taylor. She glances to her right and spots a priest and two altar boys. Now, it makes sense. She has no choice but to make her way down a side aisle to the front of the church. She slips into an empty pew just as the priest and altar boys make it to the altar.

Lizzie takes a gander around the inside of the church. There are lifelike statues everywhere. Even high up on the half-dozen pillars that support the massive roof. Statues of saints she didn't even know existed. Sure seems a little much to her, but when money is no object, this is what happens.

She hasn't been inside a church since breaking out of the Magdalene Laundries. She listens as the priest gives his sermon on the Christian theological virtues of faith, hope, and charity or as she translates it giving your fair share to the collection box.

After a while, she figures it must be time for communion and thinks this alone should be worth the price of admission. One by one, the parishioners line up in a single file, hands folded tight against their chest. She wonders what is really on their minds as she watches the long line approach the priest so reverently. Do they really believe there is somewhere we all go after death? Her face lights up and shows a slight smile when she thinks about the possibility of seeing Sam again and meeting her parents for the first time. The smile vanishes when logically she knows it's all probably just a manipulative fairy tale like the Easter bunny, Santa Clause, and the tooth fairy.

The members of the loyal congregation that pass Lizzie on their way back to their seats avoid any eye contact. Out of the corner of her eye she spots the Nolans. Lizzie thinks, *They really couldn't look more angelic and hypocritical at the same time.* After receiving communion, they both must pass in front of her. Lizzie locks her eyes on the pair. They both walk with squinted eyes like they have just been anointed by the Pope. Phil never looks Lizzie's way. Maude waits until she's almost even with Lizzie and then with a quick turn of her head, she flashes Lizzie her best go-to-hell look. Lizzie cuts her eyes toward her and maintains her stolid expression as Maude tries to stare her down.

Lizzie doesn't plan on staying until Mass is over. She just wanted to make them feel a little more uncomfortable, twist the knife, so to speak. She quietly gets up from the pew, keeps her eyes pointed straight ahead as she walks down the side aisle to the rear of the church. If looks could kill, she will die a multitude of deaths by the time she reaches the doors of the church.

Outside the church, she slips on her sunglasses, hops down the steps, and makes her way down the sidewalk. With her good looks, the scarf, and Ray-Ban sunglasses, she could easily pass for Jackie Kennedy. That is up until the point where she climbs into Emma's old Plymouth wagon.

Days later, it's Christmas Eve and a cold wet Norther is blowing outside Emma's house. Inside the home, Lizzie and Emma sit in a couple of rocking chairs in front of a warm post oak fire burning in the fireplace. The wind comes and goes with gusts that rattle the windows. The hardwood floors are cold as ice as the cold air blows under the pier and beam structure. Lizzie is snuggled under a wool blanket and appears mesmerized by the dancing flames and the red glow of the hot coals.

"Bud would be happy to see us together," says Lizzie. "He would be proud of what we're doing."

Emma abruptly quits rocking, jumps up, and says, "You're damned right he would. How about a little of Jim Beam to celebrate the night?"

"Why the hell not?" Lizzie says, giving Emma an approving wink.

Emma breaks for the kitchen in search of a bottle of whiskey. Lizzie glances over at Emma's Christmas tree perched on the hearth and sees a straight mesquite tree limb sitting upright in a gallon can filled with rocks. Emma has spray-painted the branches silver, added a string of blue lights and covered it with tinsel icicles and ornaments. Not gaudy and extravagant like Maude Nolan's tree, but delicate and creative like Emma.

About that time, Emma returns with a couple of mugs. Lizzie can see hot vapors swirling above the liquid. She hands one to Lizzie and says, "Be careful, it's hotter than a two-dollar pistol." Lizzie raises the mug to her lips and breathes in the steamy vapors given off by the brew.

"What is it?" Lizzie asks.

Emma is surprised, "You ain't never had a hot toddy?"

Lizzie shakes her head. "I can smell the whiskey. What's in it besides that?"

"Honey, lemon, water and of course about two fingers of the old demon."

Emma raises her mug, "Here's to Bud Harkins."

Lizzie and Emma click mugs. Lizzie takes a measured, careful sip, closes her eyes, savors the taste, and says, "Oh, that's good. I would say that the old demon is hitting the spot on this cold night."

"It tends to get better as the night wears on," Emma says after another sip.

Later in the evening, Emma sets two fresh hot toddies on the fireplace mantel before she grabs a fire iron and stokes the fire. Lizzie tucks her blankets around her legs and suggests, "I think we need another log."

Emma hands her the fresh mug and says, "Here's to long-awaited justice." They click mugs again and Emma adds, "No matter what ... Phil Nolan has to pay." Neither one notices Elo standing in the doorway of the kitchen, listening to their every word.

A few nights later, at the Nolan ranch, the howl of several packs of coyotes and the sudden chirping of locusts crack the silence of the cloudy, dark night. A vague figure carrying a large bag runs from the edge of the brush to a lighted window at the rear of the camp house.

At the same time, Lizzie unlocks the door to the *Timely Remarks* and steps inside. The air is still heavy with fumes left-over from the fire. She flips on the lights and pulls a chair up to her charred wooden desk.

She pulls a photograph of Pearl from a drawer, secures it to the wall with a thumbtack, and then rolls a sheet of paper into her typewriter. Lizzie folds her hands together, pops her knuckles, and begins to type.

Back at the camp house, Phil Nolan staggers over to the cooler, pulls out a bottle of Seagram's 7, and fills a whiskey glass. In the bathroom, a window high above a bathtub shimmies halfway up and then stops. A brown, toe-sack rolls into the opening. Something inside the sack moves as it flips upside down. A moment later, a huge diamondback rattlesnake slides out of the sack, and drops into the bathtub. The snake's head is the size of a coffee mug. It crawls along inside the tub poking its head up and down before slithering over the side and sneaking along the wall.

Phil Nolan pours another glass of whiskey and gulps it down. He sways from one side to the other as he staggers across the room and falls headfirst against the bathroom door. Inside the bathroom, the door suddenly flies open and smacks against the wall as the rattler coils up beside the commode.

Nolan unbuckles his belt, watches his pants and underwear fall over his bootstraps as he stumbles backward and squats over the commode. Through the numbness of the whiskey, Phil Nolan feels a sudden stabbing jab to his hip. He maneuvers around on the seat and looks down beside the commode.

The sound of the locusts is broken by a loud, blood-curdling scream from inside the camp house. The searing pain is almost instantaneous as he grabs hold of the shower curtain, pulls himself to his feet, and tries to run. He forgets his pants are around his ankles. He manages a partial step and falls flat on his face. Still screaming, he looks back to locate the rattler. To his dismay, the snake is in a tight coil with its head back, waiting for an opportunity to strike again. Nolan lunges forward and crawls on his hands and knees until he reaches the front door of the camp house. He struggles to his feet, reaches down to grab his underwear and pants, and sees red blood mixed with milky poison trickling down his outer thigh.

Phil Nolan barely manages to pull up his pants before vomiting all over himself, stumbling out onto the veranda and screaming for help.

Chapter Twenty-Three

JAILHOUSE ROCK

A month has passed, and the New Year is in full swing. Lizzie is upstairs at the *Timely Remarks*. She glances at the wall clock and sees that it's straight up noon. She flips on the television set and begins to tidy up around the kitchen when she hears, "This is the local news with KZTV and Corpus Christi's own Gene Looper with the latest."

Lizzie moseys over in front of the TV, watches, and listens as the newscaster reads the news from a set of notes. "It has been confirmed by Texas Parks and Wildlife that Seclusion ranchers Phil and Maude Nolan have donated one hundred acres in and around Artesian Falls for a future State park. More information on this to come later."

Lizzie brandishes a broad grin and turns off the television before zipping down the stairs and picking up her purse and keys. She walks to the door, steps outside, and folds her arms against her chest.

Lizzie waves to Father Juan as he accompanies the Mexican family and the pregnant girl up the courthouse steps. Lizzie steps off the curb and climbs behind the wheel of her bright blue Ford pickup and backs away from the curb. She hears tires squealing and glances into the rearview mirror in time to see Emma and her old station wagon round the street corner and pull up and stop behind her. Emma pokes her head out of the passenger side window and whistles. The rear of the wagon is crammed full of Emma's watercolor paintings. Lizzie watches her hop out of the wagon and run up to her side window. Emma leans down and looks inside at Lizzie.

"Never thought I'd see this day."

"It is a fine day," Lizzie adds as she glances back at Elo sitting behind the wheel of the wagon. "Remember, all Elo has to do is tell the truth."

About that time, another car rounds the corner and heads in their direction. Emma runs to the front of Lizzie's truck and waits for the vehicle to pass.

Lizzie is amused and leans her head out of the truck's window. "Emma, they weren't going to run you over."

Emma chuckles and informs Lizzie, "I'd rather for them to be saying, look at the cowardly bitch run ... then don't she look natural."

She eases back up beside Lizzie's window and points down the street. "You were right; there is some justice."

Lizzie shades her eyes and focuses through the windshield.

Maude Nolan helps her husband Phil along the sidewalk toward the courthouse. Phil Nolan shuffles along with the help of a cane, one arm is tucked to his side, and a patch covers one eye.

Emma turns back to Lizzie.

"Heard that old rattler pumped so much venom in him, gave him a stroke."

Lizzie smiles. "I heard that old rattler was missing his rattlers."

"Well, as you know, that's not uncommon," replies Emma with a grin. Emma motions to Elo. "Park the car … I'll walk." She turns her attention back to Lizzie, "Don't want to keep the judge waiting."

Lizzie watches as Emma's old wagon makes a U-turn and parks in front of the courthouse. Emma pats Lizzie on the back of her hand. "Thanks for setting me up with that gallery in San Antonio. They sold out all of my paintings and want more."

Lizzie gives her big grin. "See! What'd I tell you?" Emma steps back out of the way as Lizzie drives away and then struts across the street to the courthouse.

That afternoon over in Victoria, a throng of fans pack the bleachers. A warm sun takes some of the chill out of the air. Lizzie walks to the edge of the bleachers and stands against the fence. The Roughneck team stands lined up ready to take the field. The announcer's voice echoes from one side of the field to the other.

"This is the last game of the season for the home team Blackcats."

The partisan crowd cheers.

"And the Houston Roughnecks led by all-pro Butch Markowsky."

The cheers turn to boos as the Roughnecks run onto the field. The fans, mostly Black with a sprinkle of Whites on the visitors' side, chant and rhythmically stomp the wooden bleachers. From the end zone, the Victoria Blackcats sprint to the middle of the field. They wear new uniforms and shiny black-and-silver helmets donated by an anonymous donor. The Roughnecks gather around Butch in a tight circle. He tightens his hands into closed fists.

"I want more than just to win this fuckin' game."

He spits on the grass. "I wanna' put Lott and the rest of those niggers down where they belong."

Butch and the Roughnecks line up on the field. A football stands perched on the forty-yard line. Butch's oversized foot blasts the ball off the tee; he watches it tumble end-over-end and drift down into Preston's waiting arms. Preston fakes a hand off to a crossing Blackcat and then sprints up the sideline. A swarm of Roughnecks knock him out-of-bounds. The whistle blows, chalk flies into the air as Butch pounds Preston further out of bounds and way after the whistle. Butch gets in Preston's face, grunts and says, "It's gonna get rougher than this, boy."

Preston pushes him back. "If you only knew, boy."

The Blackcats huddle up. Preston squats down, looks over at his center, who is a giant of a Black man with monster arms and hands to match. Jessie Jones just moved to Victoria from a small town in the state of Alabama. Preston calls Jessie by name.

"Jessie, let bad boy through. We going to teach him some respect."

Preston strolls up behind the center and barks out the signals. Across the line of scrimmage, Butch growls and flails his arms. Jessie snaps the ball back to Preston, steps sideways, and lets Butch blow through the line and take a dead aim at Preston. Preston rears back, uncorks a tight spiral to Butch's groin. Butch's eyes cross as the pain shoots up his gut. He momentarily slumps to the ground.

The Blackcats huddle around Preston again. Preston taps Jessie on the top of his helmet. "This time, give him your famous forearm shiver."

They break the huddle and run to the line of scrimmage. Jessie left hand cradles the ball; his right fist is snug against his chest. On the other side of the line, Butch kicks the turf and mouths to Preston, "I ain't falling for that shit again. I'm gonna kill you coons."

Preston barks out the signals. Jessie snaps the ball as Butch lunges forward; Jessie's massive elbow uncoils like a spring and slams Butch under his chin. The only sound Butch can hear now is that of his own teeth cracking. He wilts to the ground as Preston gallops for a touchdown.

Later in the game, it's just more of the same. Preston fades back, dodges a defender, shakes off another, and heaves a long pass downfield into the outstretched arms of a Blackcat just as the referee fires a gun into the air and signals the end of the game.

Just as Lizzie turns to leave, she notices a tall man in a sports coat and a gray fedora step onto the field. She watches him walk over to Preston, shake his hand, and then pat him on the shoulder and hand him a small card. Lizzie doesn't recognize the well-dressed man; she turns and makes her way out of the stadium.

As the sun sets behind the stands, the scoreboard reads, 30–0 in favor of Preston and the Blackcats. Butch is still spitting out blood as he finds another dislodged tooth. The Roughnecks' uniforms are dirty and torn. Several of Preston's teammates hoist him up on their shoulders, while the fans cheer his name. Preston's eyes search the stands for Lizzie. In the back of his mind, he was hoping she would come.

Several days later, a glistening sun rises on a crisp morning as an old car turns the corner and slows in front of a farmhouse. An arm from the driver-side window launches a rolled-up newspaper onto the yard. In a cloud of dust, the car disappears down the road as a middle-aged White woman dressed in a robe covering her pajamas hurries outside and snatches up the paper. She peels off a rubber band, unfolds the *Timely Remarks*, and begins to read the newspaper. In the La Rosa Café, Laverne reads to her husband. In front of his church, Father Juan smiles as he folds the paper and steps inside. On the street, a group of Black ladies gather in a circle with a copy of the *Timely Remarks*.

Lizzie's story reads: "Pearl Lott's death did not begin in Boys Town any more than it ended there. It was born in Seclusion. In the sordid minds of some of its citizens. The corrupt that believe they have some inherited right to control the mind and body of another. I realize that I may not have changed the consciousness of this town. It is my hope that I have at least stirred the notion of equality in one or more of you. The tragic story of Pearl Lott and others before her will weigh on this community for decades to come...."

The White woman in front of the farmhouse folds the newspaper, glances around, and then rushes back inside.

Days later, on a cloudy, rainy day in Seclusion, a long whip antenna sways on the rear of a government sedan as two men step out of the car and make their way up the courthouse steps. They wear white Stetson hats and badges, and both carry sidearms.

Inside the courthouse, the door is wide open, leading into the sheriff's office. From inside the office the sheriff can be heard saying, "Something I can help you boys with?"

Sheriff Taylor's feet roll off the top of his desk and onto the floor. He stands and eases over to a filing cabinet and nervously fumbles with a set of keys.

"Don't get many visits from the Texas Rangers."

Lizzie's Ford pickup pulls away from the *Timely Remarks* and slows as it passes the government sedan. The two Rangers flank a handcuffed Sheriff Taylor as they stand beside the car.

The sheriff struggles to maintain his balance as he places one foot into the rear floorboard of the sedan. He stops, turns his head, glares inside the Ford pickup at Lizzie. Her stern expression doesn't change as she stares back at the sheriff. He ducks his head, plops down in the rear seat, and hears, "It's all his fault, him and the Nolans."

Sheriff Taylor jerks his head around to see Javelina handcuffed to the top of the door frame.

"Shut up, you fuckin' idiot."

The two Rangers open the front doors of the sedan and scoot inside. Javelina isn't about to take one for the team. "I'll tell you guys anything you want to know." Javelina leans forward pressing his nose to the metal screen that separates the two seats. "And I know it all." Sheriff Taylor kicks at him, trying to shut him up. The two Rangers look at one another and smile.

Chapter Twenty-Four

BYE BYE LOVE

Several days later, it's mid-morning in Seclusion. Lizzie peers through a light rain as the droplets bead up on the windshield of her pickup. Lizzie flips on the wipers, presses in the clutch, and then brakes to a stop and waits for a crowd of people to crisscross the street. After the light turns green, she downshifts into low gear and accelerates through the intersection.

After a few blocks, she sees Preston hoofing it down Main Street. He's carrying a single suitcase and duffel bag. He seems in a hurry. Lizzie rolls up beside him and leans her head out of the truck's open window.

"And where the hell you think you're going in such a hurry?"

Preston stops and puts the bags down.

"Bus station."

He steps back and looks at the pickup.

"New?"

"To me," Lizzie says with a grin. "How about a lift? You're going to get wet and catch a cold."

Preston pitches his bags in the bed of the truck and slides in on the passenger side. Lizzie steps on the gas pedal.

"I hoped that you would leave Seclusion."

"I am … I'm headed home," Lizzie replies.

"Where's that?"

"I've got to find it," Lizzie says as she steers the truck under the bus station's canopy.

"You played a great game the other day."

"You were there?"

"For a little while."

She then stops the pickup beside the open door of a Continental Trailways bus. The illuminated sign above the bus's windshield denotes its destination is Dallas.

"First, I have some unfinished business down in Corpus Christi with Bishop O'Malley."

"I read what you wrote about Pearl … it was nice. Hattie appreciated it, too."

Lizzie kills the engine. "Thanks; that means a lot to me." For a moment, they both just seem to be lost, each looking into one another's eyes.

"Thanks for caring about me. If you hadn't told Emma where I had gone…."

Preston unexpectedly reaches over and squeezes Lizzie's hand. Lizzie feels a sharp lump in her throat. She can't speak as she draws his hand to her lips and gently kisses his palm. She can't find the right words.

Finally, she mumbles out "Preston...." He shakes his head, pulls his hand from hers, and presses the tip of his index finger to her lips. He wants desperately to kiss her but knows it would only make the long goodbye worse.

He smiles, opens the door, and slides out. He leans down, hesitates for a moment, like his heart is telling him this might be the last time he ever sees her.

"Maybe, in another time ... another place." He says as he steps back to the bed of the pickup. All Lizzie can do is watch him as he grabs his bags and walks to the bus without looking back.

Finally, she hollers, "Maybe Artesian Falls?"

He stops on the first step of the bus, spins around, and smiles.

Lizzie feels the air being sucked out of her lungs. Tears stream down her cheeks. She dabs her face with the back of her hand, shifts the pickup into gear, and pulls away from the station. Lizzie glances into the rearview mirror and sees the bus roll out onto the street and in a black plume of diesel exhaust head off in the opposite direction.

Chapter Twenty-Five
WHO'S SORRY NOW

Later that morning, she is on her not-so-scenic drive to Corpus Christi. She can't get the thought of Preston out of her mind. Why does life have to be so unfair, people so set in their antiquated beliefs that they can't separate their biases from the truth? She turns down the truck's radio as she passes through a small farming town. A mile or so outside the town, she pulls off the road and unfolds her Texaco roadmap. She's made it this far; she doesn't want to take a wrong turn now. Wouldn't be proper to keep the Most Reverend Bishop O'Malley waiting? She surveys her surroundings and much to her dismay there is absolutely nothing on either side of the road and as far as the eye can see but miles and miles of dirt. Soil that has been plowed into neat rows, one after another, that go on forever. Far off in the distance, she makes out several tall buildings. She wonders which one belongs to the rich oilman Joe Hamilton as she steers back onto the highway and steps on the gas. Less than ten miles down the road, the scenery abruptly changes. Now she's driving on a divided highway with tall, majestic palm trees growing in the median and swaying in a southerly sea breeze. A few minutes later, she approaches the long causeway that spans Nueces Bay. She climbs up the sudden grade to the deck of the bridge and passes the Corpus Christi city limits sign.

She takes a quick glance down at the greenish-colored water and thinks how scared even the thought of it makes her feel. As she climbs to the crest of the Harbor Bridge high above the ship channel, she wonders if her old Power Wagon would have made it all the way to the top. She feels her palms getting sweaty. From atop the bridge, Lizzie can spot her destination, as shown on the map. She doesn't have far to go.

Lizzie parks in a lot adjacent to the cathedral. She glances down at her watch as she pulls open the door to the Chancery. Her watch reads 1:25 p.m. She steps through the doorway and finds herself standing in a long, wide hallway. She sniffs the air. *Why do all these places smell the same?* Kind of a mixture between incense and old leather books.

A young priest approaches her and asks in a very authoritative manner, "May I help you?" Lizzie recognizes him from the Christmas party at the Nolans' home. He acts like he doesn't remember her.

She responds with, "I have an appointment with Bishop O'Malley at 1:30."

The young priest in his best uppity tone says, "Follow me, please."

He spins around and prances down the hall. Lizzie falls in behind, taking note of his walk. She smiles and whispers to herself, *You think?*

He stops in front of an arch-shaped wooden door, knocks, and then pushes it open. He peeks inside and sees that the office is empty. The young priest steps back and turns to Lizzie. "Please wait in here."

Lizzie pokes her head inside and notices a vast room with only a table surrounded by six straight-backed leather chairs. She watches him close the door and then she pulls one of the chairs back from under the table and sits down. She takes note of the time on her wristwatch; it reads 1:30 p.m.

Lizzie squirms and scoots in the chair trying to find a way to get comfortable, but the chair keeps winning. Finally, she gets up, strolls over to the window, and looks out. She didn't realize that she was this close to the Hamilton building. She figures out there's a bank on the first level. What is it with rich people and their banks? She ponders to herself.

Lizzie looks down at her watch and sees that it's already after 2 o'clock. She's had enough of this. She marches over to the door, jerks it open, and steps out into the hall. She doesn't spot a living soul. She takes off in a rapid pace down the hall. Her eyes flash from side to side as she searches the crossing hallways for the young priest. Her leather soles make a loud tapping sound as they strike the Saltillo tile floor. Just as she rounds the next to last corner, she runs face to face with the priest. Lizzie stands her ground, gets right up in his face and points her index finger close to his nose.

"You listen to me, and you listen good. You go find Your Excellency or Most Revered or whatever the hell you call O'Malley, and you tell him if he doesn't want his name splashed

255

across every newspaper in Texas, he better be standing right here in the next five minutes."

The priest throws his head back like he's been totally insulted by Lizzie's tone and says, "I'll see what I can do."

Lizzie is now determined not to let go of the high ground. She fires back. "Five minutes."

Evidently, Bishop O'Malley was never that far away. Lizzie sees him round a corner and walk up, face her and say, "I'm pressed for time, but I'm sure that what you have to say won't take long."

Lizzie shows off her best fake smile. "You're right; it won't take long." She folds her arms against her chest. "As James Cagney would say, Bishop O'Malley, the gig is up."

The Bishop acts like he still doesn't realize the severity of the situation.

Lizzie continues, "Tomorrow, the Texas Attorney General will present evidence to a federal grand jury resulting from an investigation into the diocese, the foundation, and you, Bishop Thomas O'Malley, for crimes ranging from witness tampering to perjury. The Texas Rangers are booking Sheriff Taylor into jail as we speak. I'm sure he'll sing like a featherless canary."

Bishop O'Malley glances down at the floor and then he looks up at Lizzie.

"Why … why are you doing all this?"

"Justice would be a good starting point."

"You don't know the meaning of justice," the bishop counters in an angry tone.

"I know that they may offer you a plea deal. My advice to you would be to take it, and when you do, you'll be made to give back the land and the money to the people you stole it from. I also know this is just the tip of the iceberg and I'll promise you I am going to keep digging."

His anger is apparent on his face, but for the time being he's controlling it.

But Lizzie is not through by any means. "I'll bet you that in the coming years, there's going to be some sick and nauseating things exposed about this diocese and most of the Catholic churches in the country and you know at best you covered it up or worse are part of it."

"Ms. Fox, I am innocent, and I will fight you and win in a court of law."

"You know that's a damned line. Make sure you tell that one in your next your confession."

Lizzie can see the color leaving his face, like all the blood is draining away. She knows she's hit on a nerve. She turns, walks a few steps, turns back around, smiles, and says, "You people can't hide behind those collars anymore. They won't cover up the sick and perverted stuff you are hiding."

She marches down the hall toward the door, leaving Bishop O'Malley standing there alone with a vacant look on his face.

Chapter Twenty-Six

ALL I HAVE TO DO
IS DREAM

A couple of weeks later, Lizzie's truck pulls off the highway outside of Seclusion onto a narrow gravel road. A cloud of red dust trails the pickup to the arched entrance of the cemetery. She climbs out of the pickup and makes her way through the entrance gate. It is eerily quiet as she zig-zags through the many tombstones. She stops, gets down on her knees and places a pair of spurs in front of a red granite headstone. She runs her fingers over etched letters and numbers that read, "Samuel Michael Fox—Born 1948—Died 1960."

An unexpected gust of wind blows through the trees and begins to turn the blades of the old windmill. Water starts to trickle into the cistern and then gradually builds into a steady stream. A flock of blue herons squawks and zooms by overhead. She can hear the sounds of animals and little critters from across the fence in a green pasture. The whole place has suddenly come to life.

Lizzie knows in her heart that this is a sign, as a feeling of peace and serenity flows through her body. She gets to her feet, looks up at a blue sky, so clear, she thinks she can see into tomorrow.

She blows a kiss to her son, wipes her eyes, turns, and walks away. She opens the door to the pickup, stands up on the running board, and turns back for one last look.

In Seclusion, Lizzie takes a slow pass down Main Street. She pulls up in front of the La Rosa Café, turns off the engine, and walks up the steps. Her eyes trail up above the café's front door. She smiles when she confirms the "Whites Only," sign has been removed, leaving only the remnants of a bright outline and four rough holes in the white-painted brick.

She pauses in front of a row of newspaper racks, drops in a dime, and pulls out the latest edition of the *Corpus Christi Chronicle*. The headline reads "Bishop Thomas O'Malley Announces Sudden Retirement / The Rita E. West Foundation Dissolves."

The beginning of the article states, "According to an unnamed source, Bishop O'Malley has already left Texas for his home in County Cork, Ireland. All current board members of the foundation were forced to resign or face State and federal charges that have not yet been named."

She jerks open the front door of the café and marches over to Grover Giles standing behind the counter beside the cash register. Without saying a word, she spreads the front page out on the glass top and smooths out the wrinkles with the palm of her hand. Grover is speechless. He just stares down at the paper.

"Look at me," Lizzie says in a low voice. Grover slowly raises his head and makes eye contact. "You got off lucky. You'd better fly right because if I hear you've gone back to your old tricks, I promise you I'll be back."

Lizzie turns, swings open the door, and marches down the steps to the street. A big grin rips across her face. She can barely keep from busting out laughing. She can't believe what she just did. How cool was that? It was right out of a movie. She just can't put her finger on the title. Had to have been a John Wayne film.

She pulls open the pickup door and gives the *Timely Remarks* one last look. A sad and nostalgic feeling runs through her body when she sees the "For Sale" sign hanging in the window, but she knows it time for her to move on, find that dream, and chase it. She spots the old Black man from Pearl's funeral who gave up his seat for her. He stands on the corner, holding a copy of the *Timely Remarks*.

A picture of Pearl is blazoned across the front with a headline that reads, "Last Chapter—Justice."

Lizzie gets up behind the wheel, starts the engine, and heads out of town.

A proud smile rolls across the old man's face as he looks up and tips his hat to Lizzie as her pickup accelerates down Main Street.

Lizzie catches a glimpse of the old man in her rearview mirror. She waves good-bye as she tunes in the radio and hears,

"An oldie but goodie from 1958, brothers Don and Phil Everly with, 'All I Have to Do Is Dream.'"

The Ford pickup zooms past the Seclusion city limit sign and slowly fades into a lonely, straight stretch of Texas highway.

The End

EPILOGUE

November 17, 1963 • Abilene, Texas — A silver metallic Pontiac is ripping down Interstate 20 at seventy-five miles per hour, passing a road sign with a giant picture of a cowboy that reads, "Leaving Abilene—Come Again."

Inside the new model GTO, the radio is blaring the latest hit song "Wipeout" by the Surfaris. Lizzie takes a quick glance down at the fuel gauge. The needle is completely to the left of "E" for empty. Up ahead, she spots a large billboard sign advertising gas, barbecue, and clean restrooms. She decides that she is certainly in need of two of them. She steers the GTO into the right lane, takes the next exit, and follows the access road to Boo Green's Texas BBQ.

Lizzie pulls up next to a premium pump at the gas station/barbecue restaurant. Lying on the seat beside her is the latest edition of *Life Magazine*, with the cover showing an article written by Lizzie Fox, titled, "Exposing The Catholic Church's Magdalene Laundries."

Lizzie steps out, locks the car, and tells the attendant, "Fill her up with premium, please." She strolls up to the front of the building, spots a pay telephone booth, and decides she had better use it while it's vacant. She steps inside and pulls the folding door close. With her eyes on the attendant pumping the gas, she drops a dime into the slot and dials the operator. After the operator comes on the line, Lizzie says, "Collect call from Lizzie Fox, person-to-person, to Charlie Bauer." A little while later, Lizzie hears another person on the line say, "Where are you, Lizzie?"

"East of Abilene, Texas. I left LA late Friday."

"I've been waiting on your call. Are you sitting down?"

Lizzie glances behind her and spies a small stool attached to the back of the booth. "Metaphorically," she states while laughing.

"Well, you've got a sit-down with President and Mrs. Kennedy at the Commodore Perry Hotel in Austin at four-forty in the afternoon on Friday. Air Force One will be leaving Dallas Love Field and arriving at Bergstrom Air Force Base at three-fifteen that afternoon."

"Oh my God, this is beyond my wildest dreams."

"Well, you've only got fifteen minutes, so we have to make use of every second."

"If you're waiting on me, then you're backing up," Lizzie says with total excitement in her voice. Charlie finishes up the call, "You stay in touch, and I'll be in Austin on Tuesday."

Lizzie steps out of the booth with a grin on her face as big as Dallas. She moseys inside, pays the cashier for the fuel, and with the leftover change buys several pieces of Double Bubble. She locates the restrooms in the back of the building past the restaurant area.

When she exits the ladies restroom, she notices a large group of men, a mixture of old retired cowboys and a few wannabes, drinking beer and gathered in a semi-circle around a television set. She inches up closer behind the group and notices that they are all fixed on a football game. The television sportscaster begins to describe the action on the field.

"We're back at the Cotton Bowl in Dallas. The Cowboys have the ball on their own twenty." Lizzie turns to leave when she hears, "Meredith drops back to pass." The announcer's voice suddenly becomes very animated and loud, "He's got Lott down the sideline. No one's going to catch him."

Lizzie's eyes flash back to the screen where she sees Preston catch the ball on a dead run and race down the sideline. He crosses the goal line and flips the ball to the referee. The sportscaster, still excited, "Nobody even laid a hand on him." Another announcer chimes in with, "That's the Cowboy's new secret weapon. Coach Landry found him down in South Texas."

One of the older guys turns away from the television and says, "Hell, with Lott playing, we may win a few games."

Lizzie clears her throat to get the attention of the men. "Hey guys, is this game on the radio, too?" They spin around and size her up, before all talk over one another with the affirmative.

Lizzie moseys outside, swings herself down behind the wheel of the GTO, starts the engine, and tunes the radio into the game. She chucks a piece of Double Bubble into her mouth as she eases back up on the access road. A few hundred yards down the road, she suddenly slams on the brakes and pulls off to the side in front of a large road sign that reads, "Left Lane Dallas 188 Miles—Right Lane Austin 217 Miles."

She sits there racing the engine, drumming her fingers on the steering wheel as she whispers to herself, "Well, shit! Another fork in the fucking road. What are going to do now, Lizzie?"

Suddenly, out of nowhere and for the first time in her life, she blows a giant bubble. It surprises her; she sucks it back into her mouth and looks at herself in the rearview mirror as she blows an even bigger one. Lizzie knows it's a sign, as an ear-to-ear grin washes across her face. She stomps on the accelerator and fishtails back onto the road.

The End Again